STORYTELLERS

a novel of supernatural terror

by Julie Anne Parks

DESIGN IMAGE

THE DESIGNIMAGE GROUP, INC.

The Design Image Group, Inc.
PO Box 2325
Darien, Illinois 60561
www.designimagegroup.com

ISBN:1-891946-04-8

First Edition

THE DESIGNIMAGE GROUP, INC.

Printed In The U.S.A.

10 9 8 7 6 5 4 3 2

DEDICATION

To my family — Chuck, Michael, Shannon and Tim — who forgave late dinners, mis-matched socks, and all my eccentricities with good humor. I love you all. Nothing is more important than family.

To my friends — and particularly to the Writer's Group of the Triad — your encouragement, enthusiasm and senses of humor are invaluable. Thank you.

And to my muse, who brought me Storytellers.

"They who dream by day are cognizant of many things which escape those who dream only by night."

Eleonora (1841)
— Edgar Allan Poe

PROLOGUE

Literary agent Everett A. Palmer beamed. "It's a deal then," he said into the receiver. "Of course, he'll accept the offer. He'd be crazy not to. I'll expect a draft of the contract by fax on Tuesday afternoon, latest. Always a pleasure working with you, Steve."

Palmer dropped the receiver into its cradle, sank back in his leather chair and sighed with pleasure. His Hollywood co-agent, Steve Corbin, had just negotiated a million-dollar option for Braxton Defoe's latest novel, *Murder Mountain*. He deserved a drink. Hell, why not go for a magnum of champagne? Last week, six publishing houses had duked it out in a fiercely fought auction. Editors at five houses cried in their beer after Halcyon Press won the auction with its two-million-dollar bid.

Palmer had pulled off the coup of the year. Not bad, considering Braxton Defoe had slunk from Los Angeles eight months ago, disgraced, burnt out and broke. Palmer had given up on him, never expecting him to write again. In fact, he'd nearly thrown Defoe out of his office when his client came begging for another advance.

Everett had thought the Defoe heyday was past.

His eyes shifted to the paneled wall, his glance flickering briefly on the busts of Poe, Shakespeare and Hawthorne. Not that Defoe was in their league. His bust would never grace a literary agency wall. But copies of his royalty checks might.

He jabbed his intercom button. "Carolyn? Track down Braxton Defoe for me. I don't care what it takes — private investigators, the FBI, Sergeant Preston of the Yukon, whatever. But find him. He's got contracts to sign. Braxton Defoe has been resurrected from the dead."

"Oh, that's right. Okay then, we'll publish posthumously."

CHAPTER ONE

It seemed a sinister place, a dark and brooding landscape of steep slopes and craggy chasms. Black clouds roiled above wooded peaks, plunging the hillsides below into shadows like a spreading stain of darkness. It was a place where a creative mind might easily slip from the mundane to the macabre, where even the most unimaginative soul might be goaded into believing the unbelievable.

It was perfect.

Piper Defoe turned off the isolated road and deftly maneuvered around the potholes that cratered the driveway. The black Grand Cherokee bumped to a stop in front of a white farmhouse with black shutters. An old-fashioned covered porch swept across the entire length of the house, punctuated by pots of red geraniums.

She switched off the ignition. "Want to come with me? Or would you prefer to stay in the car and wallow in self-pity?" The last words tumbled from her mouth before she could stop them.

Braxton turned away and stared out the passenger window.

"Suit yourself." She opened the door and slid out of the car.

A young blonde stepped onto the farmhouse porch. "Are you Mrs. Defoe?" she asked.

"Yes. And you are?"

"Susannah Wyatt. Mama drove into town, but she left the key and a map to show you how to get to the cabin in case she missed you." The young woman craned her neck and squinted against the windshield's reflection, wiggling her fingers in the car's direction. "Is that Mr. Defoe?"

"Sure is. Have you read any of his books?" Piper asked. She took the key and the folded map. Susannah looked about twenty-five, so Piper guessed she was closer to seventeen. Maybe eighteen.

Piper sighed. When she was a teenager, she'd looked like one: all gangly arms and legs and teeth. But Susannah Wyatt was petite, well-filled out and carefully made up.

Ripe.

Maybe even pretty, somewhere beneath the blue eye shadow, heavy black liner and scarlet lipstick.

Susannah blushed prettily. "I saw his movies. Awesome. They gave me nightmares for days."

No sense explaining that Braxton didn't write the screenplays. "The books were better. Tell your mother I said thanks. I'm looking forward to meeting her."

"She and Daddy are planning to stop by tonight. Just to make sure you're settled in okay, show you how the gas works, all that."

"Good. We'll expect them. Thanks, Susannah."

"Sure." The girl gave a little shrug, causing the thin strap of her peach tank top to slip off her shoulder. She automatically replaced it, her eyes still peering through the windshield at Braxton. "He doesn't look like a famous author. He looks kinda...normal."

Piper laughed. "I guess it depends on how you define 'normal'. Most people don't consider horror writers normal. Bye."

Piper crossed the porch and headed back to the car, waving at Susannah as she opened the car door. The girl, with her shoulders leaning against the door jamb and her hips thrust forward in a studied pose, waved back languidly.

Braxton was in exactly the same position as when she'd left him. She followed his stare westward, across a meadow backshadowed by the hazy blue profile of the Great Smoky Mountains' northernmost reach.

Her heart swelled in her breast. She was home.

Or as close to home as she was likely to get.

She slid behind the wheel, unfolded the map and held it against the dash while she turned the car around. "Well, Brax, you've got at least one fan who's delighted you're here."

Either he didn't hear her or chose to ignore the remark. It was a measure of his oblivion; Braxton never failed to notice comely young women. Yet he continued staring through the window, silent, the *New York Times Book Review* clutched in his hand.

Ten minutes later, they pulled onto the property that would be their home for the next year. The Jeep coughed softly to a stop, and Piper stared. The log cabin was so in tune with its surroundings that it seemed more a part of the landscape than a man-made structure.

A hill framed the two-story cabin on one side, then curved behind it, climbing so drastically that she had to lean her head back to see the summit. From that angle, it seemed to be crashing down on her.

The gentle roar of water tumbling over a stony creekbed came from the far side of the property. Damp coolness rushed through her open window and brushed her cheek. The land was heavily wooded, and sunlight dappled the ground through a leafy canopy.

She hopped out of the car and strode across a porch furnished with four white wicker rocking chairs and a small round table, unlocked the door and stepped inside.

It couldn't have been more appealing.

The rustic cabin was a far cry from the six-thousand-square foot atrocity in Los Angeles that Braxton had called home and she'd called a nightmare. She could be happy here. The furniture blended as comfortably as the cabin did to its surroundings — pleasant and clean, chosen for comfort instead of fashion. Russet, ocher and wheat Indian weavings hung down the log walls, and a round wagon-wheel light fixture dangled from a vaulted ceiling. To the left of the door stood a scrubbed oak table and chairs. The dining area was separated from the small kitchen by a peninsula and the stairwell to the second floor stood directly across from the door. It was a friendly cabin, a "grab a cup of coffee and prop your feet up" kind of place.

She went back onto the porch. "Braxton, come inside. It's wonderful."

Braxton was still slumped in the front seat, his head leaning against the window. The face of her once-handsome husband was heavily lined for his years, and an unhealthy pallor accentuated darkly shadowed eyes. At the sound of her voice, he drew himself up, fumbled with the door, then stumbled across the driveway. Hand over hand, he lugged himself up the three porch steps as if he were ninety rather than forty. Shuffling through the front door, he looked around with bleak, uninterested eyes, then asked, "Where's the bed? I want to take a nap."

Piper's patience snapped. "Shake it off, Braxton. You act like you were sentenced to Death Row instead of being offered a second chance."

He rubbed his stubbled chin. "Second chance at what? At starting over? In this godforsaken place? You got what you wanted. No need to rub it in."

"I admit I never wanted to leave the mountains, but you had to be Mr. Big Shot and live life in the fast lane. That's why you're in this mess. You forgot who you are."

He glanced at her with as much apparent interest as if she were one more tree in the forest. "I'd like to forget who you are," he said, then headed up the stairs.

Her hands shook as if palsied. She stuffed them into her jeans pockets. Suddenly the cabin seemed less inviting, alien, the kind of place that would be heaven when it was shared with the right person. Or hell, shared with the wrong one.

Piper sighed, then unloaded the Jeep. It didn't take long; there wasn't much. The few things they hadn't converted to cash were being shipped from California. She set up Braxton's computer in the smaller of the two bedrooms and her art supplies in the living room, brought in their suitcases, stashed away the few groceries she'd bought on their way to the cabin, then took a cup of coffee out to the porch, kicked off her deck shoes, and plunked down into one of the rocking chairs.

What if Braxton was burned out as a writer, as one book reviewer claimed? What if he had said everything there was in him to say? What if he really didn't want to write anymore?

She pushed the thoughts away just as a white Dodge Ram clattered up the driveway. The truck pulled behind her Jeep and rattled to a stop. Three people emerged.

The woman was short and filled out her jeans with a little left over. She tugged self-consciously on the tails of her faded plaid shirt and smiled, transforming her plump features into those of sparkling prettiness. She was in her early forties, Piper guessed.

The man walking toward her from the driver's side was tall —

six three or four — and moved with sinewy grace. His hair was silver blond, extraordinarily lustrous, feather-cut, and on the long side. It hid the arch of his ears and brushed his collar. *Sleek* popped into Piper's mind, even though she found it an odd choice to describe such a large man.

Behind him, a teenager walked with the peculiar bobbing gait of a young man who wasn't used to his new height. His hair was as light as his father's, and his face was all angles and planes. He jammed his hands into his pockets and tried to look bored.

"Mrs. Defoe?" The woman extended her hand. "I'm Mary Beth Wyatt. This is my husband, Ren, and my son, Jeff. Did you have any trouble finding the cabin? Were my directions okay? I usually leave directions to Ren, but he hasn't been around much lately. It's his busy time."

"They were excellent. We came to it as straight as an arrow," Piper said, shaking Mrs. Wyatt's hand. Her fingers were as plump as little sausages, and warm.

Piper turned to Ren Wyatt. Up close he was good looking — incredibly good looking — in a rough hewn way, with chocolate brown eyes that were at odds with his otherwise fair coloring. His hand was large, the fingers surprisingly smooth, and when they shook hands, she was startled by a tiny charge. Surprise flittered across his eyes, alerting Piper that he'd felt the electricity, too.

She looked away.

"Welcome to Crooked Creek," he said. His voice was soft and without a trace of his wife's twangy accent. His hand dropped heavily to his side.

"Thanks. Won't you sit down? All I can offer you is instant coffee. I haven't done any real shopping yet, but I did pick up some soft drinks. Jeff?"

"Yes, ma'am," he answered, softly. "Thanks."

"Instant coffee is fine," Mary Beth said. "Where's Mr. Defoe? I'm so excited about meeting him I can hardly stand it. Imagine, a famous writer in our little cabin. Who'd have thought it?"

"Sorry. Braxton's napping." She went inside and put the kettle on to boil. The Wyatts followed. "Mrs. Wyatt —"

"Just plain old Mary Beth and Ren. We don't stand on formality around here."

She smiled. "Good. Call me Piper. Please don't think me rude, but I hope you haven't told anyone about Braxton being here. He needs solitude. Peace and quiet. He's hoping to avoid any autograph hounds." Piper knew Braxton would adore fans pounding on his cabin door.

Mary Beth looked as innocent as a dove. "Haven't said a word to anyone, though I admit it's a temptation. I remember that picture of him in *People* a few years back. I don't remember any other *People* celebrities visiting this neck of the woods before. But I can stay quiet. Has Mr. Defoe been ill? Or is he working on a new novel?"

"He's had a few lapses, but now he's eager to start writing again. We thought a year without distractions might help his work."

"We'll do what we can. Don't I remember reading something about you being from right here in North Carolina, Piper?"

"Not right here. Over in Blowing Rock. But it's so touristy there now, we thought this might be a little more private."

They took their coffee to the porch and settled into the rocking chairs. Jeff slumped against the railing and studied his sneakers. Piper found it refreshing to see a teenager in clothes that fit, rather than the over-sized jeans kids wore slung around their hips on the West Coast. Mary Beth prattled on like a sparrow about the cabin, about getting the phone hooked up that morning. She wrote down directions to the grocery, the bank and the library.

Ren sat quietly, seemingly content to let his wife talk while he sipped his coffee and stared into the steadily darkening woods. Piper hadn't made eye contact with him since the moment they'd shook hands, yet she suspected he was studying her, noting every movement, every twitching muscle.

Ren didn't consider himself a frivolous man, one of those guys who suffered whiplash when a pretty face passed by, so he was bewildered by the fact that he couldn't keep his eyes off Piper Defoe.

It wasn't just her appearance that mesmerized him — she was

tall, slim, and as graceful as a morning breeze stirring the leaves. But he was reacting to her on a deeper level, a primal one.

An artist might say that Piper had been drawn with an economy of line, a few fluid downstrokes of the pencil. Even her long straight hair — as black as he imagined outer space might be — moved sinuously — draping from crown to shoulders in a smooth, continual line, adding to the illusion of elegant simplicity. A thick fringe of lashes framed eyes almost as dark as her hair and tilted slightly at the outer corners. Both her coloring and sculpted cheekbones revealed Indian blood somewhere in her family tree.

Ren's evaluation stopped abruptly when a man stepped out of the cabin, his eyes baggy and bloodshot, hair disheveled. He looked disoriented.

"Braxton," Piper said. "Meet our landlords — Mary Beth and Ren Wyatt. And their son, Jeff."

An amazing metamorphosis took place. Braxton smoothed back his hair, and his sleepy expression changed into a smile that struck Ren as more of a display of teeth than friendliness. He drew himself up to his full height, straightened the sleeves of his silk shirt, and extended his hand. He seemed delighted to find an audience on his porch.

Yet Ren noticed an interesting change in Braxton's wife, too. Her muscles tightened when Braxton appeared. Her voice thinned slightly, losing its rich timbre, and when she smiled, it seemed forced. Her eyes darted about warily.

"Coffee?" Piper raised her mug.

"I'd rather have a drink," Braxton said.

"We don't have anything."

A muscle in Braxton's jaw twitched. "Coffee then."

Piper disappeared into the cabin, and Ren heard her rattling things in the kitchen.

Mary Beth "oohed" and "aahed" over Braxton, prattling a mile a minute over this book and that. The author absorbed the attention like a kitten being stroked.

Suddenly, Ren realized he'd been addressed. He jerked his attention back to the conversation. "Pardon me?"

"Piper said you're a teacher. What do you teach?" Braxton repeated.

"Mythology. At a small private college near here."

Braxton's eyebrow arched. "Mythology? They still teach that stuff?" He chuckled, then shrugged. "Pays the same, I guess. I got my B.A. in English at Welborn College and my M.F.A. from the University of North Carolina at Greensboro. Had mythology as part of my freshman year Humanities class. Pretty dry stuff. Where'd you go to school, Ren?"

"Up north."

Braxton smiled and cocked his head. "*Where* up north?"

"Massachusetts."

"Really? Which school? Boston College? U. of M.?"

"Harvard."

Braxton blinked. "Oh." His smile faded. "Need a Master's degree to teach college level, right?"

Ren nodded.

"He's got his Ph.D. in Classical Studies," Mary Beth said. "You won't get much out of him, Mr. Defoe. He's the strong silent type unless he's telling one of his stories. Then he's quite the talker."

"Stories? What kind of stories, *Dr.* Wyatt?" Braxton asked.

"He's a storyteller," Mary Beth said. "In fact, that's how he's known around here. Not Ren Wyatt, the professor. He's 'The Storyteller.' And he's the best."

Ren bit the corner of his lip.

"*The* Storyteller," Braxton said as if rolling the name around on his tongue. He lit a cigarette and looked at Ren with renewed interest through the layers of smoke. "In the old Appalachian tradition? I've read about the practice. They have festivals or something, don't they?"

Before Ren could answer, Mary Beth said, "You bet. Maybe you'd like to go? The Jonesborough Festival is the first week in October. Ren can get y'all tickets if you'd like, can't you, honey? It's a big deal nowadays. They get so many people at the festival you can barely budge. They sell tapes and books and tee shirts. Takes over the whole town of Jonesborough. Ren's done two, no, three tapes. Good ones, too. He's the best. He's THE Storyteller."

"What kind of stories?" Braxton asked again. He smoothed his hair back over his temples. It was solid silver there, in stark contrast to the rest, a rich auburn, heavily shot with gray.

Piper emerged from the house, handed Braxton his coffee, then crossed to her chair, angling it so they formed a loosely shaped horseshoe. From the interested look in her eyes as she settled herself, Ren knew she'd been listening through the open door.

Mary Beth piped up. "All kin —"

"Different kinds," Ren said, speaking over her. "Ghost stories, humorous stories about the ridiculous situations we humans get ourselves into and the messes we make trying to get back out of them. Adventure stories once in a while. Occasionally a fairy tale. But my favorites are those based on legends. Cherokee legends, mostly." He realized he'd addressed his remarks to Piper. Her eyes widened at the word "Cherokee."

"Really?" Braxton asked. "My wife is part Cherokee, aren't you, Piper? What is it, half? Quarter?"

Piper lowered her eyes. "My grandmother was full-blooded."

"Her Indian blood is what makes it impossible for her to stay in her shoes." Braxton looked pointedly at her bare feet.

She tucked them beneath her.

Braxton continued. "Of course, I imagine half-breeds are common around here, aren't they? I lived in Asheville for a year — that's where I met Piper — and half-breeds were plentiful. But they were rare in Los Angeles. Of course, with so many ethnic groups out there, it was kind of hard to tell."

Ren stiffened. "I'm a 'half-breed,' too, as you call it." He stayed focused on Braxton's face, but he felt both women's eyes on him.

"Really? I'd have guessed you for a Scandinavian. No offense, Ren. Obviously I have no problem with it, since I married one." He blew a smoke ring, watched it linger in the air till it dissipated. *"Ren.* Is that an Indian name? Don't think I've heard it before. Are you Cherokee, too?"

"It's a nickname for Renfrid. A family name. And, no, I'm not Cherokee. My mother is Tlingit. I was raised in Alaska."

Braxton grinned and held up his palm. "Okay. Strike three, I'm out. Could've sworn you were a Viking." Braxton peered at Ren. "I guess Swedes don't often have brown eyes, though, do they? My mistake."

"His daddy was part Swedish, wasn't he, Ren?" Mary Beth said.

He nodded.

"So I'm not far off base then," Braxton said. He looked pleased with himself again. "Would you be so kind as to give Piper directions to the liquor store, Mary Beth? It's uncivilized to be drinking coffee at twilight. One should see the day off with a cocktail, don't you think? I apologize for my wife's oversight. And I assure you, the next time you come to visit — as I hope you will, perhaps favoring us with one of your stories, Ren — that you'll find us in better circumstances to entertain guests properly."

"Ren would love to tell you a story, won't you, dear? It's what he does best," Mary Beth said.

"Tomorrow night? I don't think we've anything on our calendar, do we, Piper?" Braxton asked, his voice dripping sarcasm.

Mary Beth gave a delighted bounce in her chair. "We'd love to, wouldn't we, Ren? Eight o'clock all right?"

Braxton nodded.

Mary Beth scrawled on the back of an envelope she fished from her purse. "Here's our number if you have any problems with the cabin or need directions. And here," she scribbled furiously, "is how you get to the liquor store." She thrust the envelope into Braxton's hand. "We hope you'll be very happy here, Mr. Defoe."

"About the gas," Piper said. "How do I —"

"I forgot all about that," Ren said. "I'll be happy to show Braxton how to —"

Braxton waved his hand like an emperor excusing his subjects. "I'm hopeless with anything mechanical. Piper takes care of the practical matters."

Braxton turned to Jeff. "Play ball, Jeff?"

"No, sir. I'm not much interested in sports." He scuffed his sneakered toe against the porch boards.

"Ah. The intellectual type. Are you a storyteller, too?"

Jeff grinned. "No, sir, I'm not."

"Jeff is a musician," Mary Beth said. "And a good one, too. Why, this boy can play any instrument you can name and play it well. By ear!"

"Is that so? Will you give us a concert tomorrow night, Jeff?"

Jeff's blush started at the neckline of his Garth Brooks tee shirt and worked its way up, like a thermometer in July. "I just mess around with music, Mr. Defoe. I'm not all that good."

"I'd like to judge that for myself, if you don't mind," Braxton said while Ren followed Piper into the house.

Inside, Ren showed Piper where the gas water heater sat in its snug closet beneath the stairs. His knees creaked, he banged his elbows and fumbled everything he touched. A tiny glimmer of amusement flashed in Piper's eyes before she lowered them, then watched as he pointed out the valve and lit the pilot light.

She never spoke a word, only nodded when he said, "That's all there is to it," then promptly smacked his head against the door jamb as he extracted himself from the tight quarters. Embarrassed by his bumbling adolescent performance, he kept quiet as he followed her back to the porch.

A few minutes later, Braxton said his goodbyes from the comfort of his chair, and Piper walked the Wyatts to the edge of the porch. She kept her eyes downcast and said a soft, "Goodnight. I'm looking forward to your story."

Mary Beth babbled incessantly on their way back home. Ren learned years before how to skim the surface of his wife's conversation, picking up just enough key phrases to grab the gist while he indulged his own thoughts. This time he gleaned "creative people are weird"; "eccentric celebrities"; "tense couple."

The last phrase caught his attention.

"You thought they were tense?" he asked.

"Tense? You could cut it with a knife. Honestly, Ren, don't you pay attention to anything?"

"I was paying attention, and I noticed it, too. I'm just surprised we agreed. Why do you think they're tense with each other?"

"Who knows? She's kind of quiet for a celebrity's wife, don't you think? And I would have expected her to be wearing something elegant. Some designer thing, not Levi's and a tee shirt."

"To hang around a log cabin in the woods?"

She shrugged. "Well, no. Guess not. But he's so charming and articulate —"

"I bet he's a lot older than she is."

"Yeah, probably. Those celebrities always go for young snazzy wives. But she didn't seem to have much personality. Kind of boring."

Ren glanced at his wife. "She never had an opportunity to say anything. He talked almost nonstop. And you filled in the gaps."

Mary Beth glared at him.

"I think you're judging her too quickly," Ren said. "All we know about her is that she didn't buy any liquor, she's part Cherokee and she doesn't like shoes."

"You men are all alike," Mary Beth huffed.

"What's that supposed to mean?"

CHAPTER TWO

Braxton stared at the computer screen until he feared it would permanently imprint its image on his retinas. Everything he looked at from now on would be gray with a menu bar across the top and little red, blue and yellow icons beckoning him to "print," "file," "save."

Save what? His title? *Bloodlust.* One word. After almost two hours of staring at the gray, he turned off the computer, his defiance at not saving the word *Bloodlust* a shallow victory.

How long does it take to shop for groceries and stop by the package store?

Piper took off long before he'd sat down at the computer, as if she thought his effort was an exercise in futility. How many years had it been since he'd started his writing day without two Bloody Marys under his belt? Ten? Twelve? But she didn't understand. She wasn't a writer. Had no sense of the rituals necessary to free his creative spirit: setting the drink to the left of his keyboard, ashtray to the right. The thesaurus and dictionary within easy reach and his plot outline and character sketches opened to the appropriate parts — where he'd left off the day before.

Maybe the problem was he *hadn't* left off the day before; it had been months since he'd sat at the keyboard. When he'd packed up his writing materials in Los Angeles, he hadn't been able to find his outline or any of his preparation. All he could remember was the title.

He'd start fresh tomorrow, after he'd straightened out the mess she'd made of unpacking his writing things. After he'd acclimated to the cabin.

He wandered down the stairs, wondering what to do with himself. Wondering when the stuff they'd shipped from Los Angeles would arrive in North Carolina. His novel notebook would probably be in with them.

He fixed a cup of coffee, frowning at the quiver in his hands as he poured, then meandered toward the porch, stopping halfway out the screen door. A huge black bird sat on the porch railing, staring at him. The hair on the back of Braxton's neck prickled, and a shiver rippled down his spine.

He stomped his foot, almost sloshing coffee over the rim of his mug.

The bird didn't flinch.

"Shoo!"

Not a feather moved.

Braxton flapped his free arm wildly and took a threatening step toward the bird. It moved, but not as Braxton expected. It simply sidled down the rail a short way, blinking its eyes once.

Braxton turned away briefly to set his mug on the small round table.

When he turned back, the bird was gone.

He grabbed his coffee again, dropped into a rocking chair and looked across the yard, the quiet settling over him like a plastic bag placed over his head and tied around his neck. Smothering. Suffocating. Oh, the brook gurgled, a few birds twittered somewhere in the distance, and an insect droned nearby, but where were the comforting noises of doors slamming, brakes squealing or dogs barking?

Those sounds always wafted up the canyon to him in Los Angeles, muted by distance so they weren't annoying, just pleasant reminders of civilization. Even that dumpy little place he'd rented in Asheville when he was dating Piper had comforting sounds. And that's where he'd broken into publishing, where the first of his bestsellers had been born: *Street Stalker*.

This place was too cut off from the world, from the excitement of the city. Primitive.

A loud *ka-thunk* split the unnatural stillness. His hand jerked spasmodically, and the coffee splattered down his shirt front, burning the skin beneath. He twisted in his chair, heart thumping, and heard the refrigerator gurgle through the screen door. Another *ka-thunk*. Icemaker.

Jesus. This place'll drive me nuts.

The soft hum of an engine approached, growing louder. The Jeep bumped up the driveway and stopped. Piper got out of the car and walked to the back, letting the tailgate up.

She waved. "Help me unload?" she asked.

"You go to the package store?"

She nodded, so he went to help her, holding the wet part of his shirt away from his chest.

Her black hair was loosely drawn back into a ponytail, and she wore cut-off jeans and an over-size tee shirt like a teenager might. She hadn't even bothered with makeup.

He couldn't believe she'd gone to town like that. Most women her age were painstaking about their appearance. Didn't she care? Should the wife of a successful author run around in cut-offs? He shook his head, sneered and took two paper bags from her.

"How'd the writing go?" she asked moments later as she stowed away the groceries.

He began mixing a Bloody Mary without answering her.

"Quit kind of early, didn't you? You used to write from nine until five. And then quit only if I bugged you."

Braxton took a deep breath, trying to sound reasonable and pleasant. "Everything is disorganized. In the wrong place. The stuff I need is on the other side of the country. Plus, this quiet is unnerving."

"What are you missing?"

"Only my plot outline. Character sketches. All the research material. Nothing important."

"Maybe it's in the stuff we had shipped. Should be here by Friday."

"Then the writing will go better on Friday." He turned to go back onto the porch.

"I doubt it," she muttered.

He whirled around. "What'd you mean by that?"

She put down a bag of sugar and ran her hands over her eyes. Then she sighed. "Nothing. Sorry. I didn't mean to snipe. It's just that — I get tired of the excuses."

"What excuses?"

She put the canned goods away while she spoke. "You couldn't write this morning because your stuff wasn't in the right place and you didn't have all of it. A month or so ago, you didn't have that excuse. You organized your office on your own, but you still couldn't write."

"I suppose all the pressure I was under didn't count."

She turned to face him, her hand on her hip. "Now it's too quiet, too boring. In L.A., your social calendar was too full. This morning, you said you couldn't write unless you started your day off with two bloody Mary's. In L.A. —"

"Creative people have little rituals. Mine just happen to be —"

"In L.A.," she repeated, "most mornings you were too hungover from the night before to even look at a Bloody Mary until two. Then your Bloody Mary ritual lasted until three, three-thirty, till you finally went upstairs and stared at your monitor until five, then had to beat it out to the clubs to start the process all over again. Now, am I supposed to think you have the same urge to write that you used to have? Don't think so."

"Quite the analyst, aren't you?"

"I don't need to be."

"You didn't complain about the money."

Guilt flickered across Piper's face. Braxton pressed his advantage. "Sent a nice chunk of change home to Grandma every month for years. Sitting on your ass all day at home playing the artist —"

"That's not fair!" She slammed her hand down on the countertop like a gavel. "You wouldn't let me work."

"— puttering with your paints and your herb garden. And every single time I asked you to accompany me to a social function — and we both know how important *that* is in the publishing industry — it was like pulling teeth."

"All those superficial, back-stabbing —"

"You didn't want to dress up. Wanted to stay home and read. A wife like you is as much help as a concrete block and a length of chain to a drowning man."

She glared at him over her shoulder, a can of chicken-noodle soup halfway to its shelf.

For a moment, he thought she might aim it at his head.

"That's what you feel?" she asked.

"I'm right, aren't I?"

She sighed and her shoulders slumped. "I went when you asked me to, Braxton. No, I didn't want to go. The constant flow of booze. The drugs. But I went. I gritted my teeth, maybe, but I went." She put the soup on the shelf and turned to face him. "Then you stopped asking."

"Christ! I wonder why? Nothing like a bunch of people having fun, yukking it up, and one wet blanket looking down her nose at everyone else." He took a deep, satisfying swig of his drink.

"You insisted I stay home. Since I wasn't in the same celebrity league as the mighty Braxton Defoe, I wasn't qualified for a glamorous job. And you —"

"What would you do? Flip burgers? Check-out groceries? Sell your paintings?" He snorted. "I told you that degree in Fine Arts was a waste." She'd already set up her easel and paints in front of the living room's north window. When would she realize she had no gift for painting?

"But you couldn't have your wife work in an office or a gallery, could you? Too demeaning. What would people think? Always your bottom line — what would people think? Of your wife, house, car —"

"There's a responsibility that comes with fame."

"— if you didn't appear at the right party, if you didn't play the games. You got so caught up in it, you couldn't have written a decent shopping list!"

"But I sure wrote some bestsellers!" He chugged half of his drink.

"Yes, you did. Before you went 'Hollywood.' Well, Braxton, what must people think now? Everyone knows we sold the house —"

"Nobody knows."

"*Everyone* knows that we sold for less than market value because of your squandering," she said, her voice low and accusing, her lip raised in a sneer. "All those bigwigs you schmoozed up to, all the producers and directors and moguls and starlets you brown-nosed. They all know. It's a matter of public record. It was in the paper. Brax, we had to sell off your Mercedes to get out from under the payment. All those quick trips to Vegas, all those losses you kept piling up. Your agent dumped you. Harbor House refuses to give you any more advances, and the last book you had under contract was so bad they didn't even publish it. They didn't want their name on the spine."

Braxton found himself breathing in ragged gasps. His fingers clenched his glass so hard that they ached, and he wondered if the glass might shatter from the pressure, spewing Bloody Mary all over Piper's angry features.

Whirr.

A low *hum* thrummed in his head. Pressure built behind his eyes, pushing outward, as if there wasn't enough room inside his skull for all that was in there.

An image, fleeting but crystal clear, of his fingers around her throat, the delicate windpipe collapsing beneath his hands as he squeezed until she went limp, splatters of glistening red flecking her face.

Squeezing —

The image evaporated.

He felt dizzy. Depleted.

He turned and staggered to the porch, cradling his drink carefully so it didn't wind up on his shirt like the coffee had earlier.

As he emptied the glass, the screen door creaked open behind him, and his wife's feet padded softly across the decking planks.

"Braxton, I honestly felt coming here was a good idea. I thought you might be able to center yourself again if you were away from all the distractions, all the obligations you had in Los Angeles. But if we're going to be at each other's throat constantly —"

He looked up quickly, startled by her reference to the mental image he'd experienced only moments ago.

"— it's not going to work. Maybe we should just forget the whole thing. Before we hurt each other more. Before we destroy each other completely." Her eyes fluttered closed. A muscle spasmed in the hollow of her throat.

He sighed, licked the inside of his empty glass where a red smear of tomato juice remained. "We're locked into it now, Piper. Financially, there are no other choices. In case you haven't noticed, my royalty checks keep getting smaller. There's money to last a year or so. If I don't produce a saleable manuscript by then, I go belly up. And if you're thinking of leaving me, you can forget it.

You forced me to this hellhole. You'll damn well suffer through it with me."

"I wouldn't leave you when you're down, Brax. Not unless you want me to. You know that." Her voice quivered.

He looked up at her, and a wave of guilt washed over him. "I know. And you know I still love you."

She looked him in the eye, nodded, then went back inside.

CHAPTER THREE

The Wyatts pulled up next to the cabin at eight o'clock. Piper was relieved to see that Braxton was charming, friendly, talkative and seemed genuinely pleased that Jeff had accompanied his parents. She'd never seen him relate to a young person before.

Braxton arranged the rocking chairs into a circle and offered his guests wine, instructing Piper to serve them.

When she went back outside moments later, Braxton had his arm around Jeff's shoulder, and the two were engrossed in animated conversation.

"Braxton, excuse me," she said. "The cupboard is stuck. I can't get it open."

"Next to the fridge?" Ren asked.

She nodded.

"There's a trick to that. Let me show you." He followed her into the kitchen, showed her how the wood swelled on damp days and where to apply pressure at the top while pulling the cabinet knob on the bottom. "Once the heat is on, the wood will contract, and you won't have this problem."

She smiled her thanks, her gaze fixed on a small leather pouch that had worked its way out of his chambray shirt. It hung from his neck on a slender strip of rawhide.

He cupped the amulet in his hand protectively. "It is my source," he said, tucking it back into his shirt.

She saw a flash of black beadwork as he replaced his amulet. "But you said you are Tlingit, not *Ani-Yunwiya*." She couldn't stop staring at the small lump beneath his shirt button. "Not one of 'The People'," she translated, using the Cherokee phrase for their tribe.

"No, I'm not one of 'The People'. But many traditions are similar."

She looked up into his eyes. He looked back at her warily, as if daring her to ask any questions.

"It is my source," he repeated.

She was intrigued — as much by his refusal to discuss it as by his possible meaning: *my source*. She was tempted to ask him about it anyway, but her Cherokee tradition — in which her grandmother had meticulously trained her — held her back: A person's privacy was a sacred thing, and must be respected.

She nodded, took the wine glasses from the cupboard and served her guests. Ren followed her out with a soft drink for his son.

"So, Storyteller, what tale do you have for us tonight?" Braxton asked, balancing his wine glass on the arm of his chair.

Ren smiled. "With all due respect, Mr. Defoe, I would feel ridiculous telling an author of your stature one of my simple legends."

Braxton laughed heartily, obviously enjoying Ren's deference. "Thanks. But think of it as professional courtesy. Shop talk. And call me Braxton."

Ren grinned, nodded, then sipped his wine. He put his hand briefly over the minute lump in his shirt and closed his eyes for a fleeting moment. Then he lifted his head, looked at his audience and launched into a legend about the Cherokee Rose.

As he spoke, Ren's tone changed from his soft-spoken, slightly hesitant voice to a rich timbre that swirled around his audience, lifting them into the drama, then settling them gently back down with his whispers. His voice became as much an instrument of his vocation as a preacher's or an actor's. Piper felt as if she were, indeed, watching an actor, one who had slipped into his character as effortlessly as one slips into a coat. The shy, laid-back teacher had been replaced by a powerful stage presence.

"This story takes place during the time now known as The Trail of Tears," Ren began. "As the Cherokee people were being herded out of North Carolina like cattle, one young warrior, Adahy — which means 'He who lives in the woods' — wanted to stay in the mountains and fight the white soldiers rather than be forced from his homeland to the barren wastelands of Oklahoma.

"Adahy's mother, a strong-willed and conniving woman, ordered him to accompany the tribe. He refused. So Adahy's mother developed a ruse to change her son's mind. She said that the parents of a young maiden in whom he had been interested had agreed to consider him as a potential husband for her when he got to Oklahoma. Because they had already left on the Trail of Tears, Adahy was unable to confirm this.

"Adahy almost fell for his mother's story, but at the last moment, he became suspicious of this good fortune. He confronted his mother and forced an admission from her that she had lied. He became enraged. In his fury, he killed her."

Ren paused for dramatic effect. When he resumed, his voice sounded professorial, as if he were lecturing his students.

"Matricide," he explained, "is the most grievous of all murders for a person to bear. The most damaging psychologically, more so when committed by a son. Think of Norman Bates in Hitchcock's classic movie, 'Psycho.'"

Braxton blinked, then sipped his wine.

Piper was amazed at the almost tangible retreat of the professor when the actor reclaimed his spot at center stage. Even Ren's facial expressions changed as if he were taking on a new persona.

"Those few members of the tribe that still remained in North Carolina were horrified. They stripped him of all honor and cursed him. The curse decreed that he was condemned to live eternally in the mountains he had profaned, living like a beast of the forest, thinking like the lowest life form, with neither love nor companionship to comfort him, without fire to warm him, without a spirit guide to protect him. Any humans he came across would disdain him because he was a stain on humanity. He was no longer one of The People.

"Adahy scoffed at the curse, and to show his disregard for both their power and their curse, he slit open his mother's wrist, drank of her blood and spat a small portion onto the earth."

Ren crouched down, arms extended and fingers flexed as if warding off evil spirits only he could see. He revolved on his heels a quarter turn.

Piper felt the muted, rhythmic vibrations of an imaginary

drum and could almost hear the tinkle of the shaman's ankle bells.

"The shaman cried at such desecration. It was said that once a man had drunk human blood, nothing else could sustain him. Adahy had damned himself more than The People ever could.

"Adahy fled into the woods, and his people began trodding the Trail of Tears." He paused again, stood and turned his hands palms up.

When he spoke, his voice was soft and melodic. "The Cherokee mothers were so distraught at leaving their beloved homeland that they were unable to help their children survive the arduous journey. The elders prayed to the Great Spirit to send forth a sign to give the mothers strength which would, in turn, allow the young ones to live. The next day, a rose — white for their tears — grew wherever a mother's tear fell. The roses had golden centers, symbolizing the gold taken from the Cherokee land by the white men, and each flower had seven leaves on its stem, one for each of the seven Cherokee clans. On occasion, a Cherokee Rose grew with only one leaf on its stem. This was where a tear had fallen in remembrance of Adahy's mother, slain by the son she had so loved. Even today, the wild Cherokee Rose grows along the Trail of Tears from North Carolina to eastern Oklahoma."

When the last reverberations of his powerful baritone had dissipated, the Storyteller bowed his head slightly, touched the lump in his shirt again, and looked at his audience with a smile that was once again shy.

Piper glanced over at Braxton; he looked totally mesmerized and sat stunned for a moment. Then he clapped enthusiastically.

"Told you he was good, didn't I?" Mary Beth said. She beamed, her face flushed from the wine.

"Bravo!" Braxton said. "Well done. No wonder you're known as 'The Storyteller'. Was that original? Or legend?"

Piper hid her amazement; showing appreciation for others efforts had never been Braxton's strong suit.

"Both," Red answered. "I enjoy the challenge of taking true

stories, which both the origin of the Cherokee Rose and Adahy are, and weaving other stories around them."

"You mean legend — not true stories — don't you?" asked Braxton.

Ren fidgeted. "People around here accept Adahy as a true being."

Braxton snickered. "It's a Native American version of the vampire," Braxton said. "Nothing more. But I applaud your imagination."

Ren shrugged and sipped his wine.

Mary Beth piped up. "Every so often, small animals are found whose blood has been drained. It's always blamed on Adahy."

Braxton glanced quickly at Jeff, as if for confirmation. The boy nodded.

"Plus, there was a toddler," Mary Beth continued, "who disappeared from the campground four or five years ago. Never did find a trace of him."

Braxton snorted. "That sounds like a handy excuse for a hick police department. Any unsolved mysteries get chalked up to your local boogeyman."

Ren's head lifted, and his jaw squared in apparent offense.

"Ren's best friend, Frankie Madigan, is our sheriff," Mary Beth explained. "But whether you believe in Adahy or not, it's still a good story. And besides, Ren makes up most of his stories as he goes along, don't you, honey?"

Ren smiled and gave a little shrug.

"Well, you've got quite a gift." Braxton drained his glass and thrust it at Piper. "More wine for our guests." Then he turned back to Ren. "Why do you touch your chest before you start and after you finish? Are you praying?"

Ren bit his lower lip and nodded his head slowly. "Sort of. "More like a tradition. Or superstition."

Piper tried to get Ren's attention as she collected the glasses, to warn him somehow that Braxton would not understand such things. He looked everywhere but at her.

Jeff, however, changed the topic just as Braxton opened his mouth, his eyebrows arched cynically.

"How about you, Mr. Defoe? Will you give us one of your

stories?" Jeff asked.

Braxton ran his fingers quickly through his hair. "Nope. Not me. I'm a writer — not a storyteller."

"They're the same thing," Mary Beth said.

"Not at all. I need to see the words strung out in front of me. I need to be able to think about them, rearrange them, delete, type over, insert. Sometimes I shift whole pages or chapters around before I'm satisfied. A word once said aloud cannot be retracted. Do you write, Ren?"

"I've dabbled around with it. Maybe someday..."

Braxton rose from his chair, reached into his pocket and pulled out a harmonica which he held out to Jeff. "Anyway," he said, "one story gives you something to think about. Something to savor, even long after it's finished. What we need right now is music. Here, Jeff, honor me with a tune. Your mother said you could play any instrument, and I don't have a piano or a guitar laying around, so..."

Jeff flushed, then glanced quickly at his father as if seeking an "okay."

Ren nodded. But he looked displeased.

Jeff took the harmonica, thought for a moment, then launched into a melody with haunting, intricate trills and lingering notes.

Piper smiled. The boy was good. No, the boy was gifted. The strains of his music seemed to bring the very air alive, much as his father's voice had moments before. They were both artists in their chosen medium.

When Jeff finished, hanging his head shyly, all but Ren applauded with zeal. Braxton clamped him warmly on the shoulder, a look of genuine admiration on his face. "Good job, son!" he said.

Jeff mumbled a soft "thanks" and handed the harmonica back to Braxton. "You, sir?"

Braxton smiled at the boy, winked, and ripped into a simple song that he played with consummate skill.

Piper headed into the house before Braxton finished, but not before she caught the look of respect on Jeff's face. When she returned, her tray laden with Gouda cheese, some crackers and wine, Braxton was telling the Wyatts about their life in Los

Angeles.

It sounded glamorous and exciting as he told it, not the nerve-shattering, jangling existence Piper remembered. But Mary Beth hung on every word like a star-struck groupie and interrupted with frequent questions. Piper noticed that Ren smiled and nodded occasionally, but he wasn't really paying attention.

Piper didn't know *how* she knew that.

After saying goodbye to their guests, Braxton carried the tray into the kitchen and stood quietly, leaning against the refrigerator. Piper felt him watching her as she tidied up. "Amazing to be able to do that extemporaneously," he said.

"Do what?" she asked.

"Tell stories like that, off the top of your head. It's quite a gift. I wonder how big a repertoire of stories he has?"

It was a rhetorical question, and Piper treated it as such. But this seemed like a good opportunity to offer him some encouragement. "You've got quite a gift, too, Brax," she said, rinsing the glasses. "And I think that when you've gotten used to being here, after we've settled in a bit, you'll be writing the way you used to. Remember? You used to get up in the middle of the night to jot down a thought before it was lost forever." She laughed out loud. "I remember you suddenly whipping your penlight from your pocket once in a theater. You began scribbling furiously because a line in the movie had triggered an idea in your head. The usher got all huffy and tried to confiscate your penlight, remember?"

Braxton chuckled. "Yeah, the little twit. The proverbial ninety-pound weakling. But he *didn't* get the penlight, and we *did* watch the movie." Braxton leaned against the door jamb thoughtfully. After a moment, he asked, "So you really think this is going to work? You don't think I'm burned out forever?"

"I think it's going to work if you let it. I think you lost your passion in L.A." Piper wiped her hands on the dish towel, then looped it through the refrigerator handle. "Maybe Ren and his stories will inspire you. He's a lot like you used to be — intense, perhaps even obsessive, at least when he's telling a story. Maybe you should spend time with him. Become friends."

"Uh-huh. But how about that kid?" Braxton said. "He's

terrific. Talk about a talent! And it's refreshing to see a teenager who doesn't have purple hair or hoops through his nose and God only knows where else."

A look appeared on his face that stabbed Piper's memory. Wistful. Braxton had been an idealist when they'd met, with a burning passion to leave his mark on the world. He'd always seemed happiest when writing, and just as the Storyteller assumed a different persona when telling his tale, so had Braxton when writing a novel. His characters consumed his mind, eventually earning him the reputation of being one of the most character oriented authors of the decade.

"Piper, have you heard that Adahy legend before? From your grandmother or someone?"

"Not that I recall. But I do remember hearing about the Cherokee Rose. Why?"

Braxton's wistful expression vanished and his face took on the feral look she'd become accustomed to in recent years. His eyes glinted harshly from inside their dark circles. He simply said, "We'll see," in a flat monotone, turned and strode up the stairs, an aggressive man with things to accomplish.

"We'll see what?" she asked herself aloud when he'd gone.

To Piper's sleep-blurred sight, the alarm clock's numbers shone a sinister red, like animal eyes hypnotized by headlights. She rubbed the sleep away and squinted: 1:43.

What woke her?

She lay in the dark, ears straining for any noise that might have penetrated her sleep. But there was nothing out of the ordinary: the 'click' of the clock dial revolving to 1:44; the soughing of the wind through the pines outside the window; Braxton's breathing, deep and regular, beside her on their bed.

In the vague light, Braxton looked younger than at any time in recent memory; his face showed no hint of slack dissipation or the alcohol-induced gauntness that had become normal. Instead, his expression was of such boyish innocence that Piper felt a tenderness toward him that she hadn't felt in years.

She remembered how she used to snuggle up against him, molding her naked body along his and crossing her left leg over his limbs. It had been a long time since they'd shared such intimacy.

It reminded her how reassuring human touch could be — warm, sleep inducing.

But the face that rose in her mind's eye as she drifted off to sleep wasn't Braxton's.

He smelled of sunshine and pine needles, and felt as permanent as the mountains as he pulled her back against his warmth.

His tongue traced a path of wet warmth down the length of her neck and across her shoulders; his hair tickled her cheek as if he were drawing the tip of a feather lightly — teasingly — across her skin.

When his hands found her breasts, shock waves of pleasure trilled through her and a groan started at the back of her throat, then passed through her lips before she could contain it.

She sat straight up, her breath rapid and raggedy, a blast of cold air washing over her. Her hand brushed sweat-soaked hair off her forehead, then she watched the eyelet curtains snapping crisply in the breeze from the opened window.

But she'd closed the window before going to bed!

Throwing back the covers, she shivered, swung her legs over the edge of the bed...and screamed!

In the murky gray of pre-dawn, two eyes blazed at her through the darkness, the lower face hidden in deep shadow.

She gasped and propelled herself backward onto the bed, realizing just as she landed back on the pillows that it was Braxton standing in the corner, glaring.

"Jesus, Braxton! Why are you standing in the corner like that? You scared me half to death."

It was Braxton...yet it wasn't. There was something indefinably different in the eyes. Something hard. Vacant.

He tipped back his head — his gaze never leaving her face —

and drank from a glass tumbler. Her nose tingled from the smoky scent of scotch.

He slammed the empty tumbler onto the dresser and smirked as she flinched at the *clank* of glass connecting with wood. Then he turned, headed for the door and slipped out into the hallway, stopping long enough to give her an appraising once over, then disappeared.

A pungent mustiness lingered in the air.

Piper slid lower in the bed, pulled the blankets up around her neck and clutched them tightly around her, wide-eyed, watching the first fingers of light inch across the ceiling.

CHAPTER FOUR

After that night, Piper began rising earlier in the morning and striking out for long, meandering walks in the woods, a habit which annoyed Braxton at first, but which he quickly realized worked to his advantage.

He enjoyed not having her disapproving eyes there to sour the taste of his Bloody Marys. She always seemed to be hovering somewhere at a distance like a frightened little sparrow staying just out of reach of the cat. She'd toss back her long black hair casually and pretend to be engrossed in a book or her painting, but her eyes watched his every move, reproachfully. Most annoying of all, she would creep up behind him in her bare feet, and stare — at a safe distance, of course — at his monitor, then shake her head with disappointment when she'd finished reading.

But that's something I can put a stop to.

First thing this morning, he would rearrange his office. Place the desk so the backside of the monitor faced the doorway. That way, he could see her coming, could switch documents before she rounded the corner of the desk and started snooping with those black, prying eyes. But first...breakfast.

Vodka, tomato juice, a dash of Tabasco. He snapped off a stalk of celery, dunked it into the glass and used it as a swizzle stick, then ambled out the door.

It was a beautiful morning. Dew still glistened on the grass and the sun hung in a cloudless "Carolina Blue" sky. Having his Bloody Mary on the front porch had become his morning tradition. And although he still missed the excitement of Los Angeles, he was finding more than one advantage to being in Crooked Creek.

The environment actually tweaked his imagination. Morning mists, thick and gloomy woods, evening fog, even the way the thunderstorms rolled over the mountains and broke with savage intensity — these were motivating to a dark fiction writer. He didn't have to conjure up a creepy atmosphere — he lived in one.

This past week, his creativity had surged in an unstoppable stream. Piper was right — not that he'd admit it — when she'd said it was the kind of place conducive to writing. He sipped his drink thoughtfully.

Even the interminable quiet that had unhinged him when he'd first arrived now seemed calming. As he'd started having horrible nightmares beginning their first night in the cabin and continuing still, he needed calm, especially in the mornings.

They were such weird dreams, dreams from which he awoke panting — sometimes sweating as if he'd been running — dreams alive with vivid, gruesome images that lingered in his mind for hours. Maniacal eyes that followed his every movement. Terror stricken faces on bodies that were twisted into unnatural shapes. Cries for help, howls of pain, shrieks of fear. Hands pulling him this way, shoving him that way, poking and prodding and scratching.

Yet sometimes he suspected the dreams were a result of some creative breakthrough his mind was struggling over, some revelation for his novel. Something that would become clear in time. He'd jotted the dreams down, hoping to see a pattern forming, a plotline. Not yet. Soon, perhaps.

In a weak moment, still shaking from a particularly frightening nightmare, he'd stupidly told Piper about it, how he'd been trapped inside a tiny cave — barely big enough to turn around in — and someone sealed up the entrance. He had neither food nor water. He kept screaming for help, but his voice bounced back off the cavern walls, filling his own ears, but unheard by rescuers. Yet he heard someone laughing at a distance, a deranged, uncontrolled cackling laugh, as if they were laughing at him.

What on earth had possessed him to share that dream with her? How could he have been so dumb? Did she console him? Offer sympathy?

No.

The disloyal, ignorant bitch accused him of having erratic mood swings. Said his nightmares — combined with his moods and heavy drinking — were steering him toward a nervous breakdown. Him! Braxton Defoe!

He shook his head, took a cigarette from his shirt pocket, and lit it.

God! His nails looked awful. The cuticles were ragged, the nails too long and chipped in places. This place might have nice mornings, but he doubted they'd have a manicurist.

He chuckled at the absurdity of it all, raised his glass to his lips and found it empty. Damn. He hadn't really even tasted the drink. He rocked forward, planning to go inside and refill his glass when he saw it.

Saw them, rather. Blackbirds. Maybe crows. Hell, what did he know about birds? Seven — no, eight — of them, pecking the ground in front of the porch. He stood and walked to the railing.

Corn lay scattered on the grass, and the pesky birds pecked it up, taking a kernel into their mouths and throwing their heads back, their nasty little eyes gleaming black in the dappled sunlight. Piper had probably tossed the corn out, encouraging them to eat. Well, let her clean up the bird shit they'd leave. He turned to get his second Bloody Mary, and his glance settled on a pan set on the far railing.

The metal pan held bits of something like dry dog food and heels of stale bread. He swatted the pan with his hand, scattering the food into the side yard. The birds squawked at the sudden clattering of the pie plate as it clanked off a small rock and rolled toward the edge of the brook. Then they flew over and began pecking at the bread.

Braxton stomped inside and refilled his glass. He washed a stalk of celery, peeled off the strings, then ran a paring knife down its length. Holding the halved stalks together, he cut it midway on the diagonal.

The knife slipped. A thin seam of red materialized on his finger; the seam widened, welled up, then bubbled like a natural spring.

Whirr. A soft buzzing started in his head, like the soft hum of his computer.

The blood seemed hypnotic. Miraculous.

He held his finger up, vertically, in front of his eyes. The blood seeped down over the first joint of his index finger and flowed into the ridges of his knuckle. Amazing. Its color was so pure — truer than any ruby. Thick and alive. Sensuous.

He laughed out loud. Once when he'd still been smoking dope, he'd become mesmerized by a piece of burlap. He'd delighted in its rough texture, the way light and shadow played on the weave. He'd probably said "Whoa!" fifty or sixty times.

He held his finger under the cold water faucet until the bleeding stopped, then swizzled his drink with the celery stalk and headed back toward the door.

It had gotten considerably darker outside. The lawn was partially covered by dark shade, the shadow of a large cloud that had moved in from the mountain.

Strange. A few minutes ago the sky had been perfectly clear.

He returned to the porch, drink in hand, and found another large black bird perched on the same section of rail. Or was it the same one? The bird opened its ugly beak, cawed once, then flew off.

Braxton drained his second Bloody Mary faster than his first, fixed another, and took it up to his office.

His computer was on. The familiar gray screen was highlighted with two words at the top, centered and underlined: *Murder Mountain.*

Directly below it, in standard manuscript format was: by Braxton Defoe

The rest of the screen was blank.

Braxton set his drink down on the corner of the desk. He scratched his head.

I don't remember writing that.

He was always careful to save everything and shut down his computer when he finished writing for the day. He replayed the night before in his mind as he pulled out his chair and reached for his drink. *Let's see, Ren told a tale about two neighboring farmers involved in a long-term land dispute. The Wyatts left about ten-thirty. I updated my secret weapon. I must've been pretty well-plastered. I remember having a problem finding the file. Couldn't remember what name I'd saved it under.*

He quickly ran through his file list, found his secret weapon, and accessed it. Yep, he'd made his entry last night. There were a few misspellings, some format goofs. He'd been pickled, all right.

But he would never leave his computer on — not with the sudden electrical storms. It was too risky. And where did "Murder Mountain" come from? It was good. He liked it. Liked the alliterative ring. But he sure as hell didn't remember writing it. And usually he didn't start with a title, anyway. Usually the title idea came to him some two or three-hundred pages into the book. *Bloodlust* was the one exception.

Well, shit. His whole life had changed. Maybe his way of writing was changing, too. He looked through his list of files for some character sketches, plot ideas, anything he might have written last night to go along with the title, but found nothing.

Jesus, maybe I should cut back on the booze.

He saved the title page to the hard drive anyway, turned off his computer and studied the small office, trying to decide how to protect his privacy and make the most of limited square footage.

By the time Piper returned, his desk sat catty-corner in the small room, facing the doorway, his supplies all rearranged to his liking, and he had three pages done on *Murder Mountain.*

She stopped in the doorway, a look of surprise on her face, her eyes taking in the room's changes.

"Don't like it?" Braxton asked.

"I don't need to like it. It's your space. But the room is a little small to have the desk angled. You'll have to be careful getting through that tiny space." She indicated the narrow opening between the corner of the desk and his bookcase.

"Did you use my computer last night or this morning?"

"Me? No, of course not. Why?"

"It was on when I came in this morning. Something written on it that I don't remember writing."

"You were pretty well-soused last night. Probably just forgot."

He nodded. She might be lusting after the schmaltzy Storyteller, she might be thinking of betraying him, but she wasn't a liar. Never had been. He *had* been drunk last night. Probably had written the title in a stupor and forgot to shut down the computer. No harm done. Actually, now that he thought about it, he liked the title *Murder Mountain* better than *Bloodlust.*

She turned to leave.

"Piper?"

She stopped and looked back over her shoulder at him.

"Don't put food out for those damn birds anymore. They give me the willies. Nasty critters. If you feel the need to feed something, buy one of those hummingbird feeders or something."

"What birds?" she asked.

"Blackbirds. Crows. I don't know what they are, but they're ugly, and we'll have bird shit all over the porch."

He turned back to his computer. When he glanced back up, she was gone.

He wrote for a few more hours, saved his files, shut down the computer and ambled down the stairs. Piper was curled up on the couch, engrossed in a paperback. He fixed a Thermos and a drink, took the car keys off the peg by the door, then drove off. A drive sounded like a good way to unwind.

Before he knew it, he was pulling into the Wyatts' dooryard.

Susannah was on the phone with her girlfriend when she heard a vehicle pull into the driveway. She recognized the Jeep right away, saw Mr. Defoe get out from behind the wheel and look around. The garage door was open, and both stalls were empty. *Probably thinks no one's at home.* This was her chance. She wasn't going to flub it.

"Gotta go," she babbled into the phone. "Got company. Talk to you later." She slammed the phone down and raced for the front door. She stopped, glanced quickly in the hallway mirror, fluffed up her hair, tugged the neckline of her pink tank top lower, then sauntered casually onto the porch. He'd gotten back inside the car and closed his door.

"Hey there, Mr. Defoe!" she called, waving. He looked up and watched her approach, a slow smile spreading across his face.

"Hi. You *are* Mr. Defoe, aren't you?" she asked, leaning into his opened window. She didn't wait for an answer. "I'm not supposed to know a famous author is rentin' our log cabin. Mama's afraid I'll spread the news all over town and you'll be plagued with fans. But I overhear stuff. You know how it is." She smiled.

He looks a whole lot better than the day they arrived. Actually, he's kinda sexy-looking. For an old fart.

"And you are?" He returned her appraisal.

"Susannah Wyatt."

"I like the way you say that. 'Sooozannnah.' Drawn out till it has about six syllables."

She giggled. "I'm the daughter my folks probably failed to mention."

"Why anyone would want to keep someone as lovely as Susannah Wyatt a secret, I can't imagine."

She leaned farther in the window so he could see her cleavage better, and whispered. "I make them feel old. Daddy says I'm responsible for every single one of his gray hairs." She winked.

Braxton chuckled. "I bet you are, too. I take it they aren't home?"

"Not at the moment. Daddy's not due home until six-ish, but Mama'll be back any minute."

"And Jeff? That's who I really wanted to talk to," Braxton said.

"Why?"

Braxton looked surprised. "He's an interesting young man, that's why. Very talented. Is he home?"

"No. I'm talented, too."

"I'm sure. Do you play an instrument?"

"Piano," she lied. "Why don't you come inside to wait?"

He started to say something, then apparently changed his mind. "Thanks anyway, but I'd...probably better not."

She wrinkled her nose at him and smiled. "If you're thinking about 'appearances' and all that stuff, you needn't worry. My parents trust me completely. And we would, of course, leave the front door open. Or we could sit on the porch." She shrugged. "I've never gotten to talk to a celebrity before. Or anyone as... sophisticated as you are."

"If you're sure it's okay. Excuse me." He waited for her to step back so he could open the door.

They strolled up the driveway together; then Susannah led the way up the porch stairs, conscious of the effect her cut-off jeans and swaying hips had on middle-aged men. And she'd practiced often enough on these very same stairs to get the maximum amount of mileage out of seven steps. Worked every time.

Besides, she had him pegged. Defoe's interest in bed-bouncing had been the hottest headline in every gossip magazine and celebrity rag until last summer. Then the photos of Braxton and his bevy of starlets disappeared from the tabloid pages overnight, replaced by one-liners that he was in rehab, detox, and bankruptcy court. Boring shit.

If the starlets didn't want him, that was cool. Susannah didn't want his money — she wanted his contacts. The guy still had to know people, right? The kind of people who would get her out of this burg, the kind who would take some T&A in trade for a few introductions.

Oh, yeah. Braxton Defoe was fair game.

And she felt like hunting.

She held the door open and smiled slowly as he brushed past her into the refreshing coolness of her living room.

Mary Beth steered carefully past the Defoe's Jeep as she pulled her Bronco into the garage, hoping it was Piper visiting rather than Braxton. She wouldn't want to be embarrassed by her wildcat daughter.

She'd read of Defoe's reputation with the ladies. Now that she knew him in person, of course, she saw it for the petty gossip it was. Some women simply didn't recognize real charm. She'd felt herself falling under his spell once or twice: He had a way of lavishing attention on you that made you feel special, made you feel he was addressing all of his comments to you, when, in fact, he was talking to whoever was around. Most women, less worldly women than she, would misconstrue his attentions and think he was hitting on them.

Like Susannah.

The thought hit her like a sucker punch. Susannah had been in heat since she'd first sprouted boobs.

No, it would not do for Susannah to be alone with him. God

only knew what she might do.

She turned off the ignition, grabbed her purse and hurried into the house.

Susannah was sprawled on one end of the couch, one leg dangling over the end, the other stretched out atop the cushions, her polished toes wiggling at Braxton, who sat on the other end leering at her. Her daughter looked like a hooker.

Braxton's eyes were bloodshot and his gaze so glued on Susannah that he didn't even look up when Mary Beth tromped in. He was speaking, words slurred together as if he'd spent most of the afternoon drinking, and a large wet spot stained the front of his blue Ralph Lauren shirt, where his drink had dripped. "— only too happy to introduce you, Susannah, my dear. I know all the right people, and they're always looking for new talent."

"Hello, Braxton. This is a surprise," Mary Beth said.

Braxton wobbled his head around and was obviously surprised.

Susannah closed her legs.

"There you are! I've been waiting to see you," Braxton said, rising to his feet. He swayed slightly. "Your lovely daughter has been amusing me while I waited. I hope that's all right."

With her gaze riveted on Susannah, Mary Beth snapped, "Guess it depends on what she was amusing you with."

"Mama!" Susannah's cheeks turned bright red. Not with embarrassment, Mary Beth guessed, but anger.

"Sorry," Mary Beth said to Braxton. "To what do we owe the pleasure?" She tossed her purse onto the chair.

"Actually, I was hoping to get to know Jeff better. A very impressive young man. And I also wanted to arrange for some fire wood to be delivered. The nights are turning cooler, and Piper has always enjoyed having a fire. Can you recommend someone?" His eyes were glassy.

"Sure. I'll get you the number. Be just a minute. Susannah, come with me."

Mary Beth crossed the living room and took the phone book off its shelf near the breakfast nook. "Susannah!" she called again. She found Billy Dale Wilson's number and scribbled it on a piece of message paper from the cube by the phone.

Susannah sauntered into the kitchen. Her face was as surly as an Elvis impersonator's, her ruby lips curled into a sneer. "What?"

"You've been drinking!"

"I had a sip of Mr. Defoe's gin and tonic. I asked for it. Always wondered what it tasted like."

"You want to try alcohol, you ask Daddy or me. Not a strange middle-aged man. A guest in our house! What must he think? You sit down right here, young lady. I'll deal with you in a minute." Mary Beth yanked a chair out from under the breakfast table, put her hand on Susannah's shoulder and pressed her into the chair. "Stay put." She yanked up on Susannah's straps to hoist the knit top to a more modest height.

Smiling, Mary Beth went back into the living room and thrust the phone number into Braxton's hand. "Here you go," she said.

"Thanks so much. Piper and I are looking forward to you and Ren coming tomorrow night. He never runs out of stories, does he? And your daughter is welcome to join us."

"I'm sure she has plans. She wouldn't enjoy sitting around with us old folks." Mary Beth thought she'd sounded less than gracious, so she quickly added, "But thank you for asking." She walked him to the door, watched him stumble down the driveway and start the Jeep.

The Jeep's engine purred to life, and he executed a flawless three-point turnaround, then headed the car down the driveway.

Ah, jealousy rears its ugly head, even amongst the simple folks.

The daughter was a luscious peach, ripe for the picking. The mother? She'd already started to wither, the once-round curves succumbing to the laws of gravity, the flat belly now a curve itself. Susannah was short. Fully packed. Give her twenty years, and she would be as dumpy as her mother.

But at the moment, she was perfect. And now was what counted. Mary Beth knew that. That was why she was jealous. Hmmm. An interesting idea. Might be able to use it in *Bloodlust.* No, what had he decided to call it? *Murder Mountain.* Mother-daughter rivalry might provide a nice little plot twist. Might have to research that. And he knew just where to start.

Whirr.

Another image crossed his mind: Mary Beth on her hands and knees, her face streaked with tears, cowering, shaking, pleading.

Ren barely got through the door before Mary Beth spilled her concern that Susannah might embarrass them by trying to seduce Braxton.

"Look, honey," he said, tossing his briefcase onto the table, "I know Susannah's champing at the bit, and I'm not crazy about it, either. But she's not a bad kid —"

"She's not a kid, dammit. Open your eyes."

"You know what I meant."

"Streetwalkers wear more than she was when Braxton was here. And enough makeup to hide Tammy Faye Baker under. She looked like a tramp." Mary Beth slammed the pot onto the counter, rattling the canisters.

"Dressing like a tramp doesn't necessarily make you a tramp, honey. You ought to see the way the girls in my classes dress. It's shameful."

"If you're not selling, you don't advertise."

"Then do something about it, dammit! Don't just whine to me. You *are* her mother."

"And you'll back me up?"

"Absolutely. You know my feelings. She's got to get her life together. She ought to be in college, or at least working. It's unconscionable for her to lie around all day painting her nails, watching Oprah and waiting for Mr. Right to fall in her lap to take her away from all this." He grabbed a beer from the fridge and took a long gulp, then combed his hair back with his fingers while he tried to catch his breath. He didn't need this crap. Not now. "Did...did you take twenty dollars out of my wallet this morning?"

"Of course not. Why?"

"Somebody did. I thought Jeff learned his lesson the last time."

Mary Beth looked at him for a moment, then went back to

slicing carrots. "He swore he'd never do it again. You probably miscounted." She stopped slicing for a moment and gazed off. "Thank God Braxton's such a gentleman. At least we don't have to worry about him taking her up on her offer." Mary Beth turned to look at him. "We don't, do we?"

Ren loosened his tie and chose his words with care. "Whatever else he may be, Braxton isn't stupid. He's not going to get mixed up with jailbait."

"She's not jailbait anymore — she's eighteen. She just had a birthday, remember?" Mary Beth glared at him, took another beer from the refrigerator and thrust it into his hand.

"Of course, I remember." He rubbed his eyes. "A Freudian slip. Makes me feel old."

"Me, too." She patted his hand. "Anyway, I'm not going to let her go with us tomorrow night. Maybe we shouldn't go anymore, either. Maybe it's bad politics to get socially involved with your tenants."

Ren's beer stopped halfway to his mouth while he mulled that over. Finally, he took a long swig. He needed another sip to quiet the quiver in his stomach.

He pulled the amulet out of his shirt and held it for a long moment, enjoying the warmth it generated, like a rock that had absorbed the midday sun. His breathing slowed, his heartbeat returned to a rhythmic *thub-dub*, his mind erased all images. He became centered.

"Susannah will stay home tomorrow night. There's no sense in asking for trouble." Piper's face drifted across Ren's mind, soft yet strong, wise and innocent. "But we'll go as planned."

CHAPTER FIVE

The crows were back the next morning.

Braxton glared at them through the front window, watching them hop from kernel to kernel. His loathing increased with every bite they took. There was nothing pretty about them. They were scrawny, scraggly-looking things, jerking around the yard with no grace whatsoever.

He grabbed a broom and charged through the front door, brandishing it like a sword. An eerie shout ripped from his throat, a cross between a Rebel yell and a samurai's "aiiiyee," so primitive that he stopped, surprised that anything so inhuman could come out of his mouth.

But it worked. The crows squawked off in every direction, the kernels forgotten, the bread crumbs abandoned.

He exchanged the broom for his Bloody Mary and settled onto his rocking chair. Except for the pesky birds, he had a good feeling about the day. His creative juices were flowing, and he almost looked forward to heading upstairs to start work.

He swirled his drink in his glass, watching the little whirlpool it made, and smiled. The novel was going well, he had a good feeling about his new title, and that little Wyatt girl had his blood rushing; she'd all but offered herself to him on a silver platter.

Suddenly, his grin drooped.

The uncanny feeling he was being stared at hit him like a blast of cold air. He sensed movement from the corner of his eye, yet every time he turned toward it, he was just a second too late.

Another flittering shadow.

He stood, turned.

Nothing.

Shadowdancers. Movement in the corner of his left eye.

He swung his head toward it — again, nothing but the blur of rapid motion.

Nervous breakdown. He could hear Piper saying the words slowly, enunciating each syllable, "Ner-vous break-down." The words scrolled down his mind's eye like credits at the end of a movie.

No, he'd simply been drinking too much. So he took another sip — a gulp, actually. And when he opened his eyes, he was nose to beak with the large blackbird that haunted his mornings.

It was perched atop the back of a rocking chair.

He screamed. Not much of a scream. The rush of incoming air he gulped in his panic muffled any other noise.

Close-up, the bird's eyes were huge.

Glassy.

Black.

Braxton backed across the porch and smacked against the wall.

The bird pressed forward. The black eyes glittered with flecks of amber like fool's gold. They bored into him, right *through* him. They didn't blink like human eyes. Instead, they opened and closed more like a camera lens. He could almost hear it.

Click.

Freeze frame. Images frozen into eternity, forevermore.

Snap.

The lens snapped shut again and again.

The hooked beak opened, and the stench of carrion rushed at Braxton's face. The world turned gray, then black, and the flapping of wings echoed in the caverns of his mind. Silence.

His world was spinning. He felt the revolution even with his eyes closed, felt the rotation and sensation of falling. His head slammed against the floor.

When the worst of the pain passed, he opened his eyes to mere slits.

No bird.

No eyes drilling him.

Wider.

He looked around. He was alone, lying on the porch.

He lifted his head, and a wave of nausea rippled through his stomach. He tried to pull himself up using the rocking chair for leverage, but the queasiness grew worse, so he lay back down.

His shirt was sticky and wet...and red. He touched it with one finger, lifted his hand and saw the blood-red smear on his fingertip.

The Bloody Mary.

A dark stain spread across his jeans; he'd wet himself.

Braxton rolled onto his side, then his knees, looking around, trying to ignore the throbbing in his head. No sign of the beast. He sobbed with relief. Staggering to his feet, he ripped off the soaked shirt and dropped it on the porch, stumbled through the door and to the shower.

The image of the bird's eyes haunted him, glared at him even through the shower spray. A chill ran down his spine even though the small bathroom was steam-filled, the moisture dripping down the mirror.

He forced the image of the bird — of those eyes — from his mind. Had to put the bird behind him, had to think of something pretty, something soft. Something like...Susannah.

Pictured her round little ass swaying ahead of him on the porch steps. Saw her heavy young breasts straining at the pink cotton tank top, brushing against him as he passed through the doorway, nipples hard, her warm flesh radiating through the fabric. Remembered how he tingled where her hand grazed his knee, lingered on his shoulder. He could smell her all over again, as if she stood in front of him under the shower spray. Smelled her sweet teenage scents of Vanilla Fields, cherry lip gloss and Juicy Fruit gum.

Saw her in his mind's eye as she slid out of her clothes and shut the frosted glass shower doors behind her, saw her...*felt* her... materializing out of the steam, water sluicing down the cleft between her breasts, over her belly, between her fingers as she lathered up a worn bar of Ivory, reached for him, soaping him, stroking him, till his knees grew weak and his legs started to buckle and he gripped her tiny waist to stop himself from falling.

The whirling mists of steam separated, and he glimpsed the ghostly image of Susannah's face, eyes half-closed in passion, lips smiling. The mist swirled, stirred by unseen — unfelt — air currents, blurring her image, reforming it, her expression changing to bewilderment, the smile dwindling, her full lips turning down at the corners, eyes widening in fear.

Then...pain. His one hand still grasped her waist, his other had slid up to her throat. Clutching it. Stroking it. Squeezing it. Harder.

His fingers curved, claw-like, penetrating her flesh, the shower washing away the tiny trickles of blood seeping up from beneath his ever more insistent fingers. He looked down, down at her crumpling image, down at the water flowing toward the drain in pink-streaked streams.

Still he squeezed harder, the roar of the water drowning out the final squeals gurgling from Susannah's throat.

But there were other sounds, sounds louder than the water, a strange and frightening fluttering sound of wings flapping in a downpour, and the tearing, ripping, rending of hooked beaks shredding tender flesh.

The shower spray abruptly ran cold.

Frigid water stung Braxton's entire body.

The steam dissipated, and with it, the images, the scents and the touch of Susannah Wyatt. All the sounds evaporated and took the strangely arousing sensations with them.

Braxton glanced down. The water in the bottom of the tub ran clear. In his hands he clutched a mangled bar of Ivory soap.

He dried himself off quickly and dressed, feeling no cleaner than when he started.

Braxton, with shaky hands, fixed another Bloody Mary. He started up the stairs, changed his mind, turned around and fixed a pitcher of the drinks which he then carried up to his office.

His computer was on. The gray word-processing screen greeted him. The header at the top read *"Murder Mountain/ Defoe/page 32."*

The back of his neck prickled. He set the pitcher carefully on the corner of his desk, scrolled to the top of the document and began reading. On page four and without taking his eyes from the screen, he groped for the arm of his chair, pulled it into position and sat down.

When he'd finished reading, he sat back. "I *am* losing my mind," he said aloud, and the shrill sound of his voice startled him. He reached for his Bloody Mary and drained it.

He didn't remember writing a word he'd just read.

But it was good.

Better than good. It was dynamite.

Could he have written that last night? What had they done last night? He *did* come up to the computer. He remembered now, remembered turning on his desk lamp and sitting down, but damned if he remembered...

He touched the back of his head. There was a small bump where he'd smacked it on the porch when he passed out.

Braxton poured another drink, turned his printer on and keyed in the print command. The printer hummed and began chugging out pages. He saved the file and acquainted himself with his hero's name: Paul Craig. Not that he remembered coming up with that. Nothing. Not the vaguest fragment of a memory. Not —

"Brax, are you —"

"JESUS CHRIST!" Braxton leaped from his chair, knocking it over. "Sonofabitch, can't you wear shoes? Do you always have to sneak up on me?"

Piper's eyes gaped as wide open as her mouth. She stepped back, nervous, maybe even repelled. "I'm sorry, Brax. I didn't mean to startle you."

But he barely heard her over his pounding pulse. It sounded like someone running a jackhammer in his ear. He put his hand on his chest and took a deep breath. "I know. Sorry I yelled. But, my God, you scared the bejesus out of me."

"Are you okay? Your shirt was all —"

"Yeah, I know. No, I'm not okay. But I'm wonderful. Here, read this." He handed her the first printed pages of his manuscript.

"You're writing? It's started to come?" Her eyes softened, and the hint of a smile played around her lips. She lowered her eyes to page one. *"Murder Mountain?* What happened to *Bloodlust?"*

"Scrapped it. Besides, *Murder Mountain* has a nice alliterative ring, don't you think?"

"Yeah, I do. It's great." She read rapidly, turning the pages over onto the desk, carefully keeping them in order. A few times she glanced up at him, but returned her eyes to the page almost immediately.

He handed her the rest of the pages once the printer churned them out, then poured himself another drink.

When she finished, Piper looked at him with hooded eyes.

"Well?" he asked.

"Thirty-two pages, Braxton. That's a new record for you, isn't it?"

"It just kept flowing. It was all I could do to stop where I did. You can't imagine how good it feels. After that long dry spell where nothing seemed to work and now I feel — unstoppable. Piper, this is going to be the best one ever. I can feel it. Everything's coalescing all at once. The plot, the characters, the subplots, all the peaks and the valleys. Everything."

To Piper, he sounded like a Little Leaguer telling his mother about the game: how he made the triple play, how he socked another one over the fence, his teammates cheering him around the bases while his parents screamed encouragement at the top of their lungs.

"It's nothing short of a miracle," he said, his voice quivering. His eyes shone.

How could she tell him it was awful?

She couldn't. She didn't have the heart.

Not yet. Braxton still rambled on, wringing his hands, impassioned. She *couldn't* tell him it was confused, that he had characters springing out of nowhere, that he had even changed his hero's first name three times in thirty-two pages.

But he was so jubilant that she didn't shrug away from him when he put his arms around her and squeezed. It was the first hug they'd shared in what? Ten months? A year? She couldn't remember. But pressing against his chest, she remembered his shirt drenched in tomato juice on the porch.

"Braxton," she said when he finally stopped prattling about his novel. "What happened to your shirt? The one you left outside?"

He reared back from her, pushing her away. The same eyes that shimmered with excitement just a moment before grew cold. Hard. "I was attacked."

"Attacked? Here? At the cabin?"

He nodded. His lips compressed so tightly they almost disappeared; his nostrils flared. "Those goddammed birds you insist on feeding. I warned you about that."

"You were attacked by birds?"

"By birds. On the porch. I can prove it. Here, feel this." He grabbed her hand, jerked it around to the back of his head and guided it softly over a small lump about the size of a pullet egg.

"Brax, how did that happen? Let me look." He turned around, and she parted his hair, finding the ugly lump but no blood or abrasions.

He told her about the bird perched on the rocking chair. When he'd finished, she said slowly, thoughtfully, "Braxton, I'm no expert on birds, but I don't think crows get that big."

"He was enormous."

"Maybe it just seemed that way because he came so close."

"Maybe. Looming over me the way he was, he looked like the damned Empire State Building, but I've seen this bastard before." He told her about the other occasions.

"And you're sure it's the same bird?"

"Absolutely." He took another drink.

"How?"

"How what?"

"How can you be so sure it's the same exact bird? Don't they all look alike?"

"Not this one, because of the way it —" Braxton threw his head back and looked at her with a wary expression in his eyes. "You don't believe me."

"Yes, I believe you, but I don't understand how you can be so certain that —"

"You're thinking breakdown again, aren't you?" His voice got louder, hysterical. "Or that I was drunk. Hallucinating."

"You don't need to shout."

"I'll shout if I want to shout! I wasn't drunk, and I'm not crazy!" He slammed his glass down on the desk. The liquid spurted up, fanned out like an opened umbrella and splattered over the manuscript. "Look what you've done! Get the fuck out."

CHAPTER SIX

Braxton had subjected Piper to the silent treatment so often over the last few years that it was almost part of their routine.

He stayed in his office the rest of that afternoon. She heard his keyboard clacking as his fingers danced across the keys when she passed by his closed door. Occasionally, she heard the printer churning out more pages.

He came downstairs twice, both times mixing pitchers of Long Island Iced Teas, which he carried back to his office. She rapped on his door when dinner was ready.

"I'm not hungry," came his muffled reply.

When the Wyatts' headlights wobbled up the driveway, she didn't know whether to disturb him or not.

But she didn't have a chance to worry. Braxton was out the door before the Wyatts set foot on the porch, smiling, friendly, and only slightly tipsy, although he hadn't eaten anything. Piper watched in amazement as he escorted Mary Beth to a chair and asked her solicitously, "Would you rather go inside, Mary Beth? The night air is getting a little chilly."

Mary Beth seemed a little uneasy at first, kept brushing lint from the sleeve of her plaid shirt and tugging at a loose thread on her jeans, but she soon succumbed to Braxton's charm and babbled like a schoolgirl with a crush.

Braxton greeted Jeff with enthusiasm, pumping his hand and playfully punching him on the shoulder, as if he were an old Army buddy and their reunion long overdue. Jeff blushed, but looked genuinely pleased by Braxton's attention.

Piper turned to Ren to offer him a drink and felt the smile halt on her face. Something was different, something in the compelling way Ren looked at her.

A weakness started in her knees, and she felt a smooth, gentle tugging, as if she were being pulled toward him. She remembered the jolt that ran between them when they shook hands. She lowered her eyes and looked away.

A soft fluttering started in her stomach, and suddenly it was difficult to breathe evenly. Taking a deep breath, she made herself look at him and smile. "Wine?"

His eyes were fixed on hers. "Yes, thanks."

She forced herself to look away. It was like pulling one magnet away from another, by no means impossible, but requiring effort. "Mary Beth? Would you care for wine?"

Mary Beth barely glanced at her. "Sure. Thanks." Mary Beth's eyes were bright, and she was smiling at Braxton and her son.

Piper fled inside. In the kitchen, she put her hand on her forehead. It was warm. So were her cheeks. Perhaps she should change into something lighter than the knit turtleneck and jeans she'd chosen with such care.

"You're a married woman," she whispered to herself. Braxton no longer gave a damn what she wore, and it was *wrong* for her to try to make herself attractive to someone else's husband.

Still, a warm flush spread through her as she remembered the power of what she'd felt, an attraction as strong as any force field.

Think about Braxton. You've got your hands full enough without getting involved in any kind of mid-life mess.

She could barely pour the wine.

When she returned to the porch, purposely avoiding eye contact with Ren, Braxton was ranting about their "crow problem," how Piper encouraged them with food and how he'd been attacked by one monstrous and aggressive crow.

"How big was it, Braxton?" Mary Beth asked, her eyes worried circles.

"Maybe three, three and a half pounds," he answered. "Bugger was a good twenty-six, twenty-eight inches long from stem to stern." He indicated its length with his hands.

"Crows don't get that big. I'm no expert, but that sounds more like a rook or a raven. Don't you think so, Ren?" Mary Beth glanced at her husband.

Ren nodded.

"Besides," Mary Beth continued, "crows stay in flocks. They're very social. In fact, I don't remember ever seeing a lone crow. Ravens, now, that's a horse of a different color." She giggled. "Sorry. Bad joke. But ravens and rooks are loners, they even — what am I going on about? Ren should fill you in. He's the expert." Mary Beth smiled, a dimple in her plump cheek hinting at the pretty girl she'd once been.

"Expert?" Braxton asked. "So you're not only a Harvard man and a Ph.D., and *The* Storyteller — and now we learn you're a friggin' ornithologist, too. Is there no end to your accomplishments?"

If the Wyatts caught Braxton's sarcasm, they politely ignored it. But Piper could almost feel Ren's mental focus shifting away from her and redirecting itself toward Braxton.

"I'm not an expert," Ren said. "But ravens are common in mythology and important to the Tlingits as well."

"He collects raven rattles and carvings, too," Mary Beth said.

"What are those?"

Ren opened his mouth to answer, but Mary Beth beat him to it. "Tlingit things that they use in ceremonial dances. Like maracas."

"Fascinating. Love to see them some time." The look on Braxton's face said otherwise. "Do *you* think it was a raven that attacked me?"

Ren's face, usually quite open, became guarded. His gaze fixed on Braxton's, and he hesitated before answering, as if choosing his words carefully. "It's possible. They can be aggressive, but usually only against small quarry. Rodents or —"

"Then why are they important to mythology if all they do is chase around after mice and moles? Sounds like a far cry from a winged horse or griffin to me." Braxton sipped his wine.

"Magic," Ren said. "Ravens are known as 'Tricksters.' Most often they're considered ill omens." His eyes narrowed.

"Ill omen? So I've been visited by an unlucky sign, eh?" Braxton smiled nonchalantly, but his wine glass trembled as he brought it to his mouth. "So why would a rat-catcher get the status of a 'Trickster' or portent of evil?"

"Because of their importance to Odin."

"Oh, Ren, tell the Odin story," Mary Beth said. "That's such a good one." She turned back to Braxton. "It's a Scandinavian fairy tale."

"Mythology," Ren corrected.

"Never could keep them straight," Mary Beth muttered, looking into her glass.

"Piper," Braxton said. "Mary Beth needs a refill before the story."

She rose from her chair, keeping her eyes downcast so her anger at being ordered around wouldn't show. She collected the empty glasses, but when she tried to take Ren's, he refused to let go. She glanced at him, puzzled, and froze.

Time stopped. It hovered, unmoving. As if through a long tunnel, she heard the chatter between Braxton and Mary Beth. Muted. Echoey. Again she felt a gentle pull, as if she were being drawn forward. Warmth started in her stomach and spread upward, fanning out, until she felt fevered. Ren's eyes held her immobile, like when you stare at a flickering candle for too long and find it difficult to look away. His eyes lightened, amber flecks overshadowing the brown, sparking with emotion. Anger? Yes, anger. She knew, although she didn't know how she knew, that he was infuriated at the way Braxton ordered her around.

She felt herself soften, knew she was projecting her thanks for his anger on her behalf, and pulled gently on the wine glass again. He released it. The magnetic pull disappeared. Her body temperature plummeted back to normal. Time marched forward, and the conversation returned to its normal timbre. She stumbled slightly, disoriented.

When she returned with their drinks, Ren touched his amulet, then launched into his tale. Again his voice took on a resonance that wrapped them in the velvet folds of its richness.

"This story," he began, "is about Odin, the Norse god of war and death, but also the god of poetry and wisdom and the father of Thor, the king of the Norse gods. Odin had only one remaining eye that shone like the sun. He'd traded his other eye for a drink from the Well of Wisdom, which was how he'd gained his immense knowledge. He hung impaled by his own spear for nine days on the world tree where he learned to make the dead speak.

"He ruled the nine worlds from two thrones, one in Valhalla, where slain warriors were taken, and the other in Hlidskjalf. He traveled between the thrones on an eight-footed steed, accompanied by two wolves to whom he gave all his food. He consumed only wine. Two ravens perched on his shoulders: Huginn, which meant "thought," and Muninn, which meant "memory." Every morning, Odin released them. They traveled the nine worlds, returning to his shoulders at night and telling him everything they had heard and all they'd seen. On the day of the final battle —"

Braxton did the unpardonable. He interrupted the story. "So the ravens were spies, right?"

Mary Beth's head snapped around. She stared at Braxton.

Jeff looked up from his sneakers, his eyebrows arched.

Ren looked baffled, like someone being jerked from a trance.

"They were Odin's spies, weren't they?" Braxton repeated. He seemed agitated.

A muscle at the corner of Ren's eye twitched, and he bit his lower lip. His eyes changed from surprise and confusion to angry glints, then their color deepened to the blackish-brown of dark chocolate. His sense of story, of rhythm, was shattered. The mesmerizing stage presence evaporated. The resonant actor's voice dwindled to a pleasant but less-powerful baritone with a definite edge to it when he finally spoke. "Good night, Piper. Thank you for your hospitality." With neither word nor glance for Braxton and only a quick nod of his head at Jeff, he led Mary Beth to their car.

The first rumble of thunder came over the mountain as the Wyatts' tail lights disappeared. Piper turned to her husband. "How could you be so rude? You know how you hate to be interrupted when you're writing. Yet you interrupted Ren in the middle —"

"Shut up. It was a lousy story. Not original." Braxton held out his empty glass.

Piper ignored it. "That doesn't matter, and you know it. What's wrong with you? You've never been intentionally rude before to —"

Braxton turned toward her. The look on his face stopped her cold, sending a shiver through her and constricting her vocal chords.

His face was so contorted it was almost unrecognizable. His mouth drew down on one side. His nostrils flared and his eyes narrowed into glinting slits in dark shadows.

"Disappointed that lover boy left early?" He deliberately let go of the wine glass, watching as it dropped, then shattered, on the floor. "Don't worry, he'll be back."

He pushed himself out of the chair. "I'm going upstairs to write. Bring me my wine. Then I want to be left alone."

Piper was too stunned, too dazed to scream, "Get your own damn wine," which was what she wanted to do. Instead, she knelt down and picked up shards of broken glass.

When Braxton looked up from his monitor, she was there, holding his wine in front of her, a stealthy, silent apparition. The planes of her face were flooded by frequent flashes of lightning reflecting through the window that left the hollows of her face in shadow — her eye sockets, the space beneath her cheekbones and the cleft in her jaw — giving her a skeletal look. It was fascinating, yet sinister.

Hum. The buzz again, then a light flashed behind his lids — bright white, blinding light. At first, Braxton thought it was the after-flash of another lightning strike. But then his chair seemed to revolve, spinning slowly like a child's carousel, increasing, then whirling rapidly, his office — his wife — a blur. He squeezed his eyes shut tightly, trying to stop the feeling of motion. Piper's face appeared on the screen of his mind, her eyes wide with fear. A fist — his fist? — jabbed from the foreground of his vision, connected with her jaw. The impact drove her backward —

Toppling —

Plummeting —

The image disappeared. The world wound down. Stopped.

He opened his eyes. Piper still stood half in shadow, across from his desk, his wine glass held in her outstretched hand.

"Your wine." She blinked, set the stemmed glass on the corner of his desk and left.

Both hands clutched the edge of his desk, his knuckles white from the pressure he had exerted. He looked at them, bewildered. They seemed strange, as if they were someone else's appendages. Not his. Not familiar. More like talons than hands, the fingers twisted into something...claw like.

Crazy?

Breakdown?

No. They said if you questioned your sanity, you were fine. It was only part of the creative process. Just his muse at work, creating ideas for *Murder Mountain*. That was all.

The power flickered for a moment, but then stabilized. He glanced at his monitor.

Murder Mountain/Defoe/p.102.

He was in his prime.

Billy Dale Wilson took the curve a little faster than he should have, given how slick the roads were. But he was a good driver; had quick reflexes, too. He let off the gas, stayed away from the brake, and grabbed the wheel at "ten and two," ready to pull her back around when the Chevy's ass-end came out of the skid.

If anyone could drive these back roads in bad weather, it was Billy Wilson; hell, he'd been deliverin' fire wood to summer folks for his daddy since he was fourteen. Five-years and he'd never put so much as a scratch on the pick-up.

When the truck was back under control, Billy glanced at the florist box on the seat beside him, worried that his flowers had been flung to the floor during the skid. The box *had* slid to the far side of the passenger seat, but it looked okay, fresh and white, the pink satin ribbons still perky. Good thing, too. He didn't want —

Crack!

God! That was close. That bolt must've hit something right nearby. The flash and boom struck at the same time.

He didn't want to give Elenore flowers from a dirty, crumpled box with a crushed bow.

Better to play it safe, slow down a little. Especially with the rain coming as hard as it was. It wouldn't last long. No sense taking any chances.

This was their last night together before he left for Boot Camp, to learn how to 'be all he could be.' The end of an era. But after boot camp and the training that followed...well, he reckoned he'd be in a position to pop the question. And if —

Another bolt raced earthward. A large red oak by the curve some thirty feet or more down the road was profiled for a split second against a backdrop of dazzling light. The tree exploded —

Blam!

— so loud that for a moment Billy thought someone had dropped a bomb on his truck.

The night turned neon orange — brilliant, harsh, dazzling.

His pupils contracted from the brightness of the strike. Motes of red and blue and green drifted across his blurred vision. Then his eyes held nothing but darkness.

The gritty sound of gravel crunched beneath his tires. The rear-end of the Chevy whipped out.

He jerked the wheel to where he knew the road was, thought for sure the road was, where the road *should* have been — *but wasn't.*

The truck cartwheeled.

Billy's world turned inside out. Upside-down, right side-up, puke on the rise.

The roar in his head, loud as a revving jet engine, was joined by shattering glass, snapping branches, and finally the sickening screech of metal as the Chevy *slammed!* into granite.

Afraid to move, afraid to open his eyes, afraid he still would be blinded — or worse yet, afraid he'd see well enough to see death racing at him.

He tried to breathe — but not too deep, not too fast. Didn't dare move at all till he figured out where he was.

Where exactly had he gone off the road? The entire hillside was strewn with boulders, but some formed an outcropping beneath which was a sheer drop-off. If the truck was balanced on that overhang, one wrong move might send it plunging over the side...and him with it.

But the truck *felt* stable. There wasn't any movement at all.

He opened his eyes and looked around. The dash lights still glowed — that was good. It meant he could see again. They shone eerily on his hands — which seemed okay — and his legs — which felt okay. His fingers searched his face and neck for blood, and found nothing more than the sweat of his fear.

The darkness outside the window was total.

The storm was moving off. Thunder rumbled from farther to the east and the lightning — which finally showed him he was on stable ground — struck less frequently and farther away.

Flexing his shoulders and arms, and judging himself to be mostly undamaged, he tried to open the door. It was crushed, and wouldn't budge.

He crawled through the broken windshield, waited until his legs stopped trembling and he was able to breathe normally.

Jeff Wyatt's house was only a quarter-mile or so ahead. He'd call the police — and Elenore — from Jeff's house.

He stuck his hand through what remained of the passenger window, rummaged around until he found the smooth cardboard box, then took off.

It was slow going. The truck had gone only about fifty-feet down the embankment, but the pitch going back up was steep, the grass soaked and slippery, and he could barely see the ground. By the time he reached the pavement, his calves were cramping, and he had to spend a few minutes massaging his muscles before he headed up the road.

Snap!

Billy froze, jerking his head toward the sound at the far side of the road.

Silence.

Probably a raccoon. Possum. Not loud enough for a deer.

He shifted the box to the crook of his other arm, then zipped his windbreaker against the chill. He was pretty sure the box had survived the wreck okay; one end of the box felt slightly crumpled, but the bow seemed perky enough.

He started forward again, his steps quicker, his footsteps loud in the still night.

The last of the storm clouds faded, brightening the sky somewhat, and a few leftover droplets of water dripped from an overhanging branch.

Leaves behind him rustled slightly. He turned around, walked backwards while he scanned the woods.

Nothing.

He turned around again, chiding himself for being spooked by night sounds. He and his buddies always snickered at the summer people's comments about how creepy the mountains were at night, how the hovering haze made them sinister. Threatening.

He grinned at his own foolish —

Those rapid thumps *were* coming from his own heart, weren't they? It was drumming in his chest, felt like it might explode.

The back of his neck prickled. He went ice-cold all over and his knees felt weak.

It wasn't his heart.

Footsteps approached. Running footsteps.

Billy started to turn but — *Whoomph!* — something bowled into him, something so foul-smelling that bile surged up his throat and spewed out of his mouth before he slammed face first onto the asphalt. Panicked, he gulped for air.

Whatever struck him had him pinned. His neck was on fire. White-hot searing stabs of pain sliced down his neck, followed by the sickening *rip!* of fabric and flesh being torn away.

His fingers scrabbled at the road, splaying, clenching. Splay. Clench. Splay.

Searching, even as he surrendered to pain that was more consuming than fire.

When his fingers found satin, they stopped.

The ribbon glistened bright red.

CHAPTER SEVEN

Ren steered his mother and wife down the crowded brick sidewalks of Jonesborough, Tennessee. The picturesque little town was filled to capacity for the annual three-day National Storytelling Festival. Jeff ambled along behind them on the narrow brick sidewalks, his guitar thumping against his hip, his right hand clutching the embroidered strap.

Susannah had stayed at home.

Mary Beth chattered like a park squirrel about the pumpkins, cornstalks and potted mums decorating the antique stores and coffee shops, dragging her mother-in-law from one dolled-up storefront to another.

Keysa Wyatt was as quiet as Mary Beth was talkative.

Yet Ren knew her dark, rheumy eyes absorbed every detail, even subtle nuances that she would be able to recall perfectly years from now. She was a spry old girl, quick-witted, and tough. Fortunately, he'd inherited her acute powers of observation.

He settled the two women into folding chairs inside the large, open-sided tent where he would tell his first story.

Scanning the crowd, he wondered if Piper and her husband were among the throng of festival-goers seating themselves on folding chairs inside the tent or sprawling on blankets around its perimeter. He'd given the Defoes complimentary passes the morning after Braxton had apologized for interrupting his story.

Mary Beth had insisted upon it.

He didn't see the Defoes, but he did notice Jeff chatting with a cute little redhead lolling on a blanket. Nice to see his son's usually sullen features relaxed and happy.

So Ren took his seat to the left of the stage with the other storytellers and scanned the audience again for Piper.

She wasn't there.

He swallowed his disappointment and tried to focus on the first "teller", just starting his routine.

He couldn't concentrate.

Piper's face kept intruding on his thoughts, the image of her dark doe eyes lingering in his memory. He hadn't seen her in over a week; seven days that seemed more like seven months. He'd wanted to introduce her to his mother, was anxious to see his mother's reaction to both Piper and Braxton. His mother's mother had been the village shaman, and Keysa had inherited much of the power, power that enabled her to see clearly into the most multifaceted heart.

The teller to Ren's left jabbed him suddenly with her elbow. Ren looked up, and realized he'd missed his cue.

Showtime.

He grasped his amulet for a moment, head bowed, then strolled onto the stage.

"There's certainly a mixed crowd at this thing." Braxton threaded his way through the crowd at the festival's food court, pulling Piper along by her hand. There were yuppies and old folks, rednecks in flannel and suburban couples in matching Eddie Bauer sweaters and Timberlands.

The local restaurants and caterers had pitched tents around the perimeter of a parking lot and offered everything from fried dough and onion rings to haute street fair cuisine for the urbane and self-styled literati.

Braxton couldn't decide *what* to eat. All he knew was that he was ravenous even though he'd wolfed down a huge breakfast not quite two hours ago. Yet he was starved to the point where his mouth watered and his stomach growled.

Piper drew up beside him. "Can't you wait? The stories have already begun." She nodded her head in the direction of the closest tent, where the roar of audience laughter rolled across the terrain like a cresting wave. "It would be rude for us to miss Ren's performance after he gave us passes."

"He'll get over it." He skimmed the signs over the cook tents again. "Shish kabob. That's what I want. Sure you aren't hungry?" He headed toward the booth without waiting for an answer.

"What'll you have, sir?" drawled a dark-haired young woman, her pen poised above her order book.

Braxton stared past her into the stainless steel trays of cubed raw beef behind the grill. Bloody, raw cubes glistened in the sunlight.

"Sir? Made up your mind?"

His teeth and gums tingled, wanting to rip into those cubes, aching to bite down on that cold, red flesh, to feel the blood burst free and trickle down his throat.

"Sir?"

Braxton's mouth watered. "Four kabobs." He gulped several times in rapid succession to avoid drooling. "Only don't cook them. My dog likes his meat raw."

Piper wound her way through the sea of chairs toward the stage. Ren was just finishing his first story and glanced briefly at her.

Realizing how conspicuous she was with people craning to see around her, she dropped to her knees. There weren't any empty seats.

Ren seemed right at home on stage. He was made for it, she thought, noticing his easy confidence, the carefully chosen — but artfully done — gestures he used to punctuate his tale. He looked enormous from her ground level vantage point, larger than life, and incredibly magnetic. His hair, freshly cut, still grazed the top of an off-white turtleneck that strained snugly over his lean muscles.

Suddenly she realized everyone was applauding.

Ren put his hands in his jean pockets, smiled his thanks to his audience, and began another story.

She listened, watching the incredible expressiveness of his full lips, the way his eyes changed from dark to light. She felt that he was telling the story just to her, that every word was directed to her ears and hers alone. The crowd faded away until they vanished altogether, and she and Ren were alone in the tent. His voice alternately raised and lowered, swirled musically or growled menacingly with every twist and turn of the storyline; every burst of laughter or tear of pain, caressed *her*. Only her.

Suddenly, it was over. The audience's applause snapped her back to reality.

She stood there, her heart pounding, breath ragged. She shook her head as if she were trying to shake off Ren's powerful hold on her and managed to clap weakly just as the rest of the audience finished.

Ren locked his gaze on hers. A magnetic jolt shot through her, warming her. She backed through the crowd, watching as he ambled off the stage.

Ren hastened to Piper's side as the tent emptied. "I'd like you to meet my mother. Can you come now?" he asked.

Piper nodded and followed him to where Mary Beth and his mother sat. Ren made the introductions and watched closely as his mother and Piper — both of whom habitually kept their emotions off their face — sized each other up.

Oblivious, Mary Beth checked her makeup in her compact and fluffed up her hair.

Finally, the pleasantries over, Piper excused herself, saying she needed to find her husband.

Ren watched her leave, then turned to his mother. He arched an eyebrow questioningly and waited for his mother's assessment.

"Your woman has a heavy heart," she said.

"*My* woman? She's not my woman."

Keysa glanced up at him with that intense look that always unnerved him. As a child, he'd been convinced she could read every thought that flashed through his mind, as if those thoughts were spelled out on a ticker tape going in one ear and out the other.

She drew her amulet from the bodice of her cotton dress, worked the lacing at the top open and pulled out a white feather. She snapped it in half. Then she held the broken halves together, end to end. "Two halves make one whole," she said. Then she dangled it upside down, holding the widest end, wiggling it to show how solid it was; the feather had fused back together.

She tucked it back into her amulet.

▓

Braxton saw Piper approaching, fresh and stunning in a red sweater and plaid skirt that swirled around her long legs like a cover girl in a hosiery commercial. Her hair gleamed blue-black in the sun and her face was flushed.

He, on the other hand, was humiliated and filthy. His shirt clung to him, soaked with cold sweat. He'd dripped blood all over his khakis, and grass stains blotched the fabric where he'd dropped to his knees behind the dumpster when he'd started retching.

Don't let her see me.

He scurried farther back behind the dumpster.

But she spotted him. Her eyes widened, her hand went to her mouth, and she hurried toward him. "Brax, what's —"

He raised one hand, weakly. "Where the hell have you been?"

"I — what's that all over your face?"

He touched his cheek. His fingers came away tipped in red, triggering a burst of saliva in his mouth, tasting again the succulent richness of the raw beef, the tantalizing aroma of —

Piper's horrified expression brought him back to the present and he realized she was waiting for an explanation.

"I — I started to get ill. Dizzy. Thought I was going to pass out. Got up to find someplace private, and my legs gave out."

Piper's mortified expression changed to concern. She hurried to him, placing her cool hand against his warm forehead.

"You're clammy."

"I know. But I feel better now. The shish kabob wasn't cooked enough. Maybe tainted. Who knows?"

"Can I get you something?"

"Yes. Something to clean myself up with. And something to settle my stomach. A cold beer if you can find it."

"How about a glass of —"

"I *said* a beer."

"Fine." She stomped off to the front of the tent.

Once he'd washed his face and polished off the beer, he felt well enough to join Piper at the next storytelling session. Surprisingly, he found himself enjoying it. So much so that after only a few minutes, he reached into his jacket to turn on his pocket recorder.

Piper nudged him with her elbow. "What're you doing?" she asked in a whisper. "They said no recording of any kind."

He waved her off with a flip of his wrist.

Merely insurance, he assured himself. Just like when he jotted down quick outlines of Ren's stories — his "secret weapon" — notes to trigger his own imagination in case he ran into writer's block again.

After the session, while Piper braved the lines for the rest rooms, Braxton lit up a cigarette and lounged in the shade of an oak, watching the parade of people.

Two couples strolled by, heads close together: Die-hard hippies left over from the sixties — graying hair pulled back in ponytails, backpacks, long skirts, full beards; two English-major types in Docker shorts and Birkenstocks; and a lone, lovely young sweet thing whose eyes scanned left to right as if she'd become separated from her partner. A thin strap of her knit top kept dropping off her shoulder as she walked. She kept hoisting it back up with her thumb, only to have it fall a moment later.

There was something tantalizing about her, something alluring about the strap falling off her slender, tanned shoulder. His stomach fluttered pleasantly.

Whirr.

Something hypnotic in the way her sweatshirt — the sleeves knotted around her waist — accentuated the sway of her hips, the narrowness of her waist. He could hear — yes, actually *hear* that tiny bead of sweat *plop!* onto her chest and trickle downward until it disappeared into her top.

She passed by.

He felt the softness of her skin like fine silk, tasted the salty tang of her sweat, and inhaled the shampoo/sunshine/lemon-rinsed goodness of her hair.

He scented her.

His nostrils twitched, flared, as he picked up her heady aromas of food and perspiration and loneliness and desire and flesh.

Flesh.

His lips quivered. His gums ached. His teeth tingled. Saliva seeped into his mouth, flooded it so heavily he was forced to swallow. He remembered the meat, the richly red and dripping chunks of uncooked flesh he'd consumed such a short time ago, sucking the salty juice from the cubes, ripping into the slippery, fibrous beef with his teeth.

His fingers clenched and unclenched. He took an involuntary step toward the lovely young woman who had passed him by, the woman who soon would disappear from —

"*Hey, Mr. Defoe!*"

Braxton froze. Blinked. "Jeff. Uh, hi."

Jeff Wyatt ambled up the brick walkway toward him, fallen leaves scattering as he passed, his guitar slung over his shoulder.

Braxton's clenched fingers loosened. "Having a good time?"

Jeff shrugged.

Braxton nodded toward the guitar. "Performing today?" He took a handkerchief from his pocket and mopped his forehead with it.

Jeff shook his head. "Nope. Not officially, at least."

"How come? I haven't heard you on guitar, but if you're half as good as you are on the harmonica, you belong up on that stage."

Jeff blushed. The contrast of bright red skin against his silver blond hair was startling. "My father won't *allow* it." There was an edge to his voice, a slight hint of anger.

"Why?"

The boy grimaced, lowered his head, then poked at a rock with his sneakered toe. "Same old shit. We're supposed to live in a democracy, but I don't get to do squat."

Braxton suppressed a chuckle and ground out his cigarette. "Define 'squat'?"

Jeff slid the guitar strap off his shoulder, set his instrument carefully on the ground, and leaned against the oak tree. "Like the music. That's what I want to do with my life. My father — he's glad I'm musically inclined and all, but says I can't make a living at it. Just because he couldn't."

"Your father plays?"

"Yeah, he was in a band when he was a kid. But he wants me to go into education or business. Something stable."

Braxton's mother's voice whined in his ear: *Why waste your time writing these stupid stories. You can't make a living writing fairy tales! Get your grades up — go to college, be a teacher. Or else you'll wind up like your good-for-nothing father.*

Braxton's hands tingled, as if they'd been still too long. He flexed his fingers, tensed them. Then relaxed them.

"Are your grades okay?" Braxton asked.

"They suck. Every time I try to study, music starts running through my head. I can't stop it. I can't concentrate on anything else."

"Between you and me, some people just don't recognize genius." His mother's face flashed through his memory. "Don't let anyone get you down. Follow your instincts, boy."

Jeff smiled, tentatively, as if such sympathy — especially coming from an adult — was unexpected. Still, the boy's eyes remained worried.

"Something else bothering you?" Braxton asked.

Jeff lowered his head, then glanced over at a group of teenagers giggling and talking on a blanket. When he spoke, his voice was softer than usual. "They found Billy Dale Wilson two days after I got my driver's license. So now I'm not allowed out after dark. I'm sixteen! Like I can't take care of myself! I mean, I'm sorry about Billy and all, but —"

"That *was* pretty nasty stuff, Jeff." Braxton scratched his neck. "Billy was a good-sized boy, and *he* wasn't very successful at taking care of himself."

"You knew Billy?"

"Your mom gave me his phone number. He'd delivered a load of firewood to our cabin that morning, so while I didn't really *know* him, I saw how big he was. All muscle."

"Frankie said he didn't have a chance, attacked from behind like that."

"Who is Frankie?"

"The Sheriff. My father's best friend."

Braxton nodded. "Do they have any leads on who did it?"

"Not who. *What.* They found some bobcat scatter and some bear spoor nearby."

"What the hell is 'scatter'?"

Jeff grinned. "Shit. Literally. Droppings. So they think that's a possibility. Frankie said whatever took Billy down had inhuman strength."

"Hmm. Well, I'm sure that once everyone gets over the horror of Billy's death, things will get back to normal. You'll get your wheels back." He clapped Jeff on the back.

Jeff's face brightened perceptibly. "You really think so?"

"I know so. Now quit wasting your time talking to old farts like me." He gave Jeff a playful shove right into a pair of teenage girls sauntering by. The requisite giggling and blushes and mumbled "s'cuse me's" were exchanged.

"Go get 'em, kid." Braxton winked. "Before I do."

The passes Ren gave Piper and Braxton included admission to the most popular of the Storytelling Festival's events: the ghost stories. After dark, spectators huddled on blankets spread on the green of a little park, or bundled up in lawn chairs. Tonga torches blazed at strategic places around the grounds, and eerie lighting illuminated the gazebo, where the storytellers told Halloween tales.

Braxton had to admit it was cleverly done, and even the stuffiest looking old folks seemed to enjoy the tales of rattling chains and angry spirits. One teller accompanied her story, set in the Carpathian Woods, by playing "the bones" that she wielded like castanets, clacking out a rhythmic rapping to emphasize the creepier aspects of her story.

The whole effect was decidedly hokey. And wonderful. Braxton loved it. He kept himself close to a speaker and kept his hand on his mini-cassette's "record" button.

When the last cassette was full, Braxton wandered back to where Piper was on the far perimeter of the grass. Alone.

"Weren't you supposed to get me a beer?" he asked.

"Screw you."

He jumped back in mock surprise. "Uh-oh, Mama's not happy. What's the matter? Couldn't get past your storyteller's groupies?"

Piper jumped up, eyes glaring, lips trembling. She looked as though there was something she desperately wanted to say.

Then it passed. Her expression cleared. Her shoulders slumped.

"Brax, let's just go home."

CHAPTER EIGHT

He wrote most of the next night, the words gushing in an unstoppable flood. At quarter till four in the morning he turned off his computer and crept into the bedroom. Piper lay on her side, her breathing deep and regular, illuminated by the soft light shining through their opened bathroom door.

Sleeping deeply, nothing more.

He smiled to himself, and as if in answer, Piper smiled back softly. Her breathing deepened, then grew more rapid. One arm stretched languidly over her head, the back of her hand against the pillow. Her smile widened. Her eyelids fluttered softly. She rolled onto her back, and dispelling any question as to what she might be dreaming about, her hips raised slightly from the mattress while a tiny moan escaped her lips.

Whirr.

Half-breed whore.

His anger so consuming it was almost tangible, Braxton flicked off the bathroom light, ripped the blankets off his wife, and picked up his pillow.

Suddenly Piper was jerked from sleep by something — a pillow — bashing her head repeatedly. Her arms folded protectively over her face, she was further startled by a shrill inhuman scream, muffled, yet terrifying for all its muteness. She heaved herself up, still trying to ward off the blows, and rolled off the mattress at the same time.

Braxton, his eyes rolling madly, chest heaving from exertion, stood by the edge of the bed, his lips drawn back in a snarl. "Get out of my bed, slut!"

He lunged onto the mattress, crawled across it, and leaning

toward her, grabbed a hank of her hair. "Cry, goddamn you."

She moaned, bending into the pain, then tried to wriggle free.

"Maybe this will make you cry like a real woman!"

The *crack* of his fist against her jaw exploded as its force slammed her into the wall, knocking the wind out of her. Piper tasted a sweet, coppery wetness inside her mouth.

He crawled to the other side of the bed and grabbed the small ceramic lamp from the night stand, yanking the cord out of the wall. He flung his arm back, apparently planning to hit her with it, still trying to bring her to tears, when his head snapped around at the sound of a large *thump* against the window.

The glass fissured slightly.

She pushed herself up. Her only thought was to get away from him, to crawl into some dark, safe womb where he couldn't frighten her anymore, couldn't hurt her.

Braxton screamed, his eyes still riveted on the window glass.

His arm was still reared back. He swung it forward and hurled the lamp like a pitcher throwing a fast ball. It smashed into the wall next to the window.

Another *thwump* hit the glass from the outside. There was no question as to whether the glass was cracking or not: tiny fracture lines were definite.

Braxton's face went, in a split second, from stroke-toned red to the color of a shroud. "Did you see it? Did you see that thing? It's breaking in here! It's coming through the glass to get me!"

Piper slid the quilt from the bed, and on hands and knees, the blanket trailing behind her, crawled around the bottom of the bedframe and peeked at Braxton.

His gaze — wide and terrified — was riveted on the window. His mouth hung open. Small, whimpering noises sounded in the back of his throat.

Piper broke for the door.

She raced around the corner of the house, wrapping the blanket around the tee shirt and panties in which she'd been sleeping as she fled, then half-slid down the creek embankment. Her heart beat like a snare drum in a marching band as she picked her way upstream, barefoot, leaping from stone to stone when possible. The cold, rushing water numbed her feet where she waded between rocks she could not leap to. The chilled, predawn air carried the sound of shattering glass, followed by a muted scream.

Freezing, Piper lay in a hollow she'd scraped from the soft pine needles until the dawn began to dry up the early morning dew. Numb, she watched the sun rise over the mountain.

It was a long time before Piper finally worked up the courage to crawl out of the pine woods. With the blanket wrapped tightly around her, she picked her way back toward the cabin. She guessed by the sun that it might be nine-thirty or so.

She opened the front door gently, stuck her head inside and looked around. Nothing. She slid on silent feet up the stairwell, heard the gentle purr of Braxton's computer, but his office chair was empty. She stepped softly into their bedroom.

The room was trashed. Bedding lay wadded in a ball on the floor, fragments of the ceramic lamp were scattered on the rug, the floor and even on the foot of the mattress. The sheet rock was punched in where the lamp had smashed against it, and the window was shattered. But the room was vacant.

She crossed stealthily toward their bathroom door, listened, pushed it gently open. No one was inside.

Her breath whooshed out in a rush of relief. She yanked open her dresser drawer and jerked on a pair of jeans and socks. Rummaging around, she found a sweatshirt and pulled it over her head.

But as her head poked through the neck opening, her eyes filled with Braxton's face, looming in front of her.

He grabbed her shoulders, pinning her to the spot as if she were nailed to an invisible cross.

His eyes filled with tears. "I've been frantic. Where were you, for God's sake?"

She couldn't speak. She shivered, opened her mouth, but nothing came out.

"My God, Piper, I came in from writing, the bed was all torn apart, the window busted all to hell and you disappeared off the face of the — my God! What happened to your face?" He ran his finger down the line of her jaw.

"You don't remember?"

"Remember what? Did you fall? Were you attacked?"

"Yes, you sonofabitch, I was attacked. By you!"

"What? What the hell are you talking about? I've been out of my mind. Woke the Wyatts up at four-thirty this morning. Thought maybe you'd gone there. They called the sheriff. He's out looking for you now."

Piper searched his eyes. They were Braxton's eyes, bleary, bloodshot, but Braxton's.

Not that thing's, not...

"What did you do to the window, Piper? Why'd you break it? I need to know what's going on here." Braxton let her go, ran his fingers through his hair and paced back and forth in front of the dresser in short, agitated steps. "Sane people don't break their bedroom window, then wander into the woods in the middle of the night."

She finally found her voice. "You're telling me you don't remember last night? You don't remember hitting me? Throwing the lamp?"

He stopped. His expression was shocked, then confused. "Piper, I've never hit you. Never. I'm not the greatest husband in the world, but I've never struck you, and you know it."

"Then one of us is crazy, Braxton, and it isn't me. You punched me right in the jaw. Called me...names. You only stopped when you screamed that something was trying to get at you through the window. That's when I ran."

He stared at her, obviously stupefied. "If what you say is true, there should be glass all over the floor, right? But look, honey, the window was broken from the inside. The glass is on the ground out there. So why would I have said something was trying to break in and get me? Doesn't make sense."

He resumed his pacing, then turned toward her, shoving his hands in his pockets and lowering his head. "Piper, if you were — well, with someone else last night, I — I can't say too much, can I? With my track record and all. But I hope you'd have enough sense to limit your affairs to someone who would treat you better than that." His eyes went to her jaw.

"How dare you!" Her heart thumped wildly in her chest as she stepped toward him. "You were the one written up in the tabloids for having a different woman on your arm for every one of those Glitter Town Galas. Not me."

She took another step toward him, anger swelling inside and overpowering her fear. "*I* didn't snort coke with the starlets. *I* didn't rack up debts at the casinos. *I* didn't bounce from bar to bar, or from bed to bed."

She took yet another step forward. He stepped back. "That's ancient history. I admit I did some stupid things. But that part of my life is over. You don't have to keep dragging up dirty —"

"Then don't you accuse me of being unfaithful."

"Well, Pearl Pureheart is certainly having hot dreams, then. Should've seen yourself last night." He smiled.

Piper had a fleeting memory image of feathers, a flash of warmth, and she stopped.

"Who's getting you so hot and bothered in your dreams, Piper? Ren Wyatt? Think I haven't seen you watching him out of the corner of your eye? Think I haven't seen the two of you making cow eyes at each other? The best defense is a good offense, right, sweetheart?" He shrugged. "You're a piece of work, Piper. I'm going in to write. You'd better get a hold of the sheriff, tell him to call off the manhunt. Or sluthunt. Whichever." He glared at her briefly, then retreated into his office and slammed the door shut.

Piper just stood there, completely numb. She glanced at the bed. The blanket and sheet were wadded into a ball. Both pillows were on the floor underneath the window.

Something glinted in the sunbeam streaming through the remaining shards of glass dangling from the fractured pane.

Smoothing the pillowcase with trembling fingers, she touched, then lifted, a shimmering black feather.

CHAPTER NINE

Piper answered the door, her palm so sweaty it kept slipping off the knob. She finally swung the door open.

Ren stood there, blue sleepless shadows in the space between his brows and cheeks contrasting starkly with warm brown eyes. He stared at her in the blank, uncomprehending way one person looks at another he hasn't seen in a while and didn't expect to see now. Then his thoughts seemed to gel, and recognition lit up his eyes. He framed her shoulders lightly with his hands.

"Are you all right? My God, what happened?" His jaw clenched as his glance traced down her lower face. He released her right shoulder and plucked a forked pine needle from her hair with long slender fingers. He turned and called over his shoulder. "She's here, Frankie."

She peered around Ren's shoulders and saw a sandy-haired man in blue pants and a gray shirt with a badge over the left breast pocket, doffing a brimmed hat.

"Mrs. Defoe? You okay, ma'am?"

She nodded. She tried to smile, but the effort hurt her jaw. She glanced back at Ren, and for a moment, she felt closer to crying than at any time since her childhood. But her eyes remained dry.

Worry, anger, relief and concern marched across Ren's face like flash flood warnings across the bottom of a TV screen. "Can we come in?" he asked.

She nodded and stepped back.

The two men entered, the sheriff turning his hat around in his hands as if it were a steering wheel.

"Won't you sit down?" she asked, her speech still sounding thick to her ear. Her tongue felt lumpy where she'd bitten it. She gestured to the living room with her left hand.

"Piper, this is Sheriff Madigan. Frankie Madigan. He's pretty much all of the Crooked Creek Police Department. And my best friend."

Frankie nodded and extended his hand. "Mrs. Defoe, I need to ask you some questions."

She shook her head. "There's no need. I'm okay. There aren't any charges to press or anything. Sorry for all the trouble."

Frankie looked unconvinced. "What happened to your face?"

"I...I fell. My husband and I had a — disagreement. I was upset, ran from the house toward the creek and had forgotten how steep the embankment is. I slid down the bank — it was dark — and fell on a rock. I shouldn't have run off. I wasn't thinking straight."

"Frankie, mind if I have a few words alone with Piper?"

She suddenly realized Ren's stare had never left her face.

"Okay. I'll be in the car." Frankie turned to go, then paused. "Mrs. Defoe, if you change your mind, give me a call. I realize what a famous man Mr. Defoe is. Hell, I've bought all of his books myself. But what's right is right. Being a celebrity can't protect anyone from being accountable for their actions. At least not here in Crooked Creek."

Piper stared at him for a moment, not sure what she should say, how much she should admit. She decided on a simple, "Thank you. I'll call if I need to, Sheriff."

His smile was warm but with the touch of sadness that hinted he'd seen too much and it weighed on him. "Ren and I go back a long time. He said you're a friend. Call me Frankie. We're not fancy around here, and Ren tells me you're a local lady. Almost local, anyway. Blowing Rock isn't far."

"Thanks, Frankie. I appreciate that."

He winked at her and closed the door behind him.

"Where's Braxton?" Ren asked.

His voice was as soft as buttercups to her ear and she almost smiled. "Upstairs, writing. Would you like a cup of coffee?"

He shook his head. "Will you tell me what happened?"

"I did."

He didn't blink, but his eyes darkened as she looked into them. She felt the force of his personality washing over her, as powerfully as when he was telling one of his stories. Yet he didn't say a word or look away from her. He just reached for her hand, uncurled the fingers, pulled out the feather still clutched within, and held it between their two faces. "Will you tell me what happened?" he repeated, his voice as soft as the feather he held.

"How did you know the feather was there?"

He smiled. "Do you always answer a question with a question?"

"Do you?"

His smiled widened. "Would you rather I didn't?"

"Does it matter what I prefer?"

He threw back his head and laughed. "Yes. It does matter what you prefer. To me it does." He drew her into the living room, and they sat side by side on the sofa. "Tell me."

She couldn't suppress a sigh. Her first inclination was to fabricate something, to preserve their privacy, uphold her sense of loyalty to her husband and maintain some sense of dignity. But when she looked at Ren, saw the raw, honest emotion in his eyes, she realized she didn't want to lie to him. "Last night, well, actually this morning, I was sound asleep, and I woke up to him hitting me with his pillow, like an old-fashioned pillow fight. But he wasn't playing; he was wild.

"He called me names. Vile, ugly names. He had this...this horrible look on his face. Enraged. No, more than enraged. Like he was someone...*something* else altogether. Then he stopped with the pillow and —" She couldn't look at him anymore. She looked at her hands instead. "— and used his fist."

He stiffened visibly on the sofa beside her. "Does he usually —"

"No. Never before. I swear. Then there's this damn bird obsession —" She looked at him.

Ren lowered his eyes slightly and turned to look at her. "The crows? The raven he was asking about?"

She nodded.

He stared at her for a moment, then stood and began pacing, his hands jammed into his pockets. "What about them?"

"They've been giving him fits. You heard him the other night about the giant raven who 'attacked' him on the front porch. He keeps ranting and raving about how intelligent the bird is. How he can see the intelligence and cunning in its eyes."

He stopped in front of her easel. "Who's the artist?"

"I'm the painter. Not an artist."

He cocked his head to the side and studied her attempt to paint Crooked Creek gorge. No matter how hard she tried, she couldn't manage to bring her painting to life. The gorge — at least as she'd painted it — seemed flat.

"It's really not bad," he said.

She chuckled. "That's about the nicest thing that's been said about my paintings."

"They *are* intelligent."

"My painting?"

He looked at her and grinned. "No. Ravens. They're a very intelligent specie."

"Maybe so. But surely not so smart they would persecute one particular man. Braxton's obsessed with them." She proceeded to tell him about the broken window and Braxton screaming that something was trying to come through the window to get him. "I'm sure he thought it was that raven. He didn't say so, but I'd bet that's what he was thinking. Then, when I came home this morning, he asked me why I'd broken the window! Ren, he didn't remember a thing."

"Maybe he was covering up." He stopped pacing and dropped back down on the sofa.

"No, he didn't remember. He isn't a good liar. Anyway, one of the pillows was still lying on the floor beneath the window." She looked away from him, not wanting to see him look at her as if she, too, were mad. "That's where I found the feather. On top of the pillow. Maybe the bird *was* trying to get to him last night."

Piper looked at her hands. She glanced toward the front window, then panned the room, anywhere, at anything, not wanting to look into Ren's eyes, waiting for him to speak. Finally, she couldn't stand waiting any longer and abruptly shifted her eyes to his.

He sat quietly, turning the feather over in his hand. As if he'd felt her look, he turned to her. His expression was strangely still — a disquieting kind of still — like the air before a thunderstorm. "Did you dream last night?"

"Maybe. I think so. I remember something about rocks and feathers and —"

And then she did remember. Like a film zipping along in fast-forward, the whole dream flashed in front of her eyes.

Her face grew hot.

"Are you familiar with the terms incubus and succubus?" he asked.

She shook her head, relieved he'd changed the subject.

"In mythology, they are demons or spirits that force sexual intercourse upon sleeping humans."

She didn't know what to do with her hands, then ended up rubbing her forehead with her fingertips. A dull ache was starting to throb behind each temple.

"Did you dream of a raven?"

"Don't be ridiculous!"

"Did you?"

"I have no idea. Well, there was a bird. Black. Feathery. Maybe." Somehow she'd gotten to her feet. "That's all I know. So now you think I'm nuts, too, right?"

"No." His voice was so soft she barely heard him. Maybe she imagined it.

He reached over and touched her lightly on the wrist. "Was it violent? Or loving?"

"Dreams are just symbols," Piper said. "Problems, symbolized problems that your subconscious is trying to solve." She realized her foot was tapping, and she willed it to stop. "I was probably thinking about Braxton's obsession with the crows —"

"Raven."

"— whatever, and the bird became symbolic in my dream of —"

"Was the encounter violent or loving?" he repeated, his voice a shade harsher.

"Loving," she admitted, then puffed out her cheeks and expelled the air in an exasperated burst. "Loving. Wonderful. There. Happy? Think I'm a class-act pervert now?" She glanced at him to gauge his reaction, but his head was bowed slightly, and his fingers were wrapped around his amulet. He tucked the leather pouch back beneath his shirt and looked up.

"Piper, there are —"

"Don't let me interrupt you two lovebirds," Braxton said from the bottom of the stairs. "Just refilling my pitcher." He held the container up in mock salute. "But perhaps I'll do the gentlemanly thing and take a drive. Leave you two to your own devices."

He slammed the empty pitcher onto the counter and stomped out the door.

Piper and Ren exchanged glances.

"Does he often 'take a drive'?" Ren asked.

"Yes. Whenever he's upset or angry." She paused, glanced out the window at the Jeep roaring away. "No more dream interpretations, Ren. Please? They aren't important. What's important is Braxton. He was under a horrible amount of stress in California, professionally, financially too. Gambling, drinking, drugs, not eating well, staying up all night. His career blew up in his face. He became depressed." She folded her hands, rubbing them back and forth as she wondered how much she should say.

"Now I'm not sure. He doesn't seem depressed since we moved into this cabin. He's writing a lot. Even when you and Mary Beth visit, as soon as you leave, he heads straight up to his computer and stays up half the night. He's turning out reams of work. More than ever."

"So if he's not depressed and working well, what's the problem? Other than his abusing you."

She sat back down, looked at her hands, twirled the gold band on her ring finger. "He let me read the first pages, and I — well, I helped myself to a few more chapters yesterday. When he was napping. Ren, they're awful. He switches the names of the characters, confuses their personalities. The sentences are disjointed to the point of being gibberish."

"And this hasn't depressed him? That he's lost his ability to write?" Ren asked.

"That's just it. *He* thinks he's writing wonderfully. He rambles about clever plot twists he's come up with that day, or how this is the most intricate plot he's ever worked with and he can't believe how all the subplots are intertwining so cleverly."

"Writing is subjective. That doesn't mean it's bad."

"I know that. But this is barely English! I'm beginning to think he's — his mind has snapped."

Ren looked closely into her eyes, then turned and leaned his head against the sofa back. He sighed. "I know I shouldn't ask this, but I have to. Why do you stay with him?"

She stiffened. "You're right. You shouldn't ask. Why do you stay with Mary Beth?"

"I love her," he said simply. "Sure, her incessant chatter can be annoying. She's put on a few pounds over the years, and maybe she's superficial at times. But...she's the most warm-hearted person I've ever met. She's a good woman."

Piper was ashamed of herself. She'd had no right to categorize Mary Beth with Braxton. *In sickness and in health.*

"Besides," he continued, "Mary Beth never punched me in the jaw." A twinkle in his eye hinted he was trying to lighten up the conversation.

"Good point." She smiled, hoping it would convince him she wasn't being malicious with her unwarranted swipe at Mary Beth.

"Has Braxton displayed any other symptoms that might point to either a physical or emotional disorder?"

"Violent dreams. Gruesome stuff. He finds fault with everyone, everything. I don't think I've heard him say a kind word about anyone. Well, except for your son, of course. Braxton's quite taken with Jeff. They seem to have bonded."

"No offense," Ren sputtered, "but if Jeff has to bond with someone besides me, Braxton would *not* be my first choice."

"I know," she said. She wanted to ask about Ren's strained relationship with his son, but didn't want to pry. Besides, Jeff wasn't the issue at the moment.

The door swung open, and Frankie stuck his head in. "Ren, sorry to interrupt, but I've got to get back to the station. Another dispatcher quit."

Ren laughed. "What do you guys do to your help down there? Chew them up and spit them out? What's that make, three? Four?"

"Three," Frankie answered. "No, we treat them well. Just can't find anyone with a work ethic anymore. Nobody wants to earn a paycheck."

"I do," Piper said.

"You?" Frankie asked.

"Yes." She paused, her mind racing through the possibilities and the obstacles. "I need a job. I...need the money. I need something constructive."

Frankie stared at her. "You're serious, aren't you?"

"Yes, very. I've been looking at the want ads. There isn't much."

"We don't pay much," Frankie warned.

"If I can earn enough to buy the groceries and pay the utility bills, we'll be that much further ahead. Of course, I've never worked as a dispatcher. I don't know if..."

"Come in Monday morning. We'll give you a try, and you can try us on for size. If the fit isn't good, either for you or for us, by the end of the week, nobody's lost anything. Right?"

Piper smiled and offered her hand. "Right. I'll be there. What time?"

"Eight o'clock," Frankie answered, pumping her hand enthusiastically. "I can put Marge back on nights. She likes the graveyard shift better, anyway. Keep you on days. If the arrangement works out." He turned to Ren. "You ready?"

"Yeah. Just one minute more, okay?"

Frankie nodded, said his farewell and closed the door behind him.

Ren reached for his jacket. It was a dark brushed wool, soft, as soft as Piper thought his hair might feel under her touch. She stood and held it for him, inhaled the smell of him — the pine needle and mountain stream scent of him. She held her breath, giddy with his nearness.

He turned to face her, and his eyes softened, flashing warmly through her.

Then the moment was over. His eyes cleared and he took a step back.

His voice was husky, quivering. "Let — I'll try to find someone close by who can help Braxton. A counselor, perhaps. Although he should have a complete checkup first, in case there's a physiological disorder."

"He'll never go."

"I'll think of something." He headed for the door, then stopped. "Will you be all right?"

She nodded.

"I have an eleven o'clock class and a one o'clock." He reached into his pocket, drew out a pen and an old envelope and scribbled a number on it. "Here's my number at school. Promise you'll call me if anything — *anything* — happens?"

"I promise."

When the door closed behind him, the house seemed empty. More peculiarly, she seemed empty.

Piper pulled herself slowly up the stairs, feeling every one of her thirty-two years. She stopped on the landing, the gentle purr of Braxton's computer uncommonly loud in the still house.

Veering right and around the corner of his desk, her eyes glanced at the monitor.

Murder Mountain/Defoe/p. 380 across the top right of the screen.

Three hundred and eighty pages?

Impossible.

She scrolled down the screen.

"— and the horns started blaring. The cop on the street corner cry, Piper, cry, cry, cry, why can't you cry? it's not natural not to cry. maybe theres something wrong with your tear ducts or maybe theres something wrong inside your head or maybe you dont have no emotion no heart and thats why you cant ever cry cry cry cry cry. bet i can make you cry if your human that is but thats the question isn't it? Are you human if you were a normal human you would want to go to parties and be the wife of a successful author and wear designer clothes and live in a beautiful house and you could cry cry cry cry but i can make you cry just watch me make you cry you ugly half breed whore your gonna cry cry cry cry cry c —"

Piper stuffed her fist into her mouth, biting down hard. Then her stomach contracted. She ran, blindly, smashing her shoulder into the door frame, around the corner, her stomach heaving, and barely made it into the bathroom before the retching began.

CHAPTER TEN

Piper stood beneath the water, chin tucked toward her chest, hands braced against the tiles, letting the hot spray blast against the bunched up muscles in her shoulders and neck. She hoped it would soak away the hurt, the betrayal.

It didn't. The hatred Braxton had aimed at her through his monitor had found its target, and the wound was already festering.

Still feeling dirty when the water turned tepid, she gave up, towel dried her hair and pulled on a clean pair of jeans and a sweatshirt. Her fingers lingered on the telephone. Should she call Ren? She'd promised.

She snatched her hand away. Ren had his own life. He didn't need her mucking it up. And even if she'd wanted to call, he had classes till late afternoon.

She needed to immerse herself in something she had some control over. Something engrossing. Padding barefoot down the stairs, she stuck a soft rock tape into the stereo, fixed a cup of coffee, and studied her painting.

It stunk.

Braxton was right. Contrary to what they'd told her in college, she had no gift for painting, no matter how relaxing it was or how completely she could lose herself in the act of applying paint to canvas. Her perspective of the gorge was correct, the shading was realistic, yet the overall effect was...mechanical. Tightly controlled. There was none of Van Gogh's passion, none of Picasso's depth.

Perhaps because she was so tightly controlled, had kept such tight reins on her own emotions since she was a child. Stifling the hurt of an abandoning mother, trying to please the conservative, aging grandmother who raised her, then being a constant disappointment to her husband.

Piper lifted the canvas from the easel, leaned it face first against the wall and set up her large sketch book to a fresh page. Perhaps she'd start at the beginning, what her freshman art instructor had called "learning to see".

With her eyes closed, she freed her mind of all thought and images, placed her charcoal stub against the paper, and let her subconscious dictate the drawing. She felt her hand move, hesitantly at first, then wobbling across the pad. Her eyes opened after a few seconds and she continued what she'd begun.

Her charcoal flew over the canvas, the lines flowing boldly, fluid. Free, sweeping, confident strokes.

When she'd finished, she stood back and stared at what she'd almost mystically created.

A raven stared back at her, proud, haughty and omnipotent.

The sketch was good, *damned* good, the best she'd done since college.

But what perversity had made her sketch something guaranteed to antagonize Braxton? What dark corner of her mind was so cruel?

She quickly covered the sketch with a drop cloth.

More time had passed than she realized, and she was tired. She put away her art supplies, refilled her coffee, strolled onto the porch and was just propping her feet up on the rail when Ren's white truck appeared in the driveway, a rooster tail of dust fanning up behind him.

His long legs skipped the first two porch steps. "Braxton come back yet?"

"Hello to you, too."

"Hi. Sorry." He stuffed his hands in his pockets, took a deep breath as if he intended to say something, then clamped his lips together.

"What's the matter?" She set her mug down and rose from the chair.

"Nothing. Not — sorry, I didn't mean to give you the impression something had happened. It's just that I..."

He ran his fingers through his hair and swallowed. "I've had

this feeling ever since I left this morning that something was —
wasn't right."

Braxton's monitor immediately flashed in her mind, of the
hatred its words revealed. But Ren couldn't possibly...

"I almost phoned you a few times, but you'd promised to call
if anything happened." He abruptly stopped pacing and faced her.
"Piper, we need to talk."

"Okay. Have a seat."

"No, not here. I don't want Braxton to come home and find
us...together. It wouldn't look right. Let's take a walk."

Piper bit her lip for a moment. Ren was always so calm —
why was he in a flap now? "Pardon my logic if I'm wrong, but if
he comes home, sees your truck here and we're not here, don't you
think he'll assume that..."

Ren gave her a weak grin and shrugged. "You're right. I'm not
thinking straight. Do you...want to go for a ride?"

"Sure."

Fifteen minutes later, Ren's truck pulled into the parking lot
near the top of Roan Mountain. It had been a quiet ride, the
silence uncomfortable. Or maybe, Piper thought, it was just the
nearness of Ren that she had found so discomforting. They
decided to walk a small section of the Appalachian Trail.

Ren was still quiet.

"Are you going to tell me what all this is about?" Piper finally
asked. This was a whole different side of Ren than she'd seen
before. His silence struck her as ominous rather than his usual
reticence. He was obviously uneasy; his smiles had been forced,
and his face was flushed although the day was comfortable and
their walk had been slow paced.

He stopped, glanced at her, then looked around. "Let's find a
place off the main trail to talk." He pointed to a narrow path
intersecting the more heavily traveled one they were on.

A few feet through the trees, they came to a small clearing with
a spectacular view of the valley. The color of the maple trees —
already gaudy with autumn color — was even more brilliant where
the rose gold sun of late October shone down on them.

Ren sat down and leaned against a large ash, stretched out his long legs, and sighed.

Piper sat down next to him. "What's going on?"

He plucked a blade of grass from the ground beside him and flicked off little snippets of it with his nail. "The whole time we've been walking I've been trying to think of a way to explain things to you that won't make me sound like a raving lunatic. I can't come up with anything."

He took a deep breath, expelled it through puffed out cheeks, then turned to face her. "Piper, I *know* things, things other people don't know about. Except for my mother. If anything, she's even more...perceptive...that way than I am." His eyes were very intense, as if he were trying to convince her simply by the power of his gaze.

"Like second sight or something?"

"Yeah. Mostly 'or something.' Hard to explain. I don't see 'visions' or anything, and it isn't like extra sensory perception. I just get a feeling in my gut — not all the time, just occasionally — and certainly never when I *want* to sense things."

"Okay. You have some kind of gift."

"You don't believe me." His voice was flat.

Piper sat up straighter and looked at him. "Yes, I do. There are lots of things that can't be rationally explained. At least not yet. Maybe someday they will. But I don't understand why this suddenly has you in an uproar? I gather you've lived with it for a while. It hasn't just happened to you now, has it? And what could it possibly have to do with me?"

He put his finger under her chin and tilted her head up. A warm tingle spread along her jaw and her heart gave a little lurch.

"It has everything to do with you, Piper. You're in danger. I've thought about it all day. Ever since I left your house this morning, I've..."

"Danger from what?"

"I don't know. It isn't clear. But it's a very strong feeling."

"What you're saying is that you think Braxton's going to hurt me. Aren't you?"

"I didn't say that."

"No, but that's what you keep hinting."

"It's a possibility, Piper."

"He made a mistake, dammit. A bad one, granted, but a mistake. One he doesn't even remember — you've got to take his mental state into consideration. And he was so...solicitous...this morning."

She pulled away from him. How could she explain that she was incapable of thinking at all when he was so close?

She took a deep breath, drew her knees up to her chest, locked her arms around them, then gazed out across the valley. Funny how things so far away appeared so sharp and well defined when things close up were in such a muddle.

"Braxton's never been violent before," she said. "At least, not that I know of. Not with me. He's got problems, granted. Big ones. But he deserves a second chance. I owe him that much. And if he agrees to see a therapist...well..."

"Loyalty's fine, Piper, even admirable. But not blind stupidity. Braxton's delusional. You need to keep your distance from him."

She jumped to her feet, spun around and glared down at him. "You don't know that. And you have no right to talk to me about such things. There's a fine line between friendship and butting in, Ren Wyatt, and you've just crossed it."

Then he was on his feet, too, glowering down at her. "I'm only trying to protect you, dammit. I can't stand seeing you hurt. When I saw your face this morning, saw what he'd done..." He ran his hands over his face. "Piper, I'm so confused," he said, his voice barely above a whisper. "But one thing I'm not confused about: Braxton is dangerous. There's more going on than we know. You've got to get away from him."

She spun around, planning to stomp off, refusing to listen to any more.

But Ren grabbed her arm, pulled her close. Suddenly his arms were around her and she was on fire.

His lips glided across her neck like white coals. A scalding tremor ran up and down her spine like fingers flittering through the scales on a piano.

She molded herself to him, sculpted herself to every possible surface until they were so hopelessly entwined that they cast a single shadow on the ground.

There was nothing but that moment, that place. Nothing existed beyond his earthy scent and the sweet salty taste of him, the gentle strength of his hands beneath her sweater and the heat of him. There was no tomorrow, no yesterday. Just need. Frantic, unbridled need.

They struggled from their clothes like butterflies emerging from cocoons, peeling them away, not allowing enough distance between them to make the disrobing easier, fumbling with the complexities of buttons and zippers and belts by pure instinct.

Then time halted.

Her world consisted of heat, hands, and hearts thumping in unison. Somehow they went from standing up to laying down, from two entities to one, and Piper found herself careening along on a steadily increasing rush of air, until she found herself on a sudden *whoosh* as if she were rocketing through the sound barrier at Mach I to a new dimension. A new reality.

For a long time after, neither of them stirred. Piper was too emotionally drained to move more than her hand, which lazily stroked Ren's fine hair, reveling in its softness, listening to his breathing gradually return to a rhythmic, even pace. She luxuriated in his warm weight upon her, in the security of it. She felt so safe. So *linked.*

Ren turned his head toward her. His lips fluttered across her neck as softly as butterfly wings, across her cheek, her eyelids. Then he took a deep, ragged breath, and rolled off of her, washing her in sudden cold. He lay on his back, resting on the leaves and pine needles. Piper rolled toward him, kissed him once softly on his cheek and started to drape a hand across his chest.

But he slid out from underneath her arm, stood and began tugging on his clothes.

She hadn't expected that. Hadn't anticipated such an abrupt end to the warm afterglow. Her stomach contracted. Was he upset? She sat up, leaned back on her palms, felt something unexpectedly soft, velvety, beneath her left hand and glanced over at it.

She blinked.

Shifting her weight, Piper picked up the largest of several feathers, still warm from her hand. It glimmered in the sun, blue black. Luxuriantly silky. Ren was staring out at the mountains on the far side of the valley, buttoning his shirt.

"Ren, —"

"I'm sorry. I don't think I can talk about this right now. Sorry." His voice was thin, and his shirt was all askew, buttoned into the wrong holes. His hands were visibly shaking as he fumbled to straighten out the mess he'd made of his shirt.

She dropped the feather. Stood. Slid her hands up his chest and started to rest her head on his shoulder.

He moved away. "Please don't."

"Ren, don't do this," she said. "Please."

"You probably won't believe me, but I didn't plan for this to happen. I only wanted to warn you about —"

"I know."

"I would never — *never* — do anything to hurt you. Don't know what I was thinking. I wasn't thinking. That's the problem. I just...reacted."

"Is that so wrong?"

He gaped at her. "Yes. It *is* wrong. You're upset, your life is in tatters, you're in no frame of mind to judge who or what you want. And even if you were — we're both married." He caught the metal corner of his buckle in the belt loop as he jerked the leather through. He yanked, ripping the denim loop off. "Dammit!"

"Yes, but —"

"There are no buts." He turned to look at her. His eyes were wounded, filled with the confused hurt of refugees on the nightly news fleeing their homelands. "I'll never be able to look Mary Beth square in the eye again."

"You still love her?" Piper's voice sounded tiny to her own ears.

He didn't hesitate. "Of course I do. We've been together a long time. It's not...not the same as what I feel for you. *Have* felt for you, ever since that first night we met. There was never that intensity between Mary Beth and myself. That electricity."

"Then why did you marry her?"

He gazed at her with a look of unbearable sorrow, then his expression quickly changed into something unreadable. "Piper, please get dressed."

She'd forgotten she was naked, felt the heat rise in her face until she knew it must be as scarlet as the leaves beneath her feet. She quickly retrieved her underwear from the ground and struggled to get into her clothes as quickly as possible.

Pulling her long hair out from the neckline of her sweatshirt, she turned to face him.

He'd watched her dress, never took his eyes off of her while she had hurriedly tried to cover her nakedness. He looked at her now as if she were still undressed. She felt the impact of his eyes deep within her, eyes filled with tenderness and sorrow. "This can't happen again, Piper. We can't let it."

"But I can't let you go! I can't just pretend it never happened, Ren!"

"Please, Piper. Don't torment me like this. Don't torment us."

"But —"

He hushed her by putting his finger to her lips.

"There are no buts. Wrong is wrong."

She brushed his finger away. "It felt right to me. More than right. We're meant —"

"Don't say it. Please don't. We're thinking with our hearts, not our heads. Don't say anything you'll regret once the guilt starts eating away at your conscience, once the ramifications of this afternoon seep into you." He put his hands on her shoulders and stared at her intensely. "I've never felt anything remotely close to what we had a few minutes ago. But I have to forget it — somehow — and so do you. If you care about me, you will."

Forget it? Forget the most incredible moment of her life? Forget that for one brief moment she'd felt a part of someone, of something larger than herself?

He dropped his hands. "Let's go. You've got enough to think about with Braxton."

She tried to take a deep breath. It caught in her throat. She tried to speak, and couldn't. Finally, she bit her lip and simply nodded her head.

It was only later that she remembered the feathers.

CHAPTER ELEVEN

Braxton snatched frequent glances at the nubile young woman at his side, their flirtatious banter having exhausted itself to a silence he found more pleasurable than idle chatter. They strolled up an old logging trail toward a gorge Susannah had described to him as lovely.

And, more importantly, private.

Struggling up the path's steep incline, Braxton felt the beginnings of a cramp in his leg. His breath started coming a little harder.

Damned cigarettes!

Finally, the path flattened out, curved, and they were on the edge of the chasm known as Crooked Creek Gorge. The ground fell away at about a sixty-degree angle some seventy or eighty feet to the boulder-strewn water below.

The view was spectacular, but no more thrilling than the promise on Susannah's face or the movement of her breasts as she caught her breath, her gaze sweeping across the gorge. She was so young; his first thought was that the hike shouldn't have affected her at all. Then he realized that because she was so short, her tanned legs had taken two steps for every one of his.

He set down the small cooler they had packed and flexed his fingers. "How much farther to this wonderland you told me about?"

She looked up at him; her smile reflected in knowing eyes. "Hungry?"

"Starving." *But not for the fruit and cheese I bought.* "How far?"

Her smile widened. "Maybe a hundred yards, through there." Susannah pointed to a break in the trees angling away from the precipice. She picked up the cooler and took off, scrambled over a boulder, then stopped on its crest to look back over her shoulder.

"Coming?"

"Yep. Just enjoying the scenery." It wasn't the gorge he'd been watching.

Braxton had spent most of his day driving aimlessly around, trying to overcome his depression, wondering how to dispel the gloom that encompassed him. As he cruised past the Wyatt's driveway, it occurred to him that what he wanted — what he needed — was Susannah.

She was there, alone, waiting for her date to pick her up, a date whom she was only too happy to stand up when she realized she could spend time with Braxton.

Now, the first lightning bugs flashed in the graying light. Crickets chirped. Susannah picked her way down the far side of the boulder, then disappeared into the trees.

He found her a few minutes later, leaning against a large boulder that dominated the small, grassy clearing. Her silver blonde hair gleamed in the fading light. Water gurgled noisily nearby, feeding the river far below.

Susannah opened the cooler and set out the two glasses and bottle of wine. "I'm glad you suggested buyin' wine and cheese instead of the beer I started to bring." She bit her lower lip. "You must think I'm a real bumpkin. Guess I am." She held the corkscrew out to him. "Here. You do the honors."

"You're not a bumpkin, Susannah. You simply haven't been exposed to more upscale living. But I can change that. Why don't you set out the food?"

He worked the cork, then poured the wine, while she set out grapes, peaches and cheddar cheese on a small plate, and stretched luxuriously.

Invitingly.

"How are you going to expose me to...what'd you call it? Upscale living?"

He dropped down beside her, putting his arm around her shoulder and squeezing the warm, firm flesh of her upper arm. "Well, I can't do anything, of course, until I finish my novel. That won't take long. But then I'll have to fly to L.A., to take care of the business end of things. You can ride along. There's a few people I can introduce you to. That is, if you can bring yourself to leave

Crooked Creek."

She slipped out from beneath his arm, rolled over onto her knees, then sat back on her haunches, facing him. "Oh, yes," she said breathlessly. "You have no idea how bad I want to get outta here. I'd do *anything* to leave this place. Could you introduce me to a producer? Or — or whoever could help me be an actress?"

Braxton smiled. "I could. Although whether you can act or not remains to be seen. You do have other...talents, that are readily apparent." He allowed his gaze to drop to her chest, and let it linger there for a moment. As he thought she would, she sat up straighter, thrusting out her breasts as if for approval.

Oh, she was a hot little ticket.

"Actually, what I had in mind was modeling. It seems more in line with your...charms. Have you done any modeling?"

She laughed. "In Crooked Creek? Where? At the hardware store? Besides, I thought you had to be tall and thin to be a model. I'm only 5'2" and — well, not flat-chested."

He reached out and lifted a strand of hair off her shoulder. It was like champagne-colored satin, and curled delicately around his finger. "Well, that's true — for fashion models. But they prefer more feminine women to model at trade shows and such. And I understand they pay quite well." He patted the ground next to him. "Sit here. Let's watch the night fall together."

He refilled their glasses while she snuggled up next to him, then sipped his wine and watched her.

He offered her a piece of cheese; she took it daintily between her teeth, and his stomach contracted when she licked his fingertip.

Then he offered her the fruit tray; she smiled, selected, and he stared, strangely aroused, as she bit into a juicy peach with small, neat teeth. A trickle of juice ran down her chin.

He leaned over and licked it off.

It was the moment of harvest.

Under the soft gray of an October twilight, he was ready to pluck the fruit from the tree.

His fingers expertly opened the tiny buttons of her white knit shirt, then peeled it away, revealing Susannah's firm, warm flesh, soft as a peach beneath the fingers exploring her landscape. She was a willing, succulent morsel on her own merits, but the knowledge of whose daughter he was about to plunge into increased the pleasure of his feast tenfold. He cupped the heavy warmth she offered and tasted of the fruit of the tree.

It had been more like the rutting of two animals than lovemaking, Braxton thought afterward. But that was okay. He'd been satisfied, Susannah purred like a contented kitten, and the bottom line was it had been a pleasant way to pass a glorious autumn dusk. What the luscious Susannah lacked in experience, she made up for in enthusiasm and firm young flesh.

Satiated, he rolled onto his side, propped his head on his hand and sipped his wine.

So, Storyteller, what else do you have that I want?

Your son?

Your daughter?

Your precious *stories?*

He smiled, thinking for a moment about the brief summaries of every tale the storyteller had shared over the past two months, probably fifteen or twenty of them, secure both on Braxton's hard drive and backed up on disk. Those stories were his secret weapon against future writer's block.

Most likely he wouldn't need them. *Murder Mountain* would be finished by the first of November at the rate he was going. And several novel ideas had sprung from its pages, plots that would surge him to the head of the bestseller lists again. Where he belonged.

It was such a pleasure stealing from The Storyteller.

Susannah sighed contentedly, drawing Braxton's attention away from his thoughts and back to her. She rolled onto her side, stretched sensuously and arched toward him.

The peculiar *hummmm* filled his head again, softly at first, its volume steadily increasing to an annoying level, like a dentist's drill. Grating.

His muscles tensed. A nasty taste flooded his mouth. Abruptly, Susannah looked overblown somehow, rather than succulent.

Frowsy. She parted her lips in an alluring smile. A sliver of pink appeared, an invitation that suddenly seemed as appealing as a snake's tongue flicking at lightning speed, seeking a target.

His stubble had reddened her cheeks and chin; they looked like the early stages of bruising, where the flesh would become mottled and soft, then start to decay.

She reached for his hand, guided it to the curve of her waist, a waist that would someday soon disappear under rolls of flesh. She had the kind of compact, fully fleshed body that, at its peak, was ripe and sensual but would inevitably turn to fat — sagging, dimpling flesh hidden under shapeless cotton housecoats or maxing out the stretch of polyester pants.

His fingers tingled, as if their nerve endings were becoming desensitized. The flesh of her waist felt thick. Rough.

She guided his hand to her breast.

Had it been so spongy before? A gelatinous mass of white flab, iridescent in the dim light.

Repulsive.

She opened her mouth to speak, asked what was wrong with him. A fetid odor hit him, borne on her breath, the smell of demons and devils and corpses and blackness. The pink serpent's tongue lashed out at him again.

He struck.

He knocked the serpent back down the thing's throat. Its mouth spewed forth a spattering of blood as the serpent retreated. He aimed his fists for the marshmallow flesh of the beast's breasts, sank into them, into the spongy mass of decaying meat that had succured the serpent and other vile fiends.

He hammered at it, fists alternating like pistons punching the air, but these shot into the hollow at the base of the thing's throat.

Something *snapped*.

The hollow was gone, flattened, level terrain.

But his hands still fit around it, and they felt so good squeezing, kneading, like a child's modeling clay, silky, his fingers sinking into softness.

Something crumpled within, delicate *pops* and *crackles* and *crunches* accompanying the rushing of his blood.

Everything blurred together, everything pink-tinged blurs,

whirling blurs of gray, tinged with pink.

A flash of red exploded behind his eyes. He screamed in agony, his hands flying to the sides of his head as if it were detonating and he was trying to hold it together.

His scream echoed off the mountains, lingered in the thin air, then dissipated.

His eyes closed tightly to shut out the whirring. The humming.

He toppled sideways, slammed onto the ground and rolled onto his back.

When his pulse finally slowed and the hum faded to silence, he opened his eyes, nostrils flaring at a foul odor mixing with the rich aromas of pine and humus.

Damn, his fingers hurt. And he was out of breath, panting like an old man. But at least that godawful *hum* had stopped.

He held his hands above his face and opened his eyes. Blood dripped off his hands, plopped onto the bridge of his nose, tracked over the side and leaked into his eye. He blinked away the blood and stared with horror at the condition of his hands.

What the fuck happened? His hands were covered with blood. Were his fingers broken? He wouldn't be able to write. They wouldn't be able to hit the keys or hold a pen.

He flexed them, grunting his relief when they moved easily. He splayed them, then retracted them. They felt okay: tired, bruised, but okay.

He sat up, reeling a little from dizziness. When it passed, he turned his head to the side and looked straight into the jaws of hell.

"Sus — Susannah?"

Brain glitch.

This "thing" couldn't be Susannah. She couldn't be next to him, naked and bleeding and broken and — dead.

Blood trickled from her mouth, streaks of blood glistening red, smeared across her face like war paint.

Her nose was out of alignment, flattened and crooked.

The shimmery silvery hair was mostly dark red, and her front teeth were sharp jagged shards.

A fly buzzed out of somewhere and landed on the corner of her opened eye.

Dark purple-blue ovals ringed her neck, a surreal necklace. Bloody fingerprints stood out amongst the rivulets of blood on her breast, crimson against white.

He looked at his hands. He looked at Susannah's face.

He traced the fresh blood on his index finger with his other hand. He had no cuts. No abrasions. Lots of blood.

He looked at the fingerprints on her breast. He looked at his fingers.

At the purple splotches on her neck. At his fingers. At the awkward angle of her head.

At his fingers, long, strong, supple fingers that had thrown TD passes, gripped five-irons, signed autographs, tied lures, wrote best selling novels.

His fingers blurred.

Her pummeled face blurred.

Harlot.

His pulse raced.

His throat constricted.

Whore.

His nostrils flared, tickled by the scent of death.

His fingers splayed.

Tramp.

He rubbed his knuckles, brought them to his nose and sniffed them like a hound catching a scent.

He rocked back on his heels. Slowly, methodically, he licked the blood from his hands.

<hr />

Yellow light spilled out the cabin's windows, washing the ground with a warm, inviting glow. It looked like a greeting card. *From our house to your house.*

Braxton stumbled through the door. Piper was curled on the sofa, her feet tucked beneath her, an afghan draped around her shoulders. She placed her opened paperback down on the cushion, swung her legs over the edge of the sofa and stood. "Brax, are you okay?"

"Fine." It was more a growl than an answer.

"I didn't hear the car pull in."

"Had a flat. It was too dark to mess with. I'll get it in the morning."

He started up the stairs.

"What happened? It's almost two o'clock. Your clothes are a mess. And you're shaking like a wet dog on a cold night."

"Need a hot shower."

"You missed the Wyatts."

"Sorry."

"That's not like you." She made a move toward him.

"I said I was sorry, goddammit! Leave me the hell alone." He stepped on the first stair.

Blonde hair sprawling on the pine needles.

Second step.

Black hair strewn across rock.

Third step.

Red blood, white skin.

Fourth step.

Red blood, bronzed skin.

Fifth step.

Fingers sinking into flesh.

Sixth step.

Black feathers.

Seventh step.

Blurrrr.

CHAPTER TWELVE

A dull persistent thumping, like a shutter banging against the house during a windstorm, permeated Braxton's foggy mind. He clutched his head to stop the throbbing, but his hands felt as if they'd been bruised, battered.

Breathing was difficult. His chest was under enormous pressure, and the room seemed stifling. He struggled to sit upright, and a drop of sweat rolled over his brow and slid down his cheek.

He remembered sliding, tumbling toward the creek.

Creek?

When he pushed back the covers and sat up, the room spun around as if he were on one of those "Whirl and Puke" rides at a theme park. He threw his legs over the side of the bed and his foot landed in something soft, like sinking into flesh.

Sinking into flesh?

He blinked and looked down at his foot. It had landed on Piper's slipper, a fuzzy scuff.

Flesh?

Jesus, it's cold.

He ripped the blanket off the bed, wrapped it around him and tried to stand. His legs were weak; he crumpled into a heap on the floor.

I'm sick. Oh, God, I'm so sick.

Distant voices murmured through the floorboards, voices he could not identify.

A thick, phlegmy rumble started deep in his chest and erupted into a hacking cough that left him gasping and weak. He worked his way out from beneath the stifling blankets to where the air felt refreshing, knelt down, and pressed his forehead to the cool, smooth, planked floor.

Cool water, rushing water, scrubbing his hair, scrubbing his hands, scrubbing the scent of the whore off him.

What whore?

"Braxton? What's wrong? Are you all right?" Piper's voice loomed over him; then suddenly her tawny, supple hands tugged at his arms, awkwardly maneuvered him up off the floor and half-draped him across the mattress.

"S...So cold." His teeth chattered like the wind-up dentures sold in novelty shops.

"You're burning up. Here, can you push?" She nudged him the rest of the way onto the mattress and pulled the covers over him.

He coughed again, a racking, rattling sound, like BBs in an air gun.

She sat on the edge of the mattress. "Braxton, I'm sorry to hit you with this when you're sick, but have you seen Susannah Wyatt? Sheriff Madigan is downstairs. Susannah's missing."

His eyeballs felt fried. He managed to shake his head, "no." The movement hurt.

"I didn't think you had, but he wanted me to ask. It seems she never came home from her date last night, and the Wyatts are frantic." She tucked the blankets around his shoulders. "But you need to let me know where the car is. I'll get the tire fixed, or get it towed home or something."

He closed his eyes and let his head roll to the side. Better to let her think he'd just drifted off. He'd sort out his thoughts later, figure out which were real, which were dreams.

Not dreams.

Nightmares.

And, apparently, he *did* drift off. The next thing he knew, it was five-ten in the morning. The clock's digital numbers glowed eerily across the room, casting a red glow on the dresser. He was alone.

He sat up, then stood gingerly, testing the strength in his legs, then using the wall for support, made it into the bathroom. He was soaked again, but he felt a little stronger. Perhaps the fever had broken. Vague memories of hot soup, cold juice and foul-tasting medicine being spooned down his throat drifted through his mind. When he pressed the lever to flush the toilet, his left hand hurt.

Bracing himself against the wall, he rounded the bottom of the bed, pulling open his drawer to look for dry pajamas. Suddenly queasy, he felt spied upon. He glanced into the mirror above the dresser.

He thought he saw a movement in the window, a glimmer.

The glass, just replaced, was smudged, smeared with the glazier's fingerprints. It was hard to see through the streaks. He spun around, craning his neck, and squinted, trying to blot out the blurs.

A glimmering sparkle of shimmering moondust on shadow.

He stared into eyes which smoldered with rage and silent accusation. They shifted from side to side, staring, boring through him like an auger through ice.

The raven.

A stabbing pain ripped through his chest, dropping him to his knees.

It slacked off after a moment, and he looked to the window again.

Empty.

Braxton crawled on hands and knees to the window, pulled himself up by clutching the sill and closed the curtains, then flopped back onto the bed. He shivered again, trembled uncontrollably, but this time there was no fever.

He lay awake until the first gray fingers of dawn crept through a place where the curtains didn't overlap. He got up, dressed, and made his way slowly down the stairs. Piper was asleep on the sofa, her breathing deep and regular. He shut the door softly behind him. At the edge of the porch, he scanned the sky, the trees, around the corner of the house.

Nothing.

Visions...nightmares...fever...they left him weak. Drained. Just the thought of walking all the way to the lonely glen where he and Susannah had parked the car was exhausting, assuming he could even find it again.

But he'd find it.

He had to.

Piper left Braxton a note telling him she was going to the Wyatts to offer moral support, chiding herself for doing so even as she folded the note and taped it to his monitor screen. Why bother? He didn't care where she went or what she did. His monitor was dark now, but the last words she'd read on it were imprinted on her mind.

She slipped on a fleece-lined denim jacket and headed out the door.

It was a gorgeous day — sunny, crisp and cool. Not a cloud in the sky. A perfect day to walk.

But by rights, it should've been raw, dismal, with roiling storm clouds and a chill wind blowing. After all, Piper had found and lost the love of her life in the course of one afternoon. Probably a record.

But it was important to keep things in perspective. What was a broken heart compared to a missing human being? A missing daughter? God only knew what the Wyatts were going through. For her to wallow in self-pity now would be unconscionable.

Piper had to finally admit her marriage was over and it had nothing to do with Ren. She couldn't live with the hatred she'd seen on that monitor, or never knowing from one minute to the next what might happen. Braxton was too unstable. The hungry, idealistic young author she'd married no longer existed.

But she'd failed, too. Miserably. Not even counting... yesterday. With Ren. Her stomach lurched at the thought of Ren and her heart constricted. She couldn't even think about that yet. Didn't know how she'd be able to face him. How she'd ever be able to face Mary Beth again.

But she had to. They needed all the support they could get. She bent her head to the wind, thinking — not for the first time — how fortunate it was that she and Braxton didn't have children.

The door opened as Piper stepped onto the first stair tread to the Wyatts' porch and Frankie Madigan stepped out. He didn't seem surprised to see her.

"Saw you walking up the driveway," he said, holding the screen door open for her. Voices drifted through the opening.

Piper paused and kept her voice low. "Have they found Susannah yet?"

Frankie shook his head. "But her boyfriend showed up half an hour ago, drunker than a skunk and raving mad. I've got a deputy in the kitchen with him, trying to sober him up, at least get him coherent enough to answer some questions. Come in."

Piper had never been in the Wyatt house before. She stepped into a living room that reflected Mary Beth's taste, not Ren's. Ruffled lampshades, flounced pillows and "country-style" crafts — blue and mauve beribboned geese and dried flower wreaths — were everywhere.

Ren sat hunched over on a blue tweed sofa, a startling island of masculinity in a *Woman's World* room, his head in hands, elbows propped on his knees. There was no sign of Mary Beth. The voices she'd heard still seemed to come from an area past the dining table.

"Ren?"

He looked up, eyes shadowed and flat, his face gaunt. He hadn't shaved, and his whisker stubble glinted in the light coming through the window. He looked ten years older.

"I'll go see how Skip is sobering up," Frankie said. "Maybe make a fresh pot of coffee."

Piper crossed the living room and sat next to Ren. She reached for his hand, automatically sandwiching his calloused palm between both of hers. It was an instinctive gesture of sympathy that felt *right*. Natural. As if his hand belonged in hers.

What to say? Platitudes like "oh, she'll be fine," or "you know, how kids are nowadays"? Meaningless nothings that eased no ones pain, did little more than fill vacant air waves with the sound of human voices?

No. If it were her child who was missing...

"How's Mary Beth coping?" was what she decided on.

He rubbed his eyes with his free hand. "She did fine at first. Madder than hell. Figured Susannah was out partying with Skip and lost track of the time. As the night wore on, she passed 'mad' and went straight into 'ballistic.' But then when Skip showed up looking for Susannah..."

He looked away. His Adam's apple bobbled. After a long moment, he turned back toward her. "She fell apart. Went completely berserk. Frankie and I finally got some Valium down her throat which kicked in a little bit ago. She's sleeping."

"And Jeff?"

"I sent him up to my mother's. He's okay. He had the presence of mind to take his guitar along. As long as he has an instrument to make music on, he can handle anything."

Piper ignored the edgy note in Ren's voice. "Does Frankie have any theories? Did you check with her girlfriends? Maybe she spent the night —"

"She's only got one 'girlfriend' —" he tripped on the word, placing a bitter emphasis on it, "and yeah, we checked. Nothing. Seems she's got a lot of boyfriends, though." He lowered his head and looked at their hands. "I keep thinking about Billy Dale Wilson. What happened to —"

"Ren, don't. You'll make yourself crazy thinking about that. And I'm sure something like that couldn't happen again. It was a fluke. She'll turn up."

Ren looked into her eyes, opened his mouth as if to say something, then apparently changed his mind. A moment later, he asked, "Is Braxton still sick?"

"I guess not. He was gone when I woke up this morning. Guess he went to fix the tire."

"Tire?"

She nodded. "He had a flat last night. Walked home. Said it was too dark to change it then."

Ren's hand trembled slightly in hers. "Where did he leave the car?" His voice was flat. His words were clipped, a far cry from his usual rolling cadence.

For some reason she couldn't identify, she didn't want to meet his eyes. She stroked his long fingers with her own. "He didn't say." She felt a slight flutter deep inside her, then suddenly, a need to defend Braxton. "He was really sick, Ren. Fevered. Chills. So weak he could hardly stand. And a rattly cough. I'd have thought he would have stayed in bed this morning. Even if the fever broke, it would leave him too weak to walk. Or change a tire."

"Brought you two some fresh coffee," Frankie said, setting the mugs on the coffee table.

Ren slid his hand out of hers and reached for the coffee, wrapping both hands around it as if to steal its warmth.

Her own hands suddenly felt incredibly empty and cold.

"How're you making out in there?" Ren gestured toward the kitchen.

"He's coming around," Frankie said.

"Well? Is he making any sense? Does he know where she is?"

"Skip told Warren he was supposed to pick Susannah up at seven. He got here a few minutes early. No one answered the door. He waited around till seven-thirty. Still no sign of her. He says that's when he decided to leave. He said that —" Frankie stopped suddenly and looked a little confused. Then his expression cleared, and he continued. "Said she'd stood him up before and this time would be the last time. So he left."

Piper suspected Frankie was leaving something out, but she didn't question him. She was here to offer moral support, not play detective.

"Where was he last night?" Ren asked. His voice was wooden, tightly controlled. "Where did he go when he left here?"

"Cruising, he said. Looking for someone to party with." Frankie looked away. Again, Piper had the feeling he was being evasive, or if not evasive, telling parts of things rather than the whole.

A raised voice in the kitchen broke the quiet. Frankie headed toward it, disappearing.

"I need some air," Ren said. He stood and went out onto the porch. Piper followed close behind. He hunkered over the railing, his forearms resting on it, staring out toward the mountains. She joined him, soaking up the peaceful vista, wondering how it could all look so serene, so magnificent, when a daughter was missing.

Movement caught her eye, a flash of light. Then the hazy, lazy swoop of a bird drew near.

"Look, a hawk," she said, touching Ren's shoulder and pointing skyward.

They watched the bird spiral downward on its current, gliding, wings outstretched. Then it flapped its wings twice, evened out its flight path and circled the dooryard, its wingspan impressively wide.

"Raven," Ren said, fishing his amulet from his shirt and cupping it in his hand.

"You must have eyes like a hawk yourself to identify it from this distance," she said, feeling a tiny smile play on her mouth. She looked at him. Ren turned toward her, held her with his gaze, and she felt a shudder trickle down her spine. There was such a strange look in his eyes: flashing, either unseeing or seeing too much, she wasn't sure which.

Was he remembering yesterday?

He faced into the sun which highlighted the golden flecks in his brown eyes, yet he didn't squint against its brightness, but rather held fast to her gaze. She needed to look away, wanted to look away. She felt the connection forming between them again, the link, as if she were being drawn into those unfathomable depths of gold and brown.

Abruptly, he blinked, and the connection was severed. She looked away, her breath coming in shallow little flutters, and sought the bird. She wanted to watch the raven, to have something beside Ren to focus on, and was curious to see whether her sketch was as life-like when compared to the real thing as it had looked in her living room.

But the bird was gone.

She looked to the east, then was panning toward the west, trying to spot the raven, when a soft rush of air blew against her cheek and a sudden weight fell on her shoulder.

The raven perched there.

Piper froze. "R-Ren?"

"He won't hurt you," Ren assured her, watching her closely and holding his amulet.

"Didn't you say ravens are bad omens?"

He nodded. "But also birds of power. Great power. And knowledge."

By turning her head slightly toward the raven, she could see the tip of his hooked bill from the corner of her eye. She reached out tentatively with her right hand, felt the air like a blind woman, found Ren's hand and grasped it. Then she traveled up the length of his arm and touched the soft pelt of his amulet with a fingertip. Her fingers found beadwork, the kind her grandmother had spent long evenings working on, years of close work that eventually left her blind and permanently stooped.

She closed her hand, encompassing the amulet in her palm, and a surge ran down the length of her arm, a current that lasted only a fraction of a second. But when the slight shock stopped, she felt strong, at peace, more concentrated than she'd ever felt, and warm. The amulet radiated warmth like a sunbeam on a spring day. She looked at it with wondering eyes.

But Ren, shielding it from her sight with his own large hand, pried her fingers loose from the amulet and tucked it protectively back into his shirt.

"Why not?" she asked.

He shook his head, no.

"Please?"

He clasped his hands in front of him and stared at his boots.

Suddenly, her mind's eye retrieved the image of the black feathers she'd found yesterday after they had — when Ren had left her. "Ren, yesterday —"

"We can't speak of yesterday. Ever."

For a moment, everything blurred: Ren's face; the soft weight of the bird on her shoulder; even the murmured conversation from within the house. It all jumbled together. That something so beautiful as what they had shared should be made tawdry and cheap was incomprehensible. They would have to come to terms with it at some point. But now wasn't the time.

She gulped for air, for dignity. "Then at least get this raven off my shoulder."

He made no move.

She jerked her shoulder slightly, and the raven leaped off, landing with a flutter on the handrail. The bird shifted its weight from claw to claw, settling himself, then looked into her eyes, holding her mesmerized.

"What does he want from me?" she whispered. "This isn't natural. Birds aren't this friendly, this eager to be near humans." Then it dawned on her. "Could this be the same one that Braxton's obsessing over? Maybe he isn't as crazy as I thought."

"Perhaps he's *crazier* than you thought. Perhaps the raven is trying to protect you."

Her gaze still held by the power of the raven's unwavering stare, Piper stepped sideways, drawing closer to the safety of Ren.

She leaned against him, the lump of his amulet beneath her head, its warmth heating Ren's flannel shirt. But Ren immediately stiffened, pushed her slightly away from him, just enough so that loneliness washed back over her like a cold wind. Her glance finally tore loose from the raven's.

"No," he said. His hands glided up her arms and stopped at her shoulders, pinning her in place. He looked down into her eyes, gently, sadly. "There are things that are better left unsaid, no matter how large they loom in our hearts, in our souls. It cannot be. It *must* not be. Not in this lifetime."

He loosened his grip on her shoulders and walked back into the house.

She turned, disoriented, not sure what had happened, not sure what she felt. The raven still stared at her, searching her eyes, boring through her, as if it was ferreting out every secret, every image flashing through her head. Had it stopped staring when she'd turned to Ren? She didn't know; she didn't think so.

Abruptly, the raven opened his bill, *"caw-r, caw-r,"* and launched itself, flying right over her head, then gliding between the slender columns that supported the porch roof. It flapped its great wings, found its air current and took off higher and higher, circling once, seeming to look down at her, then disappeared over the trees and out of sight.

She started back into the house, thought better of it, and headed down the steps instead.

CHAPTER THIRTEEN

Ren ran his fingers through his hair and paced back and forth in front of the mantled fireplace. Fear and anger, guilt and love — all assaulted him at once.

How could his child be missing? Was it some kind of cosmic retribution for his sins? Did the pimply-faced kid in the next room know where she was? Had he harmed her? Susannah had always been headstrong, but she wasn't foolish. Or was she?

He didn't know. Ren shuddered, realizing just how little he really knew his daughter. Or his son, for that matter.

But how well do we know anyone? Really know?

He wrapped his hands around his amulet, breathed deeply and tried to use his powers to think like Susannah might think, to glean where she might have gone and why.

No good. He couldn't think like she did. He had no idea *how* she thought, what kinds of things ran through her pretty little head.

It was pointless. He might as well be tuned in to five radio stations simultaneously for all the good his powers did him when he was so upset. He had to find some peace of mind to recharge his batteries. And that meant one thing, one place.

He crept down the hallway and gently opened the door to the master bedroom. The room was dark and still; Mary Beth was asleep. She'd been sedated.

When had his sexy young wife become a middle-aged woman? Funny, you blink, and the whole world has changed. You are your father; your children are grown. You stop, at some unidentified point in time, looking to the future and start thinking of the past.

He pulled the covers around her, bent over and kissed the top of her head lightly.

Forgive me, Mary Beth, for what I've done.

He kissed her again then tiptoed from the room, heading for

the kitchen. He should tell Frankie where he was going.

"— swear to you I don't know," Skip was saying. His back was to Ren, his head in his hands. A mug half full of coffee was before him on the table. "When I left here, I went to the Pizza Keg. I mean, how many times am I supposed to let her stiff me? I bought a few drinks, and there was a good-looking redhead who wanted my company. One thing led to another and...well...you know, Sheriff. We left together. Went up to Roan Mountain, did some partying. Kerry or Terry, her name was. Sherry, maybe. Something like that."

"And you never talked to Susannah, never saw her at all?" Frankie asked. He slumped against the refrigerator, his glare never leaving Skip's face. The deputy, Warren, sat at the table with the boy.

"I swear, Sheriff. I'll swear on a stack of Bibles I didn't see her. She probably got it on with another one of those old guys she likes so much. From what Susannah says, they pay her plenty. The older the guy, the more they give her, and she —"

Ren moved like a lightning bolt.

He leaped into the room, dragged Skip out of the chair and slung him halfway across the kitchen before Frankie could react.

Ren was in the boy's face, ready to pummel him, when Frankie's arms clamped around his wrists. "Easy, Ren, calm down."

"If you're going to let him talk about my daughter that way, I'll have to shut him up," Ren said, locking eyes with Frankie.

He promptly wished he hadn't.

There was something in his friends eyes he'd never seen before. Sorrow? Sympathy?

"You think he's telling the truth?" Ren asked. "You know something I don't?"

For the first time in their long friendship, Frankie either wouldn't — or couldn't — answer.

Finally the sheriff let go of Ren's wrists. "Ren, it's probably just —"

But Ren jerked away. "Leave me alone. I'm going to the woods."

"Not now, buddy," Frankie said.

"It's either that or I take to the streets with a shotgun. I'm going nuts."

Frankie held up his hand. "Okay, okay. Anything but that. I have enough trouble without armed, pissed-off fathers scaring the shit out of the locals. Go do your thing."

Ren nodded. "You know where my spot is if you need me. If you hear anything."

Frankie nodded.

"You'll look after Mary Beth?"

"You need to ask?" Frankie said. "She'll understand. She always does."

Ren nodded his thanks, glared at the skinny, puzzled face of his daughter's sometimes boyfriend, then left.

The Jeep was parked in its customary spot when Piper got home. She gave it a perfunctory glance as she scurried around it, then stopped suddenly, gasping, not believing what she was looking at.

Between the Jeep's front end and the porch, a small doe lay on her side, eyes glazed, gray tongue lolling out of the side of her mouth. Her neck and belly were ripped open and flies swarmed over the carcass and the entrails which were strewn across the yard.

The grassy area leading from the woods was flattened, the grass blades bent toward the doe.

A predator must have been dragging its kill toward the creek, when Braxton turned into the driveway, frightening the hunter away.

"Poor deer," Piper said softly. "In your end is your beginning."

Then she turned her mind from the doe, ran toward the porch and hurried up the steps, halting abruptly at the top of the stairs.

The raven sat on the rail at the far end of the porch, its eyes fixed on her. She walked up to it, slowly, afraid of scaring it off.

It ruffled its neck feathers once as she approached.

She held out her hand. "Come here, fella," she said. "You are a male, aren't you?"

The bird blinked.

"Come." She spoke so softly she wasn't sure whether she'd spoken aloud or only thought she had.

The bird ignored her outstretched arm, flapped its wings once and soared to her left shoulder. The sharpness of his claws pricked through her shirt as it shifted around until it faced forward. Slowly, she lifted her left hand up, and with one finger stroked its chest feathers, surprised he let her pet him, and surprised by how good the simple gesture felt: wondrously soft, softer than any feather she'd felt before, as soft as a memory.

"Ren was right," she said to the bird, "you aren't a bad omen. Not for me. You're my friend — my magic bird." She ran her finger down its chest feathers again.

The raven made a rough sound in the back of its throat, a cross between a purr and a cackle, as if it agreed with her. It lifted a leg, stretched out its claws, then gently replaced it on her shoulder, repeating the gesture with its other foot.

Piper smiled. "I need a name for you. You're too majestic for something like 'Max.' Too dignified for 'Midnight' or 'Onyx.' How about 'Raven'? I like it. Do you?"

It chortled again in the back of its throat.

She laughed. "You like it. At least I know you aren't guilty of that." She pointed at the deer. "You're a big fella, but not big enough to bring down a deer. I have to go inside now, Raven. I'll see you later, okay?"

As if the bird understood, it hopped off her shoulder, flapped its wings once and settled onto the railing.

Before Piper let the screen door shut behind her, she glanced at the bird. It sat straight and dignified, never looking away from her.

As she entered the house, she scanned the living room. The ashtray was overflowing with stale cigarette butts, newspapers lay scattered on the sofa and floor along with Braxton's balled up socks, a murder mystery he'd been reading, and an empty Bloody Mary glass had left a ring on the coffee table.

But that wasn't all. Her easel lay broken in the corner, her paint box had been dumped out and her carefully organized tubes of paint were scattered in a wide swath. A knife handle protruded from her sketchbook — the blade stuck right between the eyes of her charcoal raven.

She sighed and shook her head. Shouldn't be surprised, she thought. She certainly wasn't going to make an issue of it: She'd known it would set him off. The only real surprise was that he'd been curious enough to peek under the drop cloth.

She found Braxton upstairs, tapping away at his keyboard. "How's it going?" she asked.

"Good." He didn't look up.

"Feeling better?"

"Fine."

"Brax, we need to talk."

"Not now." His fingers continued to dance over the keys, never missing a stroke, eyes staring at his monitor. He chewed on the corner of his lip. He was flushed. Sweating.

She rounded the corner of the desk and glanced at the monitor.

Page 420? Incredible!

But she didn't like the look of all that perspiration, that blotchy ruddiness on his cheek. She put her hand to his forehead.

He jerked his head away from her hand and leapt from his chair, knocking it over backward. Never looking away from her eyes, he backed away, hands behind him, feeling his way along the wall.

"Do...not...touch...me. BITCH," Braxton shouted.

"God, Braxton, I'm sorry. I didn't mean to —"

"You never mean to!" His eyes were wild. "Always sneaking up on me. Spying." Spittle sprayed from his mouth. "Trying to catch me doing something, aren't you? Driving me crazy with stupid accusations. Looking at me with those creepy, disgusting black witch eyes of yours."

"I thought your fever had returned and —"

"Don't give me any of those shitty excuses of yours. You're looking for evidence: lipstick on my collar, or smeared makeup or —"

"I was not! Your face is bright red. You don't look well." She edged toward the door.

Braxton stretched to his full height and squared his shoulders, leering at her. "Right. Always the concerned wife, aren't you?" He stepped toward her. "You're dying to ask me where I was yesterday, why I didn't come home until late, aren't you? AREN'T YOU?" He took another step.

Piper backed away, through the narrow space between the corner of the desk and the wall, smacking her hip into the sharp maple corner of the desk.

But he kept coming.

"You're wrong. I was checking for fever. I don't care *where* you were as long as you weren't with Susannah." She took another step backward, felt the door jamb on her left, stepped out into the hall.

"Susannah?" Braxton snorted. "Why would I be with Susannah? What the hell do I care about some small town slut when I could be with any woman I want? Sophisticated women. Intelligent women. Beautiful women. Not half-breed, half-witted whores happy to wander through the woods all day wearing pony tails, shapeless jeans and sweatshirts."

His face grew redder, and his eyes glittered. "I know where you were just now, Piper. You think you're so smart, trying to throw me off track. But I know better."

"What're you talking about?"

"Your note. Oh, very clever, Piper. But not clever enough. I know you were with Ren." His lips curled into a sneer.

"Of course, you know. I told you so in my note."

Confusion flickered across his face. Then it was gone. "I still have the note, Piper. You said you were going shopping."

She stared at him. "No. I said I was going to the Wyatts' to see if I could help. I never said anything about shopping."

"YOU DID!" he screamed, pawing frantically through the papers on his desk. "I have your note. I can prove it. I'm not crazy! I can read!"

Piper didn't hesitate. She sped down the stairs.

Braxton's footsteps echoed heavily behind her.

She bolted through the screen door and down the steps. Just two paces into the yard, he latched on to her arm, almost jerking it from her socket. She spun around like a crazed dance partner, crashing into his chest.

She looked into his face, at the flaring nostrils, the bloodshot eyes flickering back and forth, sideways, as if watching something only he could see. His breath came hard and fast. Warning bells rang inside her head.

Braxton leered down at her. "I was with a woman. A real woman. Not a skinny, rock-hard woman like you, but a soft woman, warm and passionate, hot-blooded —"

He began to pant. A thin stream of spittle trickled out of the drawn-down side of his mouth. He cocked his head and peered at her, as if she were a strange new toy that he wanted to wind up to see what it would do.

His arm drew back, the fascinated look still on his face. His hand clenched into a fist.

A blur came toward her, a glimpse of motion.

Her face detonated into white light, and she flew backward and crashed onto the ground.

Disoriented. Everything smeared colors, a child's finger painting — blue — yellow — red, across the surface of her eyeballs.

Warm wetness trickled from of the corner of her mouth, tracing a path to her chin.

A searing pain enveloped her tongue.

Before the colors cleared, she was lifted by the front of her shirt and hauled upward. Felt something warm on her cheek. She planted her feet firmly on the ground, but her legs buckled, and she crumpled to her knees. She wiped away the colors.

Braxton's hands grabbed her shoulders in a vise-like grip. His face was so close to hers that he blotted out the world, eyes half-closed. His tongue sensually flicked out, touched her jaw, ran up her cheek then licked the blood from her face, licking her clean.

Her stomach lurched.

Another blur hurtled toward her.

She jerked her face to the side trying to deflect the blow. Still another blur streaked into her field of vision. A raspy screech rankled in the air, like worn brake pads grinding against metal.

In the split second before Braxton's knuckles connected with her face, claws plummeted from the sky. Braxton's fist whooshed past her left ear; a thin, spine-tingling scream mixed with the raven's harsh cry.

She was free, toppling sideways, smacking the ground so hard that her teeth crashed together, and her shoulder *cracked.*

She craned her neck, looking upward.

The raven was atop Braxton's head like an eagle who has snatched up its prey, legs locked, claws extended, sunk into Braxton's scalp.

Streamlets of blood dribbled from his hairline and down his face, painting a bizarre road map of red across his features.

The bird's wings beat the air. It threw back its head, opened its hooked bill and screeched again. Then it began lifting its legs, alternating one with the other, pulling clumps of Braxton's hair out with every step. The tufts poofed into the air before drifting to the ground.

Braxton beat wildly at his head, screaming insanely. He collapsed to his knees, but the raven held fast.

Another clump of hair flew out and landed on Piper's knee. Tiny patches of scalp were still attached, glistening wetly.

The raven leaned forward and began pecking, wood-peckering into Braxton's splotchy skull.

Piper rolled to her knees. She finally found her voice. "Raven, no!" she cried.

The beak stopped drilling. The head snapped up. The bird's eyes met hers.

"Enough. ENOUGH!" She forced herself to stand, forced herself to ignore the throbbing pain in her face.

"Enough," she said again, more a whimper than a command.

Raven quieted for a moment; then it flew the short distance from Braxton's head to her shoulder. It perched there, settling its weight daintily.

She stumbled — Raven clinging fast to her shoulder — to where Braxton writhed on the ground, his fingers clamped against his tufty head, rivulets of blood seeping through the seams of his fingers. She helped him to his feet and wiped the blood from his eyes.

He looked at her, wildly, without recognition, until he saw the raven riding her shoulder. Then Braxton's eyes rolled back in his head and his mouth opened in a silent scream.

"Not one word," she cautioned, surprised at the flat calm of her voice. "I'll get you cleaned up. Then you're on your own, you perverted bastard."

Braxton gasped, then managed a smile that was almost ghoulish. "I knew I could count on you."

She looked back over her shoulder. "I'd do the same for a cat hit by a car, Brax. And you know how I feel about cats."

The raven swayed on her shoulder until they reached the screen door. As she opened it, the bird hopped onto the rocking chair then flapped to the railing, turned around and watched her intently as if to say, 'I'll be right here waiting for you.'

She nodded, glanced at the deer carcass then over at Braxton, staggering in circles. His lips moved softly as if he were praying. A soft whimper escaped the back of his throat, and his hands still clutched his head. She was certain he was in too much pain and shock to attack her again.

"Stay put," she called. The screen door banged shut behind her.

CHAPTER FOURTEEN

Ren choked back his rage as best he could. He needed to get a grip on his emotions, to regain his mental equilibrium.

Physical inertia was feeding his wrath, like throwing kindling on a fire already burning too wildly. He had to move — to act.

Right now, out-of-control, he was no good to anyone, not his daughter, not Mary Beth, Piper, not even himself. He'd slipped into system overload, where logical thought was impossible, where his mind was a jumble of images, emotions and frustration.

He bolted for the woods, avoiding those paths of least resistance.

Instead he blazed his own trail, scrambling over boulders, crashing through blackberry thickets, leaping over fallen, rotting logs and splashing through creeks, trying to deplete the surge of adrenaline his anger and fear had triggered.

After thundering over two-miles of demanding terrain like a crazed bear, his mind began to quiet, its attention diverted to the painful cramps in his legs — searing licks of discomfort that were preferable to mental torment — and his pace slowed.

He noticed his surroundings, sought landmarks, trying to orient himself, deciding the best route to his "sacred place," the place where he meditated and could tap into the hidden sources of strength within him.

His grandmother had taken him daily to a similar spot close to the house where he was raised, training him to tap into the spirituality where the wisdom of his ancestors lived. She had helped him find his spirit guide, and when his mentor had been identified, she had sewn his amulet, filling it with tokens of his guide's earthly presence. Thinking of her now warmed his heart and thawed the chill that had frosted his soul.

When grandmother had died and he brought Keysa to North

Carolina, they had found the spot above the gorge together.

As his breathing returned to normal and his heart gradually resumed its familiar rhythm, he headed toward the gorge and started sorting through his thoughts, the first step toward a plan of action.

He needed relief from the glut of confusion: did he love Piper? How could he *not* love Piper? He felt himself grow warm, breathless, remembering how magnificently unself-conscious she had been standing naked in the woods, the sunlight gold on a face still flushed from their lovemaking. As natural as a wood sprite.

How could he love Piper and still love Mary Beth? How could he ever hope to tuck Piper away into some musty corner of memory? How could he even *think* about a woman when his child was missing?

How could his child be missing? People didn't up and disappear except on television — certainly not around Crooked Creek, where everyone knew what everyone else was up to.

He changed direction, traveling slowly but deliberately, eager for the peace of mind his sacred place brought him. As he made his way through the woods, he kept the images of Piper in the far corners of his mind; the accusations about his daughter that Skip had flung around their kitchen were shoved into even farther corners. He would think his way through these problems when he had regained his peace, when he was back in his spiritual center.

But never before had his soul been so at war. Would he be able to find his center?

Braxton's head was a fireball that would not stop burning. Deep, quaking shivers rippled through him like an abused dog, and waves of nausea added to his discomfort. Piper's attempts to clean his wounds didn't help any. One moment, he thought nerves caused the queasiness; the next moment, he was convinced poison from the filthy beast was coursing through his system. And Piper hadn't said a word — not made a sympathetic sound — since the attack.

"You're sure I don't need to see a doctor?" he asked again.

"You need a doctor, all right," she said. "But not for these scalp wounds."

He bit back the retort that instantly came to mind. It would be stupid to agitate her while she still had the bottle of alcohol in her hand. In the state she was in, he wouldn't put it past her to throw it in his face.

Callous bitch.

When she'd finally finished and returned the alcohol to the tray on which she'd carried everything to the yard, she leaned back against the tree and crossed her arms. Her face showed as much compassion as a granite statue.

"Where were you last night, and who were you with?" she asked.

"Hand me some aspirin, will you?"

She shook some into his hand, placed the vial back on the tray and re-crossed her arms, her expression cold and stiff.

"Let's go back inside, Piper. Please? That damned beast hasn't taken his eyes off me for a single minute. Wish I had a shotgun."

Piper's gazed shifted to the branch above them. The filthy critter had accompanied her when she'd come back outside to Braxton, then settled himself directly over their heads.

Braxton suspected if he so much as raised his voice to Piper, the bird would attack again.

Piper looked back at him. "I'm not stupid enough to be alone with you again, Brax. I'm *not* going inside that house. Now I asked you —"

"I know what you asked. And I told you. A real woman." He pulled himself to his feet, grabbed the soda she'd brought out with her and washed down the pills with it. "Of course, you wouldn't know what a *real* woman is."

"I've got a pretty good idea of how *you* define it. And I don't care if you were with another woman. Not any more. Just promise me you weren't with Susannah Wyatt."

"Don't start that shit again. I told you, no."

"Swear."

"Why?"

"Because she's missing, that's why. Because her family is beside themselves with worry, and I need some kind of assurance that you don't know where she is. That nothing happened."

Fresh, warm blood.

He blinked and took a deep breath. "What do you think, Piper? Think I abducted her? Have her chained up in some isolated hideout to enact my fantasies on? Get real."

Flickering tongue, serpent's tongue, smooth white belly.

He massaged his temples. "Jesus, I feel awful." He groped for the tree, balanced himself against it, then staggered a few feet away. He dropped onto his knees and moaned. The jarring hurt his head.

"Swear to me," the bitch said. She'd followed him, no more willing to drop the confrontation than a hungry shark would drop a tuna.

"I swear. I swear I wasn't with the little Wyatt girl. Give me a little credit for having some common sense, not to mention taste. Happy? Do you believe me?"

Piper's eyes flickered. "I don't know. I want to believe you. God knows I want to. But you've been so crazy lately —"

Braxton rolled into a sitting position. "I've been crazy? You think *I've* been crazy?"

"No, Braxton. I think licking the blood off someone's face is perfectly normal. It's done in all the best circles. Perhaps that's something you picked up at one of your little Los Angeles soirees?"

"What are you talking about?"

"You! Right over there." She pointed at the spot where they'd battled. "Just a few minutes ago. You licked the blood off my face."

"You're crazy! That's disgusting!"

"Damn right, it's disgusting. It's downright insane."

"Insane? Don't talk to me about insanity. You're practicing some kind of witchcraft or something, and you accuse me of being nuts. You're something else, Piper. Is this an example of the best defense being a good offense?"

He stretched his legs out in front of him. The movement sent a miserable shiver through him, but it passed, and he thought he felt better. "And why don't you care any more that I was with another woman, huh? You used to care. It used to bother you a lot."

"You get used to anything that happens often enough." Piper glared at him, then clamped her lips firmly together.

"No further comment? Point well taken. However, I expect it's more that you aren't in a position to shoot off your mouth anymore about the sins of infidelity. Am I close? Is that it?"

Piper's faced drained of color. Her hands came up in a graceful gesture.

Oh, she's good. She's real good. The palms up, wide-eyed innocence. Whore.

"Yeah, sure, sweetheart. Deny it to the end." He stood up. He felt stronger. The throbbing subsided in his head somewhat, now that the aspirin had kicked in. What he needed was a drink. "Show me a smidgen of respect. Do you think I'm a complete fool? All your long, long walks in the woods. Those passionate looks between you and the Storyteller. What am I supposed to think you're doing? Picking wildflowers? Bird-watching? Well, actually, that's possible. Maybe between rendezvous —"

Piper's upper lip twitched as if it wanted to raise into a sneer and she were forcing it down. "You're sick."

"You're guilty. It's written all over your face."

"You need a psychiatrist, Braxton. I don't know whether it's your nerves, or the liquor, or you're really mentally ill."

"Starting to sound like a broken record, sweetheart."

"All this vacillating back and forth, charming one minute, beating the tar out —"

"Beating you? In your dreams. I've never laid a hand on you. Talk about vacillating. One minute you're the unjustly accused housewife, the next you're the poor, abused victim."

Piper looked stunned. "You don't remember?"

"Remember what?"

"Braxton, look at my face. You don't remember punching me?" She tapped her cheekbone. It was swollen and purplish.

"Okay, you look like shit. So what's new? You're not pinning that on me, old girl. I might not be a perfect husband, but I've never hit you. Never." Her face looked distorted, like a reflection in a fun house mirror where the middle part seemed off-center with the top and bottom. He closed his eyes, tightly, trying to refocus.

Whirr. That damned buzzing started in his head again. He pressed his palms to his ears to quiet the hum. It didn't work.

He opened his eyes. Piper's neck was opalescent, pearlized, her long curly blonde hair —

Blonde?

— fluttering, tousled. She was no longer tall and sinewy. Petite, instead. Voluptuous and round.

Like a peach.

Ripe.

He leaned forward to pluck it from the tree.

Swelling, past ripeness. Past luscious. Bloating.

Soft white flesh rippling within the cheap cotton housecoat. Turning purple, the pale blue eyes engorged. He reached, the deep purple fingerprints on her neck drawing him like a magnet. The throat...

Something beating at him. Drilling into his head.

"Get him off me! Get him off!"

But she couldn't. One of his hands still clutched her neck. He tried to beat off the attacking bird with the other.

"Braxton!" Piper was clawing at the hand — his hands.

He let go of her, screaming, *"Get him off me!"*

Sobbing, fingers at her neck, she gasped out, "Raven — stop!"

The bird looped around, landed back on his branch, and glared at Braxton, his head jerking, as if wishing he was still hammering his bill into Braxton's skull.

Braxton bent over, bracing himself with his hands against his thighs, trying to catch his breath, trying to regain his control.

If only the buzzing would stop!

He stood straight, watched Piper still fingering her neck, still gasping.

How lovely to have finally broken her stony countenance, to evoke emotion instead of that cold, controlled facade. "Why did you claw me, Piper? For Christ's sake, haven't I been through enough for one day?" He shoved his hands into his pockets and turned toward the house. "I need a drink."

"You need a straightjacket. Braxton, I swear to you, for your own good, you need to see a doctor. But I...I'm leaving you."

He stopped, then turned around to face her. "You're what?"

"I'm leaving. I can't take anymore of this."

He laughed. "Leave? You? You don't have the guts."

"Yes, I do. I'm leaving. Maybe filing for divorce. I don't know. But I'm not putting up with this — insanity of yours."

"Insanity." The word rolled around in his mouth like a marble. "Insanity. I see. You're going to have me committed, take all the money, money *I've* earned — you haven't contributed a dime — take my money and set up housekeeping with *your* lover. Is that the plan, Piper? Is that why you keep trying to convince me that I'm an alcoholic, or keep mentioning my mental state? We've made the big leap now, from 'breakdown' to full-fledged nuts!"

"There *isn't* any money, Braxton, and you know it. There's enough money to last less than a year. That's why I've got a job. To support myself."

"Job? What job?"

"With Frankie Madigan. The sheriff. I start tomorrow."

"The hell you are."

"The hell I'm not. At least it'll cover my expenses. And your money — *your* money — should last you longer than a year if it isn't supporting me, too. Unless you drink it all away." She brushed past him and started down the driveway.

"Where are you going?" he asked.

"Away."

Raven spread his wings and took off after Piper.

Something bubbled inside him. He couldn't stand the sight of her back turned toward him. How often had his mother done that? Threatened to leave, then turned her back on him. Keeping it turned until he promised to be good. Promised to do whatever she wanted.

But she'd done it once too often.

He was choking. Smothering. Whatever happened, Piper couldn't leave him. Couldn't abandon him. He wouldn't let her. "Piper, I'm sorry. I didn't mean it. Come back. Don't leave me. You can't leave me." He heard the pleading tone in his voice and cringed.

She stopped a few paces away and turned. He hurried to her and gathered her into his arms. She flinched and he felt her body stiffen.

Raven turned back, then flew in tight circles directly overhead.

"I'm not going to hurt her, you stupid bastard," he called to the bird. "Oh, God, Piper. I don't know what's wrong with me. I swear it. Sometimes everything is fine: I can write, I can function, I feel like laughing. Partying. Other times, I see — images. Sometimes they start with a blinding flash of light. Sometimes they superimpose themselves over whatever I'm looking at. Like a double exposure. Weird, sick images. Sounds. Tastes. Smells. I keep —"

No. Shove it back.

Piper pulled out of his embrace. Took a step back.

"Braxton, you need help. More than I suspected. That note I left you? It said I was going to the Wyatts' house. Somehow you garbled it when you read it. Your head garbled it. I couldn't understand what was going on with you. Couldn't understand why your manuscript is...the way it is. But if you're reading words that aren't there, well, it explains a lot. We'll find someone to help you." Piper reached out and patted him on the arm, tentatively, as if not sure she wanted to touch him or not.

Condescending bitch. Wouldn't know good writing if it slapped her upside the head.

"Oh, God, Piper. Please don't leave me. You swore you'd never leave. Remember?"

He saw her deflate, as if she were a balloon with a slow leak. Her buttons were so easy to push. All he had to do was remind her of her vows. Play a bird with the broken wing. He glanced up at the raven. He was still circling overhead, close, close enough so Braxton could see the bird watching him intently, the beady little eyes staring into him, through him.

"I don't know what's happening to me," he said, pleased with the slight quiver in his voice, trying to watch the raven from the corner of his eye. "I'm not sure I can function on my own anymore."

She stared at him, searched his eyes as if looking for answers. When she spoke, her voice was soft. He strained to hear it. "I don't want to leave you when you're down and out, but I'm not going to become a statistic."

She looked upward. "Raven, come!"

The bird dove downward and landed gently on her shoulder. He turned his ugly black head and glared at Braxton.

Piper lowered her head, and stuffed her hands into her jeans pockets. She walked slowly across the small clearing in the direction of the tree line. She pulled her hand from her pocket and stroked its chest with one finger, smiling up at the bird as she caressed it.

Witch.

✳

Piper was in awe of the bird. Logic demanded that a wild bird would not seek out one human being to protect. But so many things in life defied logic.

She stroked his chest feathers and once again was answered by the strange sound from the back of its throat. Contentment? She almost chuckled. Nice to have someone she could count on, even if it *was* only a bird.

Then her thoughts returned to Ren. Her feelings for him should not be cheapened by such as ugly word as adultery. There was an indefinable connection to Ren. A belonging. As if they shared the same pulse. A link that transcended parameters of law, boundaries of convention.

A link Ren chose to deny. Or ignore.

There wasn't much she could do about it. Life would go on, somehow.

Braxton? She had to find someone to help him. She couldn't leave a mental invalid to his own destructive devices, but she wouldn't continue to be his victim. Even if the abuse was a manifestation of his illness. It was a symptom, like a cough to a cold. Not the actual virus.

She sighed, wishing for the zillionth time that she could indulge in a good, soul-cleansing cry and be done with it all.

CHAPTER FIFTEEN

Late afternoon sun streamed through the bedroom window when Mary Beth finally awoke, groggy from her long, Valium-induced nap. Her mouth was dry, her tongue thick and sluggish. She padded out to the living room, found it abandoned, then stumbled into her kitchen. The coffee pot had been left on; a disgusting sludgy residue lay in the bottom of the carafe. Its scorched tang tickled her nostrils.

The sink was filled with unwashed mugs. As she rinsed then loaded them carefully into the dishwasher, she spotted Susannah's Disney World mug on the top rack. The sight of Cinderella's castle upside down brought her grief of the last twenty-four hours rushing back to her, flooding her mind. Within seconds, her tears dripped onto the dirty mugs.

When she'd wiped away the last of her tears, she automatically searched the refrigerator for a note. Ren was usually good about leaving word as to where he might be reached. Nothing.

She tidied up the kitchen, finding comfort in menial, familiar chores, then sat at her breakfast table, trying to figure out where Ren might be.

Ren had started acting strange even before they realized Susannah was missing. Withdrawn, preoccupied, jumpy. She was worried about him, not sure how well he'd handle a missing child.

Well, hell, how was anyone supposed to handle a missing child "well"?

He'd found someone to take his classes so he wouldn't be at school, limiting the possibilities to his mother's, with Frankie, or possibly went to the Defoes.

She called her mother-in-law; Keysa hadn't seen him.

She dialed Frankie's house. No answer.

Should she call the sheriff's department? No. They'd call her if they knew something. The sheriff's office was probably in turmoil. No sense pissing them off.

Should she call the Defoes? She drummed her fingers against the telephone. She still had a teensy suspicion that Braxton might have succumbed to Susannah's charms. It would be typical behavior for a man that age, wouldn't it? To find the attentions of a star-struck, attractive young woman irresistible?

She'd take a spin over there and gauge for herself. At least she'd be with someone. She didn't like being alone at the best of times, and this wasn't the best of times. She needed moral support.

She snatched up her car keys and headed out the door.

Within a short time, she was rapping on the door to the log cabin.

Braxton answered, his hair standing in isolated tufts on his head, looking like one of the walking wounded. She was so surprised by his battered appearance that she forgot to ask about the dead deer on his lawn.

"What happened to you? You look awful!" she exclaimed. His face was the color of mottled concrete, dirty-gray splotched with white, with faded pink streaks tracked across his forehead and on his cheek. Or was it a trick of the light?

"I was attacked by that bird again," Braxton said, swinging the door open wide. "Only this time, he won. Come in, Mary Beth. Is Ren with you?" He poked his head through the open door and looked around.

"No. I was hoping he was here." Mary Beth felt the tears welling up again and willed them not to disgrace her.

Braxton shook his head. "Sorry. Haven't seen hide nor hair of him. Any word on Susannah?"

She shook her head. "Not that I know of. Ren gave me a sedative so I've been asleep most of the day. When I woke up, the house was deserted. I don't know what's going on."

"How awful. Come, sit down. I'll get you a glass of wine."

Before she could protest, he was pouring the liquid into a stemmed glass. He handed it to her and with a sweep of his hand gestured her into the living room.

"Seems to me your husband would stay by your side during such a crisis. To offer moral support, if nothing else." He sat down on the sofa and patted the cushion beside him.

She tried to find the energy to be clever, to start the ball rolling toward a conversation that might shed some light on any relationship Braxton might have had with her daughter. But exhaustion numbed her. Her mind was sluggish, still laboring under the false serenity of the drug.

She intended to drop daintily onto the sofa; instead, gravity exerted its power, and she plunged downward, sinking gratefully back into the softness of the pillows. But she didn't spill a drop of her wine.

Braxton was right. Ren *should* be with her. It was their daughter who was missing, for God's sake. Did he expect her to cope with this situation alone? Not knowing if they'd found out anything?

She should've checked the answering machine. Lately, Ren had been pushing the little blue "memo" button on the recorder and leaving messages for her there rather than scribbling out a note and sticking it on the fridge. She must still be dopey not to have checked the machine. Too late now.

She sipped at her wine. It was particularly savory tonight, soothing her parched throat. She could almost believe everything was going to be okay, that Susannah was simply playing a thoughtless prank.

She took another sip, deeper.

Suddenly, she knew where Ren was. "He's in the woods," she said, noticing how tinny with surprise her voice sounded.

"The woods? Why? Searching for Susannah?"

She shook her head. "It was stupid of me not to realize it earlier. Guess I've just been too frightened to think straight." She rubbed her eyes. "It's an Indian thing. Whenever he's upset — pissed off, unsure of what to do — he heads for a special spot. Meditates. Searches his heart for guidance. That sort of thing. Never understood it myself, but he gets something out of it." Of course that's where he was. How typically Ren. She felt better already. "This is exceptionally good wine, Braxton."

"I'm glad you like it. Piper likes that meditation stuff, too. You must be right. It must be an Indian thing. I prefer to think my problems through logically rather than resorting to hocus-

pocus. But Piper heads for the trees at the first sign of trouble."
He swirled the dregs of his wine in the bottom of the glass. "But
Ren — that surprises me. He doesn't believe that crap, does he?
An educated man like himself?"

"Deep down inside he doesn't," she answered. "Maybe he likes
to cover all his bases, just in case." She smiled. "But then again,
his mother believes it. You met her at the festival — no, you
didn't. Piper met her. I remember now. Anyway, she's a dark and
dreary woman, believes all the old legends. Ren said she and his
grandmother were shamans in his village, sort of like witch doctors
or something. Actually, the old woman does pull off some pretty
spectacular magic tricks. Only she says they aren't magic. Listen
to me chatter on. My point is that Ren was raised with that Indian
hocus-pocus, so it's become a part of him."

"The acorn doesn't fall far from the tree?"

"Maybe. Or maybe he's only trying to please his mother, keep
the old traditions going. I don't know." She drained the last of her
wine.

"And Jeff? Does he follow that branch of the family?"

She smiled. "You and Jeff really are fond of each other, aren't
you? No, Jeff must be a throwback to some unknown ancestor.
He's definitely his own person. More so since knowing you. But
he's close to Ren's mother. He doesn't buy into the Native
American thing, but they're still very close."

Braxton was heading into the kitchen with their empty glasses,
so she had to turn around to continue talking to him. "Ren and
Piper," she said, "are a lot alike, more than just the Indian business.
Personality-wise. Perhaps that's why they get along so well."

Braxton brought their glasses and the bottle back from the
kitchen. "You're right, of course. Perhaps that's why they're so —
cozy."

"Cozy?" She sipped at her newly refilled glass. Something in
his tone of voice bothered her, something she couldn't quite
identify. "What do you mean...cozy?"

Braxton hesitated, then shook his head. "Nothing, nothing at
all. Still, I'm sorry he isn't here for you. I can't begin to imagine
what you're going through."

She glanced quickly at him. His eyes brimmed with

compassion. Her own eyes grew damp in response. How could she have doubted him?

He leaned over and rapped her softly on her forearm with his fingertips. "We weren't blessed with any children, of course, so I can't completely put myself in your shoes. But there's nothing quite so frustrating, is there, as feeling helpless? As if you've no control over the situation. Especially when the 'situation,' if you will, concerns your only daughter."

Her tears won. They slid down her cheek and her lip quivered. "Absolutely."

He patted her hand, then topped off her glass. "Rest assured, our thoughts are with you. And we're praying for Susannah. But I'm convinced she's fine. She's a singularly level-headed young woman. Sure, she's going through that self-conscious stage. Assumes everyone notices everything she does. But beneath all that fluff, you've got a rational daughter."

"You really think so?"

"Really. I was impressed with the quality of her mind. We all went through that angst. So she's trying a little too hard to be more worldly than she is — it's natural."

Mary Beth groaned inwardly, remembering her own behavior at Susannah's age. *If that kid even gets into half of what I got into* — "Pardon me?"

"When I told her that with her looks she could have a future in Hollywood, she considered it for a moment, then said she'd like to consider something like that in the future, but she wasn't ready for it yet. Is that mature thinking or what?"

"Well, yes, but —"

"I know. She wears more makeup than you approve of. Dresses too provocatively, I suspect. But she has to compete, doesn't she? I've read about the competition between mothers and daughters. Perhaps —"

"Oh, please!" she giggled. "She is not competing with me. Fifteen years and twenty pounds ago, I might've agreed. But not now." She daintily sipped her wine.

"Teenage boys might like their girls reed thin. But grown men want something a little rounder, not rock hard and flat-bellied. More womanly. Like yourself, if I may say so." Braxton looked shyly at his wine, refusing to meet her eyes.

He finds me attractive?

She took a healthy slug of her wine. How was she to respond to such a comment? She didn't fault his reasoning, but she surely didn't know what to say. The longer the silence stretched, the more difficulty she had thinking of a response.

Then she didn't have to worry about a clever answer. The door opened, and Piper walked in, flushed with the cool evening air. As soon as Piper's eyes met hers, Piper's face drained of color.

"Mary Beth! Any news?"

Mary Beth shook her head.

"Would you care for wine, dear?" Braxton asked. Then he smiled, rose and brushed his lips across Piper's forehead and muttered, "Knew you'd be back." He headed for the kitchen before Piper could answer.

What a gentleman, Mary Beth thought. Whatever possessed me to think he might fall victim to Susannah?

Piper walked into the living room and sat opposite Mary Beth. Mary Beth tried to smile, Susannah in the forefront of her mind again, and spotted the contusion on Piper's cheek.

"What on earth happened? You look almost as bad as Braxton."

Piper shrugged, still pale. "I tripped in the dark. Fell. Smacked my face on a rock."

"Well, you're quite the pair."

Braxton returned with a glass for Piper, took the bottle from the coffee table and filled it. "Mary Beth?" He held the bottle up.

"No, thanks. I'd better get home in case Susannah shows up or Frankie calls. Or maybe I was wrong about Ren."

"Ren? What about Ren?" Piper asked. She looked suddenly interested.

"Gone. I imagine he's gone into the woods to meditate. He goes up there when he's pressured. But he might have gone looking for Susannah. I don't know."

"I'm sure that's it," Braxton said. "He wouldn't be so selfish as to indulge himself in this meditation crap when his daughter's missing."

"No, you wouldn't think so. But he doesn't look at it as selfish.

It's hard to explain. It's his way of coping with things he has no control over."

"To each his own, I guess. But if I were in his shoes, I'd want to be where I could be reached. And giving my wife all the moral support I could."

Mary Beth caught the stunned look on Piper's face, but couldn't understand it. *Doesn't Piper realize how lucky she is?*

Braxton walked Mary Beth to the door. "Don't hesitate to call if we can do anything, even if it's only to offer a sympathetic ear. But, remember, Susannah's a level-headed young woman. She's probably following in Ren's footsteps, needs to be alone for a while."

"You're probably right."

Braxton engulfed Mary Beth in a neighborly hug. "Keep us posted."

Mary Beth smiled as she drew away. "And you watch out for those damned birds."

When she'd left, Braxton strolled back into the living room and drained the rest of the wine into his glass.

"You certainly had her eating out of your hand," Piper said.

"It's called kindness, my dear. Try it sometime. You might find it more effective than your usual frigid routine. The poor woman was distraught. She woke up from a nap and found herself all alone. No one to tell her if there'd been any news. No one to hold her hand or give her moral support."

"And you gave her moral support?"

"I tried. I'm sure you don't find anything odd about Ren leaving his wife alone during this crisis to go commune with nature, but I think it's appalling."

Braxton caught the brief flicker on Piper's usually unreadable face and smiled to himself.

CHAPTER SIXTEEN

Ren sucked the mountain air into his lungs as if it might cleanse him, or at least purge the fears that swarmed inside his mind like a cloud of teeming gnats, denying him rest. His calf muscles tightened as he trekked up the path by the gorge, and his breath seemed less plentiful than the last time he'd climbed. His sedentary lifestyle was eroding him.

He turned into the woods, eager now, certain he would find the peace of mind he sought, sure the spirits of his ancestors would once again work their magic. His feet flew over the path as he deftly dodged fallen logs and fist-sized rocks that had toppled from higher elevations. Relief swelled inside him when he saw the first flicker of the clearing that served as the landmark before his sacred place, some twenty yards farther down the path.

The relief promptly died.

He stopped abruptly, almost as if he had rammed into an invisible barrier. Something niggled at the back of his consciousness, a kind of warning. He turned off the path and, as if being compelled, turned into the clearing. He leaned against a poplar tree and scanned the enclosed meadow.

Everything seemed normal. Why, then, was there a flutter in his chest?

He stepped past the tree. The flutter grew stronger. Two brittle brown leaves blew across his boot toe and settled into a depression in the ground. The woods were still, empty of any lazy insect sounds, devoid of bird song. A whisper of water rushing down the gorge and a slight rustling of trees in the wind were the only noises. Yet there was something else.

He started across the clearing to a spot awash in sunlight, the vague sense of apprehension increasing with every step. Leaning against a boulder as tall as he was, he slid down its surface until he was on his haunches, dropped onto the ground and stretched his legs out ahead of him. The anxiety grew stronger.

He pulled his amulet out of his shirt. For the first time he could remember, it was cold.

The tremor in his belly became more insistent; it turned to a pounding that traveled up into his brain and back down into his intestines. Stomach acid burned, and churned the digestive juices into bile that backed up and filled his mouth, the searing acidity making him salivate.

He swallowed and brought his knees up to his chest. Something was wrong here. Very wrong.

His nostrils flared, as if they encountered a sinister smell, evil. Something like hot metal, like a frying pan just off the burner. Or a penny lying on an August sidewalk. Hot copper. The coppery smell of blood flooded his mouth with saliva and bile again.

His hand, lying on his kneecap, quivered, and a cold sweat sheened over him, making him clammy. He rubbed his hands together. They felt like partially thawed, skinned chicken breasts, slimy, moist. Cold.

The tree's whispers echoed and he became suddenly aware of the earth's revolutions, or something revolving.

The ground tilted crazily up to meet him. The echoes grew louder, until they were almost deafening. He covered his ears with his clammy raw-chicken hands, trying to muffle the sounds. No luck.

He scrabbled to his hands and knees and started crawling back across the clearing, only to be thrown off-balance by the tilting, heaving ground, like a ship pitching in heavy seas. Something crawled over his back, a light tickle, as if gossamer spider legs inched their way across his skin, down his side, over his chest, raising bumples.

He stopped and swatted, rubbed his chest, but the feeling was as elusive as walking into a cobweb. He forced himself onward.

He finally made it to the edge of the clearing.

The ground stilled.

Silence settled over him like a warm quilt and stopped the quivering, muffled the smell of evil, dimmed the roar and warmed his skin.

He scrambled onto the path, stood and turned, and looked back into the maelstrom of the clearing with disbelieving eyes.

🔳

"It's like being held hostage," Braxton said, peering through the curtains into the yard. "The damned thing is still out there."

"He's adopted me," Piper said, smiling. She folded a sweater and tucked it neatly into her suitcase.

"Maybe it's your familiar," he said.

"What?"

"Your familiar." He dropped the curtains and walked toward her. "You know, all witches have 'familiars' — animals enslaved by witches to serve them. Or sometimes guard them."

Piper stuffed some socks into the suitcase and glared at him, her eyes piercingly bright. "I knew I should've waited until you were gone to get my things. If you're going to start that crap again, I'll come back for the rest of my stuff later."

He grasped her shoulders lightly and pulled her to him, putting his arms around her. "I'm sorry, Piper. You shouldn't be so sensitive. I don't want you to leave at all. I can't bear the thought of you walking out on me. How will I exist without you? We can work this out. We always have before. Piper, we've been a team for so long...I was only kidding about the witch stuff."

She drew back and stared up at him as if gauging his sincerity. "I can't tell when you're serious and when you aren't anymore, Brax."

He hugged her close and rested his chin on the top of her head. Her hair smelled like sunshine and piney woods. "Lighten up, kid. You're too serious."

She muttered something, her words muffled by his chest.

"What?"

She pulled her head back. "Life *has* been serious lately. Or haven't you noticed?"

He dropped his arms and took a deep breath. He cupped her chin in his hands, lifting it so she was looking straight into his eyes. "Look, I know things have been rough. I've been a little nuts — okay, okay, very nuts. And you've caught the worst of it."

Suddenly, his eyes grew moist. "I'm sorry, honey. I don't know what's wrong with me." He swiped at his eyes with the back of his hand.

"Braxton, look at your fingernails!"

He glanced at his hand. "They're awful, aren't they? I must've contracted one of those nail funguses they talk about on television." His nails had thickened and yellowed. They were heavily ridged, the edges ragged and chipped. And they were appallingly long.

His tears spilled over and tracked down his face. "I'm falling apart, Piper."

She looked at him, stunned.

She wrapped him into her arms as a mother might do when comforting a child. He spoke into her hair, the words rushing from him like a burst damn, unstoppable. "It's like my whole world has turned upside down. Those thoughts I mentioned, those — visions, unspeakable visions. Overpowering. But so real! Like dreams from which you awaken not sure you were dreaming —"

"But what kinds of visions? You were so vague."

His mind went blank. He tried to pull at least one of the visions up from his memory bank, but his mind was empty. He felt as if he were groping around in an empty paper sack.

"I don't know," he said. "I can't remember them now that you've asked. But I know they're horrible." He swallowed; his throat felt plugged. He swallowed again. "I — I need help, Piper. I don't know what's happening to me."

"We'll get it, Braxton. I promised you, we'll find a doctor. But today's Sunday. Can't do much today. Tomorrow I'll ask Frankie who to..."

Her words drifted off as if on a breeze. He stroked her black hair, lifted strands of it and watched as they wafted back down, diaphanous, sleek. Like long cat fur. Soft as feathers.

Raven feathers.

Metallic rainbows around black feathers, rose and blue and green.

His fingers slid down, onto the curve of her shoulder, over her collar bone, up onto the nape of her neck. Warm skin, smooth as heavy cream.

And he wondered what kind of *snap* it would make if he twisted it? A crunching snap like biting into a potato chip? Or a smooth, clean, crisp *snap* like when you break a pencil in two?

Ren opened the door to his mother's house and found her in the kitchen, skinning tomatoes for canning. She turned from her work and looked him up and down, turned back to the stove and plunged a basket full of tomatoes into a pot of boiling water.

"You look terrible. Any word on Susannah?" she asked.

"No. Nothing. Where's Jeff?"

"He went to his friend's. To play music. If not Susannah, then what?" she asked. She lifted the basket out of the pot, set it to drain as she slipped off the tomato skins.

"I went to the woods to meditate. Something was wrong."

His voice must have betrayed his fear. She dropped a tomato into the sink and turned to him, her watery eyes fixing on his. She waited.

He pulled a chair out from the table and dropped onto it. He felt battered, depleted in the same way he used to feel back in college after ramming into the tackling dummy over and over at football practice. Only this time, the emotional exhaustion was worse than the physical.

Keysa's eyes never wavered. She put her knife down and shuffled across the small room, pulled out another chair and sat down. Her nose wrinkled slightly, and she sniffed. She held her hand out to him, palm up, and leaned close.

He fished his amulet from under his shirt and without taking it from around his neck, placed it in her hand. She squeezed it briefly, then let it drop.

"It's cold," she said.

He nodded.

"I smell blood."

He sniffed the air. Nothing. He shook his head.

"I smell it," she insisted. "Tell me."

He told her all that had happened in the clearing, how he'd been overwhelmed by sensory perceptions so powerful that he had begun to think he was hallucinating. "Could my spirits have left? Gone to another place? Is that possible?"

She reached into the bodice of her dress and pulled out her own amulet. Her eyes closed, her gnarled fingers clamped around the leather pouch, and she rocked back and forth on the chair in the gentle cadence of old women. She stopped abruptly, and her eyes sprang open.

"You sent your spirit away."

"Temporarily. So he could guard someone. Someone needing protection."

"But he has left you," Keysa said. "That's why his warmth is missing from your amulet. You've put yourself in danger." Her voice was a flat monotone. Her fingers continued to squeeze, then release, her amulet. Squeeze. Release.

"But the spirits of the wise ones? They would desert me, too?"

"No. Never. But if your sacred place has been desecrated, they won't return. You will have to seek them again. Find where they've gone." Squeeze. Release. "Call back your spirit guide before it's too late."

"I can't do that, mother. He's guarding someone in great danger."

"Your woman is not in danger right now. You are."

"She's not *my* woman."

Keysa leveled her gaze on him. "Deny it to yourself if you must. You can't deny it to me. My son, you must recall your spirit guide. We are surrounded by evil — a great blackness."

"How do I know if it's been desecrated?"

Keysa's eyes closed, and she started rocking once more. Squeeze. Release. In a moment, she began keening, a thin, warbly sound from the back of her throat. "My granddaughter's blood feeds the earth of that spot."

A chill swept over him, like a breeze washing across a beach when you've first emerged from the water, cold enough to turn your lips blue and the beds of your nails white. "No," he whispered.

"My granddaughter's spirit nourishes the grass of that defiled place."

"No."

"My granddaughter's body feeds the animals that graze that place, the birds flying over it, the worms crawling beneath it." Squeeze. Release.

"No! Never!" he shouted, leaping from his chair and knocking it backward. He stared at his mother, appalled at her words, horrified by the images she'd conjured up. Yet he'd never known her to be wrong.

Her eyes sprang open. He'd never seen his mother cry before, but she did so now, although she seemed unaware of her tears. She stared at him, rocking gently, squeezing and releasing. "Call back your spirit before you return there to bring back Susannah's body. You need his protection. There is great blackness around what was once your sacred place."

Her tears stopped, and she seemed to shrivel into herself. "When the sun rises tomorrow, you will call back your spirit, and you will bring back my granddaughter."

"I'll go now," he said and started out of his chair.

"No."

"Why not?"

"It will be dark before you can get back there. Only a fool would knowingly confront evil unprepared. And you are not a fool."

Ren held his head in his hands. "Not a fool, perhaps, but a lousy father."

She reached across the table and placed her hand on his hair. "Not a lousy father. Only a blind one."

"Blind?"

"You saw only that which you wanted to see. It is a fault we all share."

He looked at his mother. "You knew? You knew what kind of girl Susannah was? And it didn't bother you?"

"Yes, it bothered me. I didn't love her any less because of her ways, but the ways bothered me. She would have learned, eventually. I had no influence over that child. No one did. She had no spirit guide."

"Dark or not, I can't sit here. I'll go crazy. I'm going back up there."

"No. Tonight is for the living. Tonight you will call your wife and let her know you are here with me if she needs you. Tonight you will spend time with your son and reestablish your connection to him."

"Should I tell Mary Beth what you've said? That Susannah is — dead?" The word came out garbled. He'd never expected to use it in conjunction with one of his children's names.

"No. Let her sleep well tonight. She will need to gather herself, too. Deep down in her mother's heart, she already knows this. She is not accepting it yet. Let her rest while she can."

Mary Beth fussed a little when he called to say he was staying at his mother's, but she calmed when he explained that Keysa was so stressed he was concerned about her heart acting up again.

After he hung up the phone, Keysa nodded toward Jeff, as if silently urging Ren to go to the boy who was staring through the picture window into the night, one foot propped on the windowsill.

Ren watched his son, wondering why he looked incomplete, as though parts of him were missing, an unfinished portrait. He realized, after a moment, it was the absence of a guitar by his side or a harmonica peeking out of his shirt pocket that caused the strange illusion.

Ren shot a quick glance at his mother, then approached Jeff, clamping him on the shoulder. "How are you holding out, Jeff?"

The boy blinked, and his Adam's apple hopped up and down a couple times like a fisherman's float-bobber, alerting the angler to something nibbling on the hook. "Okay," he answered.

"Strange to see you standing around without a guitar in your hand."

Jeff's glance darted toward his guitar. The base of the sound box was on the floor, and the neck rested against the end of the windowsill. He reached for it, as if he thought Ren might try to take it. He cradled it in his arms and slipped the strap around his neck.

"I wasn't going to take it," Ren snapped. "I didn't even know it was there, for God's sake."

Jeff said nothing.

"Why don't you play something?" Keysa asked, carrying a plate of sliced pound cake into the small living room. She set it on the coffee table and shot Ren a scowling look. "Music will give us something else to think about."

"No sense in pissing dad off any more than he already is," Jeff said.

"I'm not pissed off —" Ren began, then realized he was almost shouting. He ran his fingers through his hair. "Look, Jeff," he said, careful to keep his voice well-modulated, "I'm not the bad guy here. I'm not anti-music. I was in a band myself, for God's sake. I only want to make sure you —"

"I know, I know. Make sure I have something to fall back on, like a teaching degree, so I can support myself when I come to my senses and realize I have two chances to play professionally — slim and none. Except for some smokey nightclub or beer joint. Heard it before."

"Excuse me for caring. By the way, did you filch another twenty..."

No. Don't go there.

He didn't have the energy to fight over a lousy twenty dollar bill. There were more important things to think about at the moment. He rubbed his eyes. "Never mind that — play some music for your grandmother."

Jeff shot his father a scathing look and promptly launched into a funeral dirge.

CHAPTER SEVENTEEN

Piper woke refreshed for the first time in months. Perhaps it was because she'd felt secure in the small motel room. But more than likely, it was because of Braxton. She felt at peace, confident, as if a black cloud hanging over her had finally drifted past. He'd admitted his problems.

Last night as he watched her pack some clothes, Braxton was the shy, sensitive boy she'd married, replacing — for a few hours at least — the ogre he'd become. She'd find someone who could help Brax deal with whatever was causing the "visions" he suffered, because now he was confronting them and seeking help. That was ninety percent of the battle.

What about Ren? She asked herself as she slipped into a corduroy dress, took it off again and decided slacks and a shirt would be more appropriate. *Can I so easily displace the feelings I have for him?*

No, she couldn't. There was something there, something she'd never dreamed possible, something beyond definition, as if they'd been long-time lovers instead of having shared one all-too-brief encounter.

She looked uncertainly at her reflection in the mirror. The slacks were baggy. She slid them off, and rummaged through her clothes again, finally settling on a blue wool dress that was neither too dressy nor too casual.

It was just like Ren himself said. It couldn't be.

Could it?

The dress was *too* casual.

Off came the dress. On went a tartan skirt in greens, browns and off-white, with an ecru sweater. She slipped into brown high heels, brushed her hair and grabbed her purse.

Two steps out the motel room door, Raven swooped onto her

shoulder, evidently happy to ride along on the soft perch, to accompany her wherever she might go. Unfortunately, she went only as far as the Jeep.

"Forgive me, Raven," she said as she opened the car door. "You can't come. I don't think you'd fit in at the Sheriff's office. But I'll see you this afternoon."

It flew off, and she watched it settle in the oak trees at the far edge of the parking lot.

By the time she arrived at the Sheriff's office, she'd lost her cheerful disposition. Her feet hurt, no longer used to the constriction of high heels. Her nerves were jangling. What if she couldn't do it? What if she screwed everything up? What if they didn't like her? It had been so long since she'd had a real job — she didn't know how to use e-mail or fax machines.

A police department.

What on earth had she been thinking?

But she forced herself out of the car, forced her feet down the sidewalk and through the door.

Marge had come in to run through the routine. She was a friendly woman, unpretentious, with short, unruly hair that she periodically blew out of her eyes.

Marge's management style fell in the "maternal" category: Frankie and his deputies were her "boys", so she cleaned up the messes they left and put them in their place when they got unruly. Piper suspected she might get her own knuckles rapped if she reached across the desk for something without asking. She felt quickly at ease.

The office was somewhat nicer than Piper had anticipated. The walls shone soft gray rather than the drab green Piper associated with government offices and hospitals. Wood-look Formica desks were a little battered but not depressingly so, and several closed doors with frosted windows opened off the back wall of the main office.

Marge settled Piper at a desk closest to the front and drew up a chair. Her first official act was to nudge off her shoes.

Frankie looked almost surprised to see her. "I really didn't think you'd show up."

"I said I would."

"Sure, but your husband..."

"He knows where I am." She changed the subject. "Any word on Susannah?"

Frankie shook his head.

"Well, no news is good news, isn't it?" she asked.

"Not in this business," he said, then took refuge in his office.

It was an hour later when Marge let Piper take her first call.

"Sheriff's Office," Piper said into the telephone mouthpiece. She listened intently to the caller, and scribbled notes on a green-lined steno pad. But her pen froze when the caller said something Piper was sure she misunderstood.

"Pardon me? Did you say *Adahy?*"

Marge reached over and flipped a switch so she could listen in.

"Who is this, please?" Marge asked. She scribbled down the name. "On the Overlook Road? Okay. I know the place. What makes you think it was Adahy?" She wrote furiously. "Okay, Mr. Canton. We'll send up an officer," she said, then disconnected the call.

"I don't believe it," Piper said.

"Let me give this to Frankie, then I'll explain Adahy to you." Marge pushed back her chair and went in to Frankie's office.

When she returned, Piper said, "I know about the legend. I guess I thought it was just that. A legend."

"Occasionally we get an 'Adahy' call, usually just like this one," Marge said, fidgeting in her seat. "A farmer who's lost some stock, someone finds a dog or cat that's been...well, *drained.*"

Frankie came out of his office, zipping up his jacket. "Up to Overlook Road, ladies, and I'm taking the portable with me so you can reach me while I'm out in the pasture." He took a pocket-sized flip phone off its charger. "Call if you hear anything on Susannah Wyatt."

Marge gave him a little two-fingered salute, then turned back to Piper. "But it's amazing how many times campers or hunters come back from the woods and claim to have found small animals — a fox, or a raccoon or a squirrel — who are Adahy's victims."

"How do they do it?"

"How does *who* do *what?*"

"Whoever kills those animals? Do they shoot them?"

Marge scrunched up her mouth and shook her head. "Usually stun them with something — you know, hit the animal over the head. A couple of times, its been animals caught in traps. Then they make an 'X' incision in the neck and drain the blood. Which is why —" Marge leaned close, as if there were somebody around to overhear, " — we in law enforcement can't buy into the 'Adahy legend.'"

"I don't get it."

"I mean even excluding the fact that Adahy would be over a hundred-years-old. If some old Indian demon was wandering through the woods sucking the blood from his victims, do you think he'd make a surgical-type incision? With a scalpel?"

"Well, he might have found a knife. A fisherman's knife, maybe. Mary Beth told us a toddler was taken from the campground. She alluded to the fact that perhaps Adahy had stolen the child. If Adahy *was* in the campground, perhaps he found the knife there. When he snatched the child."

Marge's creased and crinkled face glowered. "That little fella simply disappeared. Frankie and the boys never found a shred of evidence pointing to foul play. Not a drop of blood, not a piece of torn clothing. Nothing. His mama just didn't watch him good enough, and he toddled off. Maybe fell into the gorge, maybe met up with a she-bear, although they never found evidence of that, either." Marge looked at Piper from the corner of her eye. "You, uh, believe in Indian demons? That sort of thing?"

Piper felt her face grow flushed. "No, of course not. But if some hermit's holed up in the woods somewhere, there's no reason he couldn't have a knife." She squirmed uncomfortably in her chair. "Just the other day I...we found a deer carcass just off the front porch."

"Had its neck been slit? Bled?"

Piper shook her head. "No. The throat was ripped open. Belly, too."

Marge grimaced then flicked her wrist. "Don't confuse a natural kill with an Adahy-type kill." She grunted, leaned back in her chair and drummed her fingers on the desk. "Nope, I think we got us a Satanic cult around here. Last summer, there was a pentagram spray-painted on one of the boulders in the gorge. The sicko's use the Adahy legend as an excuse to cover their tracks. Or maybe one of those vampire cults. Occasionally we see kids running around with black lipstick and enough holes in their bodies to cast a polka-dotted shadow."

A few hours later, Frankie returned from the farmer's field and reported the calf's neck had, indeed, been cut with a sharp instrument. He'd also relieved Cramer's Grocery of a shoplifter and cleared up a fender-bender on the Old Mountain Road.

At the end of the day, as Marge was showing Piper how to switch the phones over to the night lines, Deputy Warren called in and said for them to notify Frankie he was bringing Skip Townsend, Susannah's boyfriend, in for questioning. Warren had found a pink blouse, covered with blood, in the trunk of Skip's car. He was trying to find Mary Beth Wyatt to identify the blouse.

"Should we stay?" Piper asked.

"Nope. They'll take him down to Taylorsville if they decide to book him. Your day is done. So, what do you think, Piper? Think you can handle the job?"

Piper nodded. "I like it. I was afraid it was going to be all high-tech equipment that I wouldn't know how to use —"

Marge snorted. "In Crooked Creek?"

Piper turned back from the door and smiled. "— but I think I can handle phones, a radio and a copy machine. I'll see you tomorrow, Marge. And thanks. Thanks for being so patient with me." Piper turned to go and stopped. "I thought Frankie said you preferred working nights."

"Yeah, I do. So?"

"So who is working nights while you're here training me?"

"I am."

"Huh? You're working a twenty-four hour shift?"

Marge smiled. "When we switched the phones over to night ring? It rings into my house. I usually man the night shift in my jammies and slippers."

It was unseasonably warm for late October. Piper shed her jacket, then climbed into the Jeep and drove back to the motel with the windows open. Raven swooped down from the trees as she parked, then settled in its favorite spot on her shoulder.

She went in her motel room, Raven having fluttered up to the rainspout, changed into jeans, tee shirt and sneakers and pulled on a sweatshirt. She went back out. "It's too pretty to stay inside." The only bad thing she could think of about working for Frankie was being trapped indoors on days such as this. "Let's take a walk," she said to the raven.

He immediately flew down and perched on her shoulder.

Should she call Braxton? See if he was okay before she went for her walk?

No. Who knew what kind of mood she might find him in?

It only took her a few minutes to reach the outskirts of town, to where she could climb up to the ridge overlooking Crooked Creek. She traveled the ridge that ran behind their cabin. Looking from her vantage point into the crotch of the mountains where a few low-hanging clouds hovered over the valleys, she felt it was just like being in heaven, looking down at the top of the clouds.

Soon she came to the pathway that flanked Crooked Creek Gorge. "What do you think, Raven? Want to scramble down there on my shoulder? Or would you feel safer flying down?"

Raven made a raspy chortling sound in the back of his throat, then shifted his weight from foot to foot in his now familiar gesture.

"Okay," she laughed. "Here we go."

Using the scruffy bushes that grew in the thin soil of the gorge banks as hand holds, Piper carefully made her way down into the ravine. She thought the bird seemed tense, as if waiting for her to slip. But it kept its perch and, after a few moments, she was scrabbling over the boulders that lined the gorge.

It was cooler near the water, but she'd worked up a sweat. She peeled off her sweatshirt and tied the arms around her waist.

Water kissed with silver sunlight rushed over the rocky river bed, sparkling its way downstream. Here and there, the creek eddied, little pools cradled by boulders that lay humped in the water like fossilized dinosaurs at their final resting place. The air smelled clean, wet, piney and, for a moment, vaguely familiar.

Wind whistled through the chasm, rippling the surface of any still water, wrinkling her reflection. The trees were scrawny, misshapen, and bent under the prevailing winds that whipped through the gorge in winter.

Piper jumped from rock to rock until she was in the center of the river. A large boulder with a slightly pinkish cast had been whittled away by millions of years of rushing water into a lounge-like shape. Using the high part as a windbreak, she sprawled out on the rock and turned her face to the sun. Raven flit from her shoulder to the high point of the boulder, keeping watch, its neck feathers ruffling in the breeze.

The sun was warm, mesmerizing her. Shading her eyes with her hands, she looked downstream. The trees seemed like an impressionist painting that used the warm tones from God's own paint box: russet and umber and ocher and gold. Crosscurrents of cold, clear water splashed near her head, close enough so she could feel their refreshing breeze, far enough away to keep her dry. Lulled by the sense that all was right with the world, except for that niggling sense of déjà vù that she could not put to rest, she found herself floating in the gray area between sleep and wakefulness.

She must have dozed off.

The next thing she knew, Raven ripped her from sleep with a harsh cry, like the sounds of boxcars being uncoupled from each other. She looked up, disoriented, startled out of her warm and fuzzy nap.

The bird was agitated, and it shifted weight from one foot to the other in rapid succession, then flapped his wings. Its head swung eerily left to right, neck feathers ruffled. Then it gave a long, grating shriek, bobbled its head once in her direction, and launched itself into the air.

Piper sat straight up. "No. Raven, come back."

Flap, flap, soar. It circled once, gazing down at her, then disappeared over the bank.

Piper looked around.

She was alone.

The gorge lost its magic. It became a desolate, windswept, barren gash in the earth.

She pulled on her sweatshirt and rock-hopped her way back to shore. With only the vaguest sense of why she was doing it, she clipped some snippings of cedar from the trees growing along the banks with her fingernail, and stuffed the flat, aromatic fronds into her pocket.

Blood runs deep, she thought, remembering how her tribal elders had gathered wild herbs for use in meditation. Spotting a patch of wild sage halfway up the bank, she pinched off several sprigs. The pungent fragrance brought her grandmother's face to mind.

Suddenly, she knew where she was going and knew why she'd been gathering the herbs.

CHAPTER EIGHTEEN

"That was a new one, wasn't it, mother?" Ren asked, staring into his empty tea cup. "Definitely not a Tlingit remedy. Never had any black cherry back home that I heard of." One minute he'd been ranting and raving at Jeff and sipping Keysa's tea. The next thing he knew, sixteen hours had passed. He'd woken up on the couch, groggy and thick-tongued.

"Me and the ladies at the Bingo Hall swap remedies sometimes," she'd answered, laying her knitting in her lap. "But you're right. We used burdock root at home. Never worked as long as this Cherokee cure."

He'd hauled himself to his feet, feeling queasy. "I wanted to be up and gone at first light."

"You needed your rest. Susannah ain't going anywhere. You'll find her. Besides, like I said —" she wrinkled up her already heavily corrugated face apologetically and shrugged. "— I didn't know it would last so long." Her eyes twinkled. "Dropped you like a rock, it did. Good stuff."

Half an hour later, with the late afternoon sun spot-lighting the world in gold, Ren charged through the woods as if all the demons in hell were nipping at his heels. Snippets of memory cartwheeled across his mind, skimming the surface of his thoughts like a child skipping stones across a river.

Susannah on Christmas morning with her first baby doll.

Susannah proudly pushing baby Jeff in his stroller.

Fly-up ceremony from Brownies to Girl Scouts.

Training wheels and first high heels.

Blue eye-shadow and enough mascara for all the hookers in New York.

Susannah racing out the door to an Asheville rock concert, her shorts leaving nothing to the imagination.

Then stumbling back in at 2:00 AM, a necklace of hickeys around her throat.

Paralleling the gorge, an inhuman sound penetrated his consciousness, one that teased his skin to goosebumps and sent a shiver down his torso. Bit by bit, he realized he'd been screaming, and his cry had spread across the rocks, ricocheting back at him from the other side of the chasm.

Moments later, a shadow glided over the ground in front of him. He raised his eyes to the swooping blackness of the raven, wings spread majestically, protectively, circling the sky above.

Ren absorbed strength and determination from the very sight of his spirit guide, fortified by the simple knowledge he was no longer alone.

Ren careened away from the gorge with restored energy, plunged through the woods and within moments, exploded into the clearing. He stopped and reached for his amulet. Its heat warmed his hand and he felt the power surging within him, power that came from his spirit guide's return. The raven.

The sounds of the earth magnified again and became a thunderous roar. The ground rushed at him, heaving in undulating waves, receding, lifting again. He planted his feet shoulder-width apart to balance himself against the earth's convulsions.

The sunlight intensified, blinding him. He squinted against its brilliance, shaded his eyes with his hands, and scoured the clearing with eyes as sharp as an eagle's. Susannah wasn't here, but Keysa was right — his daughter's blood had nourished this grass, and the defilement of his sanctuary had evicted his spirits.

He stumbled backward, choking back the rage that shot off before his eyes like fireworks. His feet found the path.

Rather than turn back toward the gorge, he followed the trail deeper into the woods. The bark of a poplar on his right had been gently rubbed; farther along, a dry stalk of weed had been snapped, lying over in the direction he headed, pointing as clear as an arrow. Part of a footprint compressed the earth where the drizzle of the previous evening had not reached to wash it away. A boot print.

His nostrils quivered. He smelled blood. His eyes, seeing more clearly than they had in years, found tiny flecks of red on blades of grass that still leaned slightly from where they'd been trampled.

And then he saw the buzzard. Twenty-yards ahead on the edge of a small, rock-strewn gully.

Another circled lazily overhead, waiting.

Ren rushed headlong, a strangled cry erupting from his throat.

The first buzzard launched himself skyward.

A flash of honey-colored movement into the brush.

A scrabbling streak of gray fur.

The stones skipped the surface of realization no longer. They plummeted into the depths of his conscience and into his very soul as he found the remains of his child. As Keysa had seen, his daughter fed the animals that grazed, the birds that flew over her carcass and the worms that crawled beneath it.

His humanity deserted him. His screams scattered all the creatures of the mountain.

Keysa answered her door, knowing even before she opened it who was waiting on the other side.

She motioned Piper inside and took the woman's offering of cedar and sage with a nod of her head. *The woman has been well brought up.*

Keysa tied the boughs together and hung them from the hook in her kitchen. She took dried, shriveled branches from a neighboring hook and motioned the woman outside. There she lit a small fire and threw the dry herbs into it.

The two women sat across from each other, the fire between them. Keysa fanned the flames with her hands, chanting the ancient invocations learned at her own grandmother's knee. She looked at the younger woman and saw that, while Piper did not understand the Tlingit words, she understood their meaning.

The fragrant smoke purified their hearts and their minds. After they were cleansed, Keysa spoke to her guest. "You have lost your protector?"

"Yes, grandmother."

Keysa allowed her mouth to show a hint of a smile, acknowledging the younger woman's respectful use of the honorary "grandmother." She nodded her head slightly. "My son has recalled his spirit."

"I don't understand."

"It is not for us to understand everything." Keysa added more herbs to the smoldering fire.

"But the search for knowledge is what sets us apart from the beasts."

Good argument.

Keysa allowed herself another small smile. "My people believe the human spirit takes many forms."

"You're saying Ren is the raven?"

"And the raven is my son. So is the butterfly and the wolf, the robin and the rattlesnake. What form it takes is not important. What is important is that my son has gone into the mountains to face evil. To do so, and to be victorious, he must have his spirit intact. His spirit must not be scattered. It must be whole, and it must be in here," she tapped her chest, "as well as here." Keysa tapped her temple, then folded her hands together and placed them in her lap. "A man cannot have strength without spirit."

"But I thought he went to the mountains to meditate."

"He has gone to reclaim the body of my granddaughter."

Piper's hand flew to her mouth. "I'm sorry, I didn't know."

Not as well-trained as I thought. Perhaps the Cherokee were not as well-educated as the Tlingit. *Her* people were trained from early childhood to keep their emotions to themselves. To wear your weaknesses on your face was to give your enemies a map to your jugular.

"We are not meant to understand everything," Keysa repeated. "Nor are we meant to show everything."

Piper looked puzzled for a moment, then as understanding came to her mind, Keysa saw her struggle to erase her feelings from her face. In a moment, she was unreadable.

Perhaps it was just a momentary lapse.

Suddenly a cold hand gripped Keysa's heart. Her sight clouded, grayed, as it often did when she began to have a vision. She leaned forward and sniffed the air. The piquant smell of the burning herbs was replaced by something harsh. Evil.

The evil hung around the woman like a mantle. It surrounded her.

Keysa sat back. She didn't know what to make of this. The woman herself was good-hearted. Piper was not the source of the evil, but something dark was connected to her. Or someone.

Like fog rising off a river, Keysa's vision cleared. The clarity did not reveal the source of evil, but the result. Instinctively, she clutched her amulet through her dress. "My son," she cried.

The madness passed at twilight, that shadowy gloaming where shapes grow subtly less distinguishable, melding into each other in varying shades of gray.

Ren sat, weakened by his tears. He was drained, robotic.

He took off his jacket and shirt and draped them over his daughter's body. He had to block the corpse from his sight.

He gathered Susannah's body into his arms and retraced his steps. Raven followed, circling now and then to maintain Ren's slower pace.

"There is nothing you can do for me now," Ren shouted into the wind. "Return to the woman. Protect her."

Raven dipped his wings and banked into a last circle. Then it cawed its ugly cry and followed the gorge. Flap, flap, glide. Flap, flap, glide.

When Ren's first footfall landed on the path that followed the gorge, the back of his neck prickled.

He felt eyes. Staring, predatory eyes.

He stopped and looked behind him.

Nothing.

He looked to his right.

Empty.

Swiveling his head to the left, he locked on to malicious yellow eyes that appraised his every move. They were penetrating eyes, the eyes of a hunter, glinting with fury.

A mountain lion hunkered down on his haunches, balanced atop a large boulder, completely still except for the slight telling twitch of his whiskers.

The cat's muscles were taut, bunched beneath the tawny coat. The eyes blinked once, golden orbs of hate split by black oblong slits. His muzzle was flecked with blood.

Ren understood.

He'd interrupted the cat's feeding.

Never taking his eyes off his opponent, he set Susannah's body down on the path's edge. He rose to a half-crouch, his arms extending from his sides like wings, his long fingers splayed. His amulet bumped against his bare chest, imparting a brief, gentle nudge of warmth on his cold skin.

Warm? Shouldn't be.

He blinked the thought away. He had to stay focused, had to think like his adversary.

The cat's golden eyes narrowed ever so slightly.

It was a waiting game, now.

And his opponent had the first move.

The cat leaped, a tawny blur tearing through the air.

Ren jumped back. He tried to focus on movement faster than his eye could follow, but saw only a fawn-colored smear of rippling muscles rushing toward him.

Extended claws.

Fangs and fetid breath.

A hot, rank smell washed over him as the airborne cat smashed into him, bulldozing him backward.

He rolled to protect his jugular from gnashing, snapping teeth. His head slammed into the earth. His mouth filled with dirt.

The world spun sickeningly as they tumbled over and over, gouging the earth into little volcanoes of dirt scuffing skyward, only to fall back in Ren's eyes, blinding him.

A scorching, searing pain shot through him as claws gouged their way across the tender white flesh of his belly and then — a ridge of earth in the middle of his back, his upper torso unsupported.

He was falling.

Rocky banks, sculpted trees and water cartwheeled crazily over and over.

Above him, an open sky appeared, empty except for four flailing paws scrabbling for something solid to hold on to.

A streak of black feathers sliced down through the sky, clutched the tip of a small cedar, and yanked it straight out beneath Ren's plummeting body.

The sapling couldn't stop Ren's fall. Neither the raven nor tree were strong enough.

But the sapling *did* break Ren's trajectory, deflecting him toward the bank.

He ricocheted off the bank and flipped over yet again. A careening leg crashed onto the raven's back, spinning the bird out of control and slamming it onto the shore.

CHAPTER NINETEEN

At four-thirty, Braxton came downstairs to fix himself a drink and caught a flash of movement outside the kitchen window. He peeked through the curtains, and saw Jeff Wyatt, guitar slung over his shoulder, wobbling down the rutted driveway on his mountain bike.

He hurried to the front door and waved.

Jeff dismounted and leaned the bike against the oak tree.

"Hi," Jeff said. "In the mood for some company?"

"If you're the company, I am," Braxton answered. "I was just about to have a drink. Can I fix you something?"

"Sure. Anything cold."

They walked in easy silence to the kitchen. Braxton tossed Jeff a frosty can of beer and fixed himself a vodka gimlet. Jeff looked at the beer, then glanced at Braxton. "Just don't tell your folks," Braxton said. Then he winked.

"Cool. Thanks," Jeff said, and popped the top.

"What are you doing out this way?" Braxton asked, heading back to the porch. Jeff followed.

"On my way back from school. I'm staying at my grandmother's while all this flap is going on. Until Susannah comes home."

Braxton slid his rocking chair closer to the railing and propped his feet on it. He scanned the trees closest to the cabin, looking for that damned raven, but all seemed safe. "Any news?"

"Yes, sir. Mama called me at school. Said they found Susannah's shirt in the trunk of Skip's car. It was all bloody."

"Damn," Braxton said softly. "Sorry to hear that, kid. Now what?"

"Mama said they were sending it to a lab. I think they've arrested Skip." Jeff looked at Braxton. His eyes were puzzled.

"You know, I don't think Skip's done anything. He's a jerk, but I don't think he'd hurt anybody. Even Susannah."

"What do you mean, 'even Susannah'?"

"Well, she's my sister, and I love her and all, but —" Jeff groped for words. "But she's asking for trouble. Wild as the wind. Talk at school is that she sleeps around. Wants to find a rich husband to take her away from here."

"She's a pretty little thing," Braxton murmured.

— Silver blonde curls glinting in the twilight —

Huh?

"How's the family taking all this?"

"Mama *was* doing okay. But she didn't sound so good on the phone when she told me about Susannah's shirt. She told me to go back to Gran's after school. My father spent the night at Gran's last night with me. He was all fired up. Like he knew something, but didn't want to talk about it. At least, not with me."

"You and your dad getting along any better?" Braxton asked. He drained the last of his drink and lit a cigarette.

Jeff grimaced and swung his head slightly from side to side. "Sort of. I guess. But he still thinks I ought to just work small-time gigs on nights or weekends for fun, like he does with his storytelling, and teach for a living. That's the last thing I want."

"To thine own self be true," Braxton said. "*My* mother felt that way. Told me I was wasting my life writing silly stories that no one would want to read. That I should study hard. Be a teacher. So don't take it too seriously. Ready for a refill?"

Jeff followed him into the kitchen. "What does she think now that you're a famous author? Did she ever tell you she was sorry she was wrong?"

"Well, noooo. She died. When I was ten."

"Oh. Sorry." Jeff looked around, stuffed one hand into his pocket, plucked at his tee shirt with the other, tapped his foot.

Braxton almost laughed aloud. He remembered that awful feeling of committing a horrendous blunder and not having any idea in hell how to correct it. He patted Jeff on the back and said, "S'okay."

Jeff's relief was almost tangible. "Is Mrs. Defoe home?"

"Nope. Why?" He poured vodka into the cocktail shaker.

"Just wanted to say hello. She's a nice lady."

"Yeah. Piper's a real peach."

— plucking the fruit from the tree —

He splashed another ounce of vodka into the shaker. "Help yourself to another beer, Jeff. And while you're in the fridge, get me another lime, please. Drawer on the right. And after we've had our drink, I expect another concert. How about it?"

Jeff found the limes and tossed him one. "Only if it's a duet. Deal?"

"Deal," Braxton agreed. He cut the lime into eighths with a sharp paring knife, picked up one sliver and began peeling the meat away from the rind to make his "twist," nicking his finger in the process. The lime juice instantly stung his severed flesh.

"Dammit!" He popped his finger into his mouth, and the stinging was replaced by a sweet, metallic warmth that sent a shock wave of pleasure through him.

Whirr.

His breath became shallow and rapid. Heat spread through his groin. He glanced sideways, but Jeff was still rooting through the refrigerator for another beer.

Braxton turned away slightly so the boy wouldn't notice his sudden erection.

No, please.

He turned on the faucet and plunged his hand beneath the stream of icy water, refusing to look at it in case he saw the blood, in case he lost control and slipped back into...

It took all his willpower. When he felt he was at least partially in control, he glanced at his finger, at the pink-tinged stream of water. A yearning flashed through him, stronger than any desire he'd ever felt before.

He jerked his arm up, and with as much force as he could muster, he brought the point of his elbow crashing down onto the rim of the stainless steel sink.

"Shit!" he shouted. The pain trilled through him like a lightning bolt.

"What happened?" Jeff hollered. He backed out of the fridge, catching a jug of orange juice with his arm. The top flew off as it landed on the floor and splattered in a three-foot radius. Jeff's eyes were huge.

But it worked. The pain wiped out Braxton's erection. "Hit my funny bone. It's okay now. Sorry I startled you." He reached for the paper towels and began mopping.

After they'd cleaned up the mess and gotten their drinks, Braxton grabbed his harmonica, and the two returned to the porch.

Braxton didn't kid himself as to who was keeping up with whom. No way did he have Jeff's ear for music, nor the boy's talent. But they reached success on a few pieces, and as the late afternoon sun softened, Braxton imagined the strains of their music drifted across the mountains, audible for miles.

When he grew tired of trying to compete, he fixed another drink. "Since you arrived on two wheels, I guess your folks still aren't letting you drive, huh?"

Jeff scowled. "No, sir, they're not. But stayin' up at Gran's, I'd have to use my bike anyway. It's not like I have my own car or anything."

"What's your grandmother like?"

"She's pretty cool, actually. For an old lady. She's always talking about curses and legends and spirits and weird stuff like that. She's full-blooded Indian, you know."

"Yeah, I heard. 'Tunklup' or something. Not Cherokee, right?"

Jeff smiled. "Tlingit. But she knows some pretty cool stuff. Like how to tan hides, and she can make all kinds of medicines from stuff she finds in the woods. She could probably live in the woods for a year without ever going to the grocery store."

"A natural born survivalist."

"Yeah. Do you have any kids?"

"No. We always wanted them, but it never worked out for us."

Jeff started looking uncomfortable again, so Braxton clapped him on the back. "But if I *did* have a son, I'd want him to be exactly like you."

Jeff glanced up at him, startled. Then his lips stretched into a tentative smile as he reddened. He turned his head quickly away.

But not before Braxton saw the tears welling up in his eyes.

CHAPTER TWENTY

Jeff finally took off for his grandmother's and Braxton spat out the ice cube on which he'd been munching just for the sake of having something to chew. He was ravenous, the kind of all-consuming hunger that had hit him at the Storytelling Festival. Braxton went into his kitchen and began to feed.

He crammed an apple into his mouth as he ransacked the fridge searching for meat. That's what he wanted — meat. Red, glistening, raw, dripping beef.

There wasn't any. He found a package of sliced ham, spat the apple onto the floor and devoured the ham. An unopened package of bacon was on the back of the shelf; he tore through the plastic wrap and stuffed the bacon into his mouth, two pieces at a time. The cold grease was soothing on his throat. He washed it down with a half-bottle of red wine.

But his stomach still growled. Still needed more. He squatted down in front of the refrigerator and pulled fruit, vegetables and condiments out, tossing them to the floor in his search for flesh.

Finally, he found two thawed chicken breasts. Cold, slimy, dripping. He was just finishing the second breast when he heard a car engine.

Piper! Shit!

She must have come back for more clothes.

He dashed his face on the dish towel, kicked wrappers and jars and produce into the corner of the kitchen and slid the trash can in front of the pile so it wouldn't be quickly noticeable. Then he went to the window.

Mary Beth Wyatt was getting out of her Bronco.

Braxton hurried to the door to greet his guest, switching the overhead light off on his way.

"Mary Beth, you poor woman. Jeff just left a while ago. He

told me about Susannah's shirt." He swung the door wider so she could enter. "Any other news?"

Her eyes were puffy, bloodshot, and red-rimmed, surrounded by purple shadows. She shook her head and bit her lip, as if doing so might stop the silent tears dripping down her face.

Braxton wrapped his arms around her and patted her back. "I'm so sorry you're going through this hell. Is there anything I can do? Has Ren come back yet?"

"No," she answered, her voice trembly. "Actually, that's why I'm here. To ask a favor."

"Anything. Have a seat." He pulled out a chair for her.

She shook her head. "Frankie's tied up with the investigation. Said not to worry about Ren. But I can't help it. I have a bad feeling. He called me from Keysa's last night. He stayed with her. Was worried about her heart. I can't ask her to help me find him. She's too old, too frail. I wondered if you — if you'd go up the mountain with me."

"Up the mountain?"

"I'm —" She looked down, embarrassed. "I'm afraid to go alone." Mary Beth wrung her hands together. "I know you're busy and all, but everyone else I know has a job —" She stammered, "I — I mean a day job. Like in an office or something."

His back stiffened. He was used to these remarks.

"Do you have any idea where to begin looking?" he asked in his most soothing voice.

Her face flooded with relief. "I know he's gone to his sacred place to meditate. I've never been there, but I know the general vicinity."

He patted her pudgy little forearm. "Of course I'll go. What are friends for? Just let me round up a flashlight and a few other things, first."

He was back in a moment with a black canvas gym bag dangling from his shoulder. "So, where do we begin?"

Piper left the old woman's house, not knowing where to go, not even knowing where to start.

Ren was in danger, that much she knew.

But she could get no further information from Keysa Wyatt. The old woman just kept repeating "My son! My son!", clutching her amulet and rocking back and forth, tears streaming over the weathered landscape of her face.

From Keysa's front yard, Piper scanned the trees, hoping to catch sight of Raven. But the trees were empty. The skies were vacant, too, as empty as the void inside her, as if someone had ripped out her insides, leaving her an empty shell. She remembered the doe at the cabin, fleetingly envied her the quick death she'd probably been given, one that saved her the horror of being emptied. Seeing the doe lying there in her mind's eye, between the porch and the Jeep, triggered the obvious in her head. She needed her car.

She headed for the motel to pick up her Jeep. She'd cover more territory in a vehicle than on foot. At least until dark.

And it would be dark soon.

She arrived at the motel a short time later, and realized she'd need a jacket if she was returning to the mountains so late in the day. She'd have to swing by the cabin to get one.

Ten minutes later, she pulled into the log cabin's driveway. At least the deer carcass was gone. But the cabin's front door hung open.

Something was wrong.

She crossed the front porch, her eyes darting left and right, her instincts on full alert.

The house was empty.

Running up the stairs, she heard the soft whir of Braxton's computer. She edged through the narrow space between the desk and wall, clipping two opened reference books with her hip and knocking them to the floor.

She ignored them. Her eyes were fixed on the monitor. The header read *Murder Mountain/Defoe/page 535*. Amazing. She scrolled down the screen. What met her gaze wasn't even English; there were no spaces between words, no paragraph indentations. She couldn't make out a single word other than the header and a footer halfway down the page, centered: The End.

Finished?

Then she saw one of Braxton's padded manuscript mailing envelopes, filled, sealed and neatly labeled. It was addressed to Everett A. Palmer, Braxton's former agent.

She picked up the books she'd knocked off the corner of the desk: *Bartlett's Familiar Quotations* and Braxton's much used *The Character Naming Sourcebook.* The sourcebook had fallen open to a bookmarked page. Highlighted in yellow were the English names "Ranfield, Renfield," meaning "from the raven's field." A few lines below, also highlighted, was "Rans, Raven, Rand, Ren" — raven.

Piper closed the book and replaced it on the desk, numb.

She found herself careening down the stairs, bursting through the door, then speeding for the woods with one word coursing through her mind.

Raven.

Piper tried to listen to her instincts, tried to remember those long hours at her grandmother's knee as the old woman had tried to pass along the wisdom of the ancients.

But too much time had passed, too many years of living in Los Angeles thinking with her head rather than with her body or heart.

She wandered aimlessly, changing directions, unsure of how to begin, where to start. And the more she meandered in circles, the more angry she became. Her jaw began to ache, and she realized she'd been grinding her teeth.

Piper stopped, closed her eyes, then took several deep breaths.

The image of the gorge rose in her mind's eye.

She only took a few steps before it hit her that she'd never make it before dark. Indecision froze her feet again, till she calmed herself, worked it all out in her head.

She spun around and headed back to the cabin.

CHAPTER TWENTY-ONE

Mary Beth blotted her eyes with a tissue and swallowed a sob. She didn't want to irritate Braxton; he was going to a lot of trouble on her behalf. The least she could do was to remain calm.

Braxton smiled at her from behind the wheel.

"Why are you grinning?" she asked.

"It's fascinating — the effects of the dash board lights on your face. You look so much like Susannah in this light. It highlights your essence, your mystery. Surrounds you with a glow that is almost surreal — red, green and white. Enchanting."

What the hell was he talking about? Was it a compliment? The lights reflected off his face, too, but she found the effect chilling. They emphasized the shadows, made the hollows of his eyes larger, darker, almost ghoulish.

Good grief.

Her imagination was stuck on high-speed, a symptom of stress. "I'm sorry, Braxton. What did you say?"

"Nothing." He smiled again. "Penny for your thoughts." He turned his eyes back to the road.

"I was just thinking how awful I feel about dragging you away from home. Interrupting your dinner, your writing, God knows what else. But Keysa scared me to death with her morbid visions."

"I know. Why do you think I'm driving? You're in no condition. You'd put us in a ditch somewhere. Calm down. Things will work out for the best, dear. Besides, you can't change anything by worrying about it."

"I know. Turn on that dirt road up there. I just want my daughter back. My husband, too. I want life to return to norm — Braxton, you missed the turn!"

"I know a better way."

"How? You don't even know where we're going."

"Don't bet on it."

The temperature plummeted along with the sun, leaving Piper chilled.

As soon as she turned toward the kitchen and saw the light spilling from the refrigerator, she knew something was wrong. She flipped on the overhead light and gaped, shocked at the carnage.

Empty boxes and plastic wrappers littered the floor. Smears of congealed grease and wine splotched the countertop. Mustard dripped down the wallpaper. Crumbs were sprinkled everywhere. A chicken bone crunched beneath her foot.

Braxton had gone on a rampage.

She jabbed Frankie's number onto the telephone keypad, sobbing in frustration when her call was answered by his machine. Her message came out garbled and confused.

She took a few deep breaths, dialed again and tried to leave a more succinct message.

She put water on for coffee, swept the floor and cleaned up the counter. Finished, she decided she needed something stronger than coffee. A little liquid courage, enough to take the edge off. It worked for Braxton. Maybe a Scotch and water would calm her down, too. She turned off the kettle and poured her Scotch, decided against adding water at the last minute.

What would she do if Braxton came back in a rage?

Maybe she ought to just go back to the motel. But she'd told Frankie to call her at the cabin.

She'd wait a while.

The phone rang, startling her so that she jumped, sloshing her drink. She fumbled with the receiver.

It was Frankie. He told her to hang tight; he'd be right over.

Mary Beth's Bronco bumped to a stop in a small clearing, a good half-mile off the paved road and then another quarter-mile off a rutted track that would bottom out all but the most rugged four-wheel-drive vehicles.

Mary Beth couldn't stop talking, even though, judging by the look on Braxton's face, it was getting on his nerves. "Are you sure about this place, Braxton? I'd swear we've gone too far north. I've never been back in here. I don't have the best sense of direction, but I think we've overshot where we need to be."

"Trust me."

"I do, I assure you. What are you doing?"

He twisted in the seat, reached into the back for the black canvas bag he'd brought. He looked at her briefly, and she had the strangest sensation he wasn't even seeing *her,* but someone else. His eyes were puzzled, he cocked his head questioningly.

"W-what's wrong, Braxton? Is something wrong?"

His expression cleared and he smiled, although in the dashboard lights it was more of a grimace than grin. "Everything's fine. You really do look lovely tonight. Soft light becomes you. Now stop being so edgy."

For once, instead of being flattered by his compliments, they gave her the creeps. Maybe because she knew there was no way she could look lovely. Not tonight. Not with eyes puffy from crying and unwashed hair. She was a mess.

I'm really coming unglued.

She ought to be grateful to Braxton. He was only being kind — he'd noticed she looked like hell and was probably just trying to cheer her up.

"What's in the bag?" she asked, trying to sound friendlier.

"Just things I thought we might need. Things my heroes might take with them when tromping through the woods at night searching for lost husbands."

She forced a grin. "Like what?"

He unzipped the bag. "Items number one and two: flashlights, so we don't break our necks." He smiled and snapped one on to show her its strong, wide swath of light. "Item number three: rope."

"What for?"

"I'm not sure," he said, shrugging, "but heroes always carry rope. Maybe to make a leash for the reluctant husband, the better to drag him home with my dear."

She chuckled.

"And last but not least, a knife. For cutting the rope into appropriate lengths. Feel better now? Knowing that we're well-stocked?"

She nodded. "Much better, thanks." She patted his arm.

"Don't get too relaxed. It's time to go. Head 'em out." Braxton snapped off the interior lights, yanked the keys from the ignition and got out. "And button up. It's chilly out here!"

She turned her collar up, grabbed the flashlight he'd given her and when the door slammed shut behind her, found herself in the blackest black she'd ever experienced.

Her good mood evaporated. Dark clouds covered the moon. Miles from any streetlights, there was nothing to break the pitch of the overhanging trees that felt as if they were closing in on her. She'd been plunged into a world made up of varying intensities of black, none of which were light enough to qualify as 'gray'. It was like being totally blind.

Mary Beth had never shared Ren's enthusiasm for the great outdoors, and this experience really reinforced her dislike.

Suddenly, she heard a *click,* in unison with being able to see. Braxton — on the other side of the Bronco — had switched on his flashlight. The beam of light bobbled along the edge of the clearing. He pointed toward a break in the trees. "I believe the path is over there. Save your batteries. We'll use mine." He rounded the front end of the Bronco, cupped her elbow in his hand and guided her toward the path, shining his light in front of them so that they could spot rocks and uneven ground.

The thick woods lasted only a short distance. As the path meandered up to a higher elevation, massive oaks gave way to slender birches, then to pines and scraggly saplings permanently bent by the force of prevailing winds.

She tried to talk, needed the pretense that things were at least somewhat normal. But the wind whipped her words away and she soon gave up.

The path was steep. She started to pant, her breath fast and ragged, and knew she had to stop. Braxton waited a few yards up the path while she rested, playing his flashlight over the rocky terrain around them.

Finally, she thought she could go on and signaled him with her hand. He took off again.

The trail became steeper still, blocked in many places by fallen boulders and felled trees. But occasionally the moon would peek through the clouds and offer some natural light. It was reassuring, somehow, dim as it was, and even Mary Beth had to admit it was pretty. Too bad the moonlight didn't last longer.

Something *snapped* in the woods to the right of the path.

She stopped, her heart pounding. Waited.

Nothing moved, so she took a few more steps before realizing she was lagging too far behind Braxton for comfort. She switched on her own flashlight and flashed its beam on his back, trying to draw his attention.

He turned around and came back for her, careful to keep his flashlight shining away from them both.

"What's wrong now?" he asked. He sounded impatient.

"Something crashed in the woods over there," she said, pointing her flashlight to the right.

He sighed, drew his lower lip inside his mouth for a moment. "Probably a deer or raccoon or something. You're bound to hear things," he snapped. "These woods are full of wildlife."

"Well, yes I know, but —"

He turned his back on her and started retracing his steps up the path.

How rude!

Still, there was nothing to do but catch up to him, so she hurried on.

A few yards later, she slipped on some small stones and lost her footing. Her flashlight went rolling down the trail.

Braxton loomed over her and held out his hand to give her a lift up.

The clouds were scuttling quickly now. The moon broke through again, washing them in silver light. Mary Beth reached up to take Braxton's hand, and...

Froze! His nails were long, ragged, and slightly curved. Why hadn't she noticed that before?

Simple. They *hadn't* been like that. The other evening, when Ren had been telling a story, Braxton had handed her a glass of wine. She'd noticed how smooth his fingers were, how meticulously manicured. Artistic hands. Hands that never stacked wood or pulled weeds or developed the fingertip callouses of guitar playing.

Now they were scruffy, unkempt —

Impatient, he grabbed her hand and jerked her to her feet. "Okay now?" he asked. She looked up into his eyes.

Very strange. It must have been a trick of the moonlight, the way it washed over him making him look almost...sinister. His eyes glittered metallically and for a second she thought —

They were suddenly plunged into darkness, except for the reflection of Braxton's flashlight, pointed into the woods. The clouds had covered the moon again.

"I asked if you were okay?" Braxton repeated. Gone was the gentle voice. He sounded angry. Gruff.

"Braxton, I — let's just go back to the car. This was a stupid idea. I want —"

"We're going on," he said, grabbed her hand and tugged her forward.

"No." She planted her feet. "I've changed my mind. We're going home."

His hand clamped around her wrist like a pit bull on a bone. "No we won't. You dragged me out here. We're going to find your dumb-ass husband and put an end to this foolishness."

"You're hurting me!" *What had gotten into him?*

He loosened his grip. His voice became soothing. Cajoling. "I'm sorry, Mary Beth. Forgot my own strength for a moment." He rubbed her wrist, as if to restore her circulation. "Better?"

She sniffed. "Yes. I'm okay. Now let's get out of here." Better to simply agree with him and get the hell back to civilization. "Let's go."

"No, we need to find Ren. I —" his voice became softer, persuasive. "I didn't want to mention this before, didn't want to alarm you, but...well, I've got a really bad feeling about this."

"About Ren?"

"Yes. Has his...meditation...ever kept him in the woods after dark before?"

"No, no it hasn't. You think something's happened?"

No answer.

"Ren's an expert woodsman. What could possibly happen? He knows these woods like the back of his hand. He and Jeff have camped all over the place. Hunted. Fished." It was unthinkable that something might have happened to her husband, especially now, especially with Susannah...

"Lots can happen, even to *'expert woodsmen'*." Braxton's voice was clipped. Guttural. "Snake bite. Bear. Might've tripped, busted a leg. Gotten sick, passed out, fallen into the gorge." Suddenly she could feel Braxton's warm breath on her face. "All kinds of things could happen to a man alone in these woods." There was a satisfied smirk in his voice now.

"Stop it. You're scaring me."

"Then let's finish what we started. Let's find him."

"What about my flashlight?"

"Don't need it. I've still got mine. You'll just have to keep up."

She'd only gone a few feet when an owl — she *guessed* it was an owl — hooted from behind them, and a few times she thought she heard something scuffling through dried leaves in the woods. But she kept her mouth shut and tried not to think of what Braxton had said.

Within a short distance, Braxton half-dragging her onward, her throat started to burn. She couldn't catch a full breath and her leg muscles felt as if they were on fire. She yanked on Braxton's sleeve. "I've got to stop. Rest." She dropped onto the ground and clasped her knees.

He nodded. "I'll go on ahead. I just want to see how much farther it is. I'll be right back."

She was too busy gulping for air to argue. But how could he see how much farther "it" was when he'd never seen "it" to begin with? For that matter, how would she know when they'd arrived at Ren's favorite place?

He had taken off and within seconds the glow of his flashlight had disappeared.

The blackness was all-consuming. Total. It closed in on her. Tiny noises sounded in every direction: scratchy autumn crisp leaves scuttled across hard-packed ground; snuffling noises; the wind soughing through the pines at the top of the ridge, mournful;

the distant roar of the creek.

The moon broke through the clouds again, giving her an all too brief respite from the darkness — a few seconds only — before plunging her back into blindness.

Where was he? Her breathing was back to normal. He should be back by now, even though she wasn't sure she really wanted him back. She rubbed her wrist. He shouldn't have worried her about Ren that way. She would never have believed he could be so cruel.

She looked down the trail, saw no dim glow of her lost flashlight, nothing to indicate where it had rolled to. She'd break her neck if she went back down that path to look for it without some light.

The smart thing to do was to stay put. Wait until dawn if she had to.

But the night was all-encompassing. Smothering. Her breath was ragged again — not from exertion. She felt a sob welling inside of her, tried to stifle it, tried to contain her fear. "B-Braxton?" she called.

He wouldn't be able to hear her over the wind.

She waited another five — maybe ten — minutes, before standing up, starting tentatively up the path, feeling for loose stones with the toe of her canvas sneaker before trusting her weight on it. "Braxton?" she called. "Brax-ton!"

Nothing.

She was shivering now, her hands shaking uncontrollably and her molars rat-a-tat-tatting together. Another step, another —

Sound.

Off to her left. A kind of feral growl.

Savage.

The moon reappeared. Braxton stood about twenty feet from her.

"Thank, Go —"

The words died in her throat.

W-was it...*Braxton?*

His features were twisted, his mouth drawn down at one corner, his upper lip curled in a snarl. Spittle glistened at the corner of his lip.

His eyes were vacant, black voids in the wash of moonlight,

and he was hunched over, his head hunkered down on chest, his shoulders bunched up, and his arms bent, hanging ape-like at his sides.

Mary Beth wanted to scream, tried to scream, but her voice caught in her throat as she backed away from that...that thing.

Her chest constricted, as if she'd been caught in a giant clamp, squeezing, forcing the air out of her lungs, crushing her ribcage.

Blackness. The moon was gone again.

And over the pulsing of her blood in her ears was another sound, a thumping sound, the sound of running feet approaching her.

She backed into something, fell backward, legs splayed, crashed her lower back onto something solid, smashed the side of her face against a rock.

Still she scrabbled across the dirt on her butt, crab-like. Legs and arms propelled her backward as fast as they could. She ignored the blood trickling down her face, dismissed the taste of it in her mouth, rebuffed the pressure in her chest.

The Braxton-thing loomed over her, head cocked.

Everything stopped.

Total silence. No scuttling leaves, no roaring river. Even her breath halted.

His eyes narrowed, mesmerized, as he looked at her face — not at her eyes, at her face. He moistened his lips with his tongue. Squatting back on his haunches, he lifted his hand and with his long fingernail, traced the line of her jaw, gently, like a lover would. But she felt the warm wetness of her blood that his finger tracked through.

He grunted, an animal "hoomph" from the back of his throat. His eyes changed. Softened. Grew lusty. Bedroom eyes, the look of passion, of need.

She caught a fast blur of movement, and realized just before it caught her in the middle of her head that it was the arc of a silver flashlight.

Adahy's arm ached. He gasped for air. The kill had not been

a clean one.

He brought his fingers to his mouth and washed them as fastidiously as a large cat at the end of its feast.

CHAPTER TWENTY-TWO

Piper was curled up on the sofa in the dark when Frankie arrived.

"Okay, what's so urgent, Piper? Why don't you have any lights on?"

"I don't want Braxton to know I'm here."

"I'm here now. It's okay." He turned on a lamp, highlighting the exhaustion that had taken a toll on his face. His eyes were puffy and shot with red; his skin was sallow. "What were you babbling about food wrappers in your message? Take a sip of your drink and tell me about it. And start at the beginning." He slipped out of his jacket and perched on an ottoman.

"Would you like one?" she asked, holding up her glass.

He shook his head. "Talk to me."

"There's more than just the food. Over there —" she pointed to an artist's easel in the corner. It sat lopsided, one of its three legs broken off a quarter of the way down and the easel was propped against the wall for support. "Go look at my sketch pad."

Frankie walked over to it and stepped back as people do when studying art. He stood motionless for a long time, then asked without turning around to face her, "You drew this?"

"Yes."

He looked at her then, his brow crumpled in a frown. "And who...?"

She went over to him and stared at her work. The knife still protruded from between the raven's eyes, but smears of red had been streaked across the paper, like finger painting. "Braxton."

Frankie met her gaze. His eyes were clearly puzzled. "Why? Why would he —"

"I lied to you. The morning Braxton reported me missing, and you asked about my face. I lied. Braxton did it."

Frankie's face softened. "I know, you'd be amazed at how many battered women I see. Go on."

She took another sip while she returned to the sofa, then started her tale, beginning with their move to California, the beginning of the end of both his career and their marriage. She ended with the mess in the kitchen.

Frankie stared at her in silence for a long moment. He rubbed his hand over his jaw, thoughtfully. "What about his background? His childhood? What's his family like?"

She twirled an ice cube around in her glass. "You're not going to get Freudian on me, are you?"

He shook his head.

"He was an only child. Never knew his father. In fact, he's always suspected his mother wasn't sure who his father was, although she denied it when he asked. All she told him was that his father was a no-good, do-nothing drifter. He's never said so, but I always got the impression he didn't like her."

"His mother? Why?"

"He was introverted as a child. Said he spent a lot of time in his room, reading, writing, playing his harmonica. She made fun of him for it. Ridiculed him, even in front of other people. Said he'd end up like his father — trash. It's always been a point of pride with him that he proved her wrong by becoming famous."

"Did she ever tell him she was sorry? That she was wrong?"

Piper shook her head. "She died when he was young. In fact, if you're looking for traumatic events, her death was the only one he's ever mentioned."

"What happened?"

"They lived way up in the mountains. Dirt poor — we both grew up poor. They didn't have a phone, a television, not even a radio. Anyway, there was a blizzard, the roads were impassable, and she had an accident. He couldn't call for help, couldn't even get to a neighbor. He had to stay locked up with a dead woman until the storm was over."

"Cause of death?"

"She fell down a flight of stairs. Broke her neck."

"Who raised him then?"

"The state. He became a foster child. Lived with four different foster families. He couldn't adjust."

Again, Frankie became quiet. He rested his head in his hands for a moment, then straightened up and began rubbing his temple in a small, circular motion with his fingertips. When he spoke, his words rolled out with precision, as if he were choosing them with care. His voice was a monotone. "Has Braxton ever displayed any preoccupation with pornography? Any —"

"No! Certainly not."

"Any tendency to harm animals?"

"No."

"Any forms of deviant behavior besides the dramatic mood swings and these violent 'visions' he claims to have had?"

She hesitated, and Frankie apparently noticed. His head snapped up, and he said, "Well?"

"There was — he, er — the day he was attacked by the bird. When he punched me and I was — he, well, he licked my face."

"What?"

"He licked my face. Licked the blood off it. You could tell he...*enjoyed* it." She shuddered.

She couldn't bear the horrified look on Frankie's face. He stared at her, his mouth slightly open and his upper lip wrinkling into a grimace of disgust. She looked away.

"Why the hell didn't you tell me this before?" The sheriff didn't try to conceal his urgency now.

"It was humiliating. I was...scared. And embarrassed."

Frankie sprang to his feet and started pacing back and forth. The muscles in his neck twitched, and he was breathing rapidly. A thin line of sweat sprang out on his upper lip.

"These are classic symptoms, Piper."

"Classic symptoms? Of what?"

"Pack a bag. Whatever you need for the night. For tomorrow. Hurry up."

"But most of my stuff is at the motel in town. I've been staying there the past few nights."

"Does Braxton know where you're staying?"

She nodded. "Of course he does."

"If there's anything you need from here, get it *now.*"

Frankie guided Piper up the stairs. Turning into Braxton's office, he realized his mistake, switched off the light, then wheeled her into the bedroom. "Where's a suitcase?"

She pointed toward the closet.

He crossed the room, flung the door open, grabbed a duffel bag and tossed it on the bed. "Now. Come on. I want you out of here before Braxton gets back."

"Where are we going? She opened a drawer and pulled out some clothes. "I'll have to stop by the motel and get my other stuff."

"No problem. I'm taking you to Marge's house." Frankie grabbed the clothes from her hands and tossed them into the bag. "Have you heard from Mary Beth at all?"

"Me? No, not since last night. Why?" she asked.

"She's not answering her phone. You'd think she'd stay close to home in case there was any news about Susannah."

"When I came home to get some of my things last night, she was here talking with Braxton. I left a few minutes after she did." Piper stopped rummaging through the dresser and looked at Frankie. "What about Ren?" Her voice quivered on his name. "Keysa said he was in danger. Do you believe her?"

"Keysa's a terrific old lady, but she goes off the deep end with that Indian hocus-pocus. Ren's fine. He likes to be alone when he gets rattled, and God knows he's got enough to be rattled about right now. But I don't like this — Mary Beth not being home, Ren wandering around." He zipped the duffel closed, hoisted it onto his shoulder and grabbed Piper's hand. "No, I don't like this at all."

He led her out of the room.

The patrol car's headlights sliced through the dark and the fog creeping in from both sides of the road. "Shouldn't I have taken the Jeep?" Piper asked.

"Don't worry about it."

Piper stared into the blackness looming outside her window. "What about Susannah?" she asked. "What do you think happened to her?"

Frankie licked his lip. "If you'd asked me two days ago, I'd have said she finally found herself a Sugar Daddy and took off with him. But now..."

"The bloody blouse?"

Frankie shrugged. "I'm ninety-nine percent certain Skip told us the truth. He said he took Susannah to a party a month or so ago. They blew a little dope, drank a lot. Susannah got stoned or high or whatever, tripped, fell and got a bloody nose. Skip gave her a tee shirt to wear home, threw her blouse in his trunk and forgot about it. Until my deputy found it in the wheel well. And the blouse *did* have grease smears on it, like it had been used as a rag."

He turned onto the paved road. "We sent the blouse to the lab. They'll be able to tell us how old the blood is, if it's human, and the blood-type. We can't identify it as being Susannah's, because we have nothing to match it to. But we'll know tomorrow if Skip was lying when we get the lab results." He glanced at Piper. "Do you think Braxton was messing around with Susannah?"

She shook her head. "I don't think so. I asked him straight out. He said 'no'. But..."

"But what?"

"I already told you. He was out the night Susannah disappeared."

"And you swear he never physically abused you before you moved into this cabin?"

"*Never*, Frankie. I think he's just...snapped. Braxton has plenty of faults, but until lately, he's never been the violent type. Not that I know of."

The squad car pulled up in front of a modest brick split level house. Frankie unlocked the front door and ushered her in like it was his own place.

"I hate putting Marge out like this," Piper said. "Won't she mind having unexpected company?"

"Nope." Frankie switched on the light, and Piper found herself in a small, cozy foyer.

She shot him a quick glance, then looked away. It wasn't any of her business why he had a key to the dispatcher's house.

"We don't often have to put people up. But it's not the first time and it probably won't be the last," he said.

"Does she know I'm coming?"

"No. But she'll hear us and be down in a minute." He put his key ring on a hall table, and as he did so, the stairwell light flicked on. "Frankie?"

"Yep, it's me. You've got company."

"I don't feel right about this," Piper whispered.

"It's fine. You'll see."

Marge, still tying the sash of a bright pink bathrobe around her waist, appeared on the stairs. "Piper?" Marge's glance took in the duffel bag in Frankie's hands. "Staying the night?"

Frankie nodded.

"I'm so sorry —" Piper began, but Marge cut her off.

"Nonsense. It's no trouble. Frankie, put the water on for hot chocolate, and I'll make up the guest bed." Marge spun on her heel and disappeared back up the stairs.

Piper followed Frankie into Marge's kitchen, watching him set out cups, spoons and cocoa mix after he'd turned the burner on beneath a copper tea kettle. As he pulled out a chair for Piper, Marge reappeared.

"Margie, where's that book on criminal psychoses?"

Marge shot Frankie a surprised and questioning look. "I'll get it." She disappeared through an archway, then quickly returned to the kitchen and handed a book to Frankie. "What's happened?"

He ignored her and began thumbing through the book. "Piper will need a place to stay for a night or two."

"No problem," Marge answered. The kettle started to whistle, and she fixed the hot chocolate.

"Frankie, please tell me what's going on," Piper said. "What's that book got to do with me?"

"Just following a hunch. A long shot. Give me a few minutes, please." Taking the book, he wandered into the other room.

Ten minutes or so later, with his finger marking his page, Frankie walked back into the kitchen and sighed as he looked at her. "What you told me about Braxton — well, it rang some bells. I wanted to check a few things out, make sure I remembered correctly."

"Criminal psychoses?" Piper realized she sounded a little incredulous, but didn't care. "Those 'classic symptoms' you mentioned back at the cabin are some sort of psychosis?"

Frankie looked uncomfortable, like a man whose collar was too tight. He started to say something, apparently changed his mind, bit his lip, then began again. "There is a disorder called 'haematodipsia' which seems it might fit Braxton's behavior. At least, as you described it."

"What, the mood swings?"

"No, the, uh...licking the blood off your face."

Marge dropped the spoon with a clatter. Eyes wide, she turned to look at Frankie. She quickly lowered them and returned to making the cocoa.

"What is it?" Piper asked.

"It's defined as a sexual compulsion — a need — to see, taste and touch blood. It's a form of necrophilia."

"Necrophilia!"

"Not uncommon in, er...serial killers."

"What?" Piper jumped to her feet. "That's preposterous. Braxton's not a serial killer. He's disturbed, but he's not a killer."

"Calm down. I didn't say he was. I'm only saying it's common in serial killers. There are, to oversimplify, two types of serial killers. Those motivated by greed and those motivated by a desire for power or danger. Greed probably doesn't fit into this situation, so it could be — I said *could* be — the second. It's basically what defines the killer as a vampire."

"Vampires?" Piper screeched.

Frankie looked at her sympathetically, then looked away. "Yes," he said softly. "Vampires. These real-life vampires share a need for blood with the Dracula-type vampires, only the real vampires don't need blood to sustain them; they need it for sexual satisfaction."

"That's sick," Piper said, not trying to contain her anger. "And even if Braxton has some sort of...of blood fetish, that doesn't mean he's a serial killer. Or any other kind of killer."

"I'm not accusing him. But I've got one young woman missing whose mother has mysteriously vanished and an abusive husband with possible — *possible* — symptoms of haematodipsia who can't be accounted for at the time the young woman disappeared. What would you make of it?"

Piper thought for a moment, then sputtered, "Coincidence."

"I don't believe in coincidence."

"You're not a doctor. You've no right to be making a diagnosis."

"You're right. That's why I want him examined as soon as possible."

"What about Ren? Aren't you at all concerned about him? Why doesn't he appear on your list of missing persons? Don't you find it peculiar that he'd go commune with nature when his daughter is missing? And besides, you told me yourself you thought she's probably run off with someone."

Frankie rubbed his face in his hands. "Piper, calm down. I know you're upset. I shouldn't have mentioned anything about serial killers. That's a major stretch and uncalled for. But surely you can see why I'm concerned? A psychotic moves into the area, and people start disappearing."

"Frankie!" Marge glared at him. "I don't know the whole story here, but Piper's upset and you're exhausted. You can have this conversation tomorrow, don't you think?"

Piper watched the two stare each other down until Frankie blinked and turned away.

"You're right, Marge. Sorry, Piper."

Marge set a mug of cocoa in front of each of them. "He is concerned about Ren, honey. But he's totally drained. Look at him..."

Frankie's eyes looked even worse than before. Blearier. He had a thick stubble on his lower face and looked as if he hadn't slept in a week. She felt herself softening.

"Drink up," Marge ordered. "Then I'll show Piper her room, and you get yourself on home and get some sleep."

A few minutes later, lulled by the hot chocolate and a sense of temporary safety, Piper trudged up the stairs behind her hostess, growing wearier with each step. How could Frankie rush to judgment like that? Okay, Braxton had problems, severe ones. Still...

Her last thought before she fell asleep was that come hell or high water, she was going to find Ren tomorrow.

CHAPTER TWENTY-THREE

Piper awoke disoriented in the strange bedroom. It took her a few seconds until she remembered being ushered into Marge's house and sent to bed like an exhausted child.

It was still early. Gray light filtered through the window, and when she looked out, the sun was only beginning to appear above the ridge.

She pulled on jeans and a sweatshirt, quietly opened the door and tiptoed down the long stairway. She was surprised to find Marge sipping coffee at her kitchen table.

"Good morning," Marge said.

"Morning. I'm not used to anyone else being up this early," Piper said.

"I wanted to stop you before you slipped out and headed for work," Marge said, folding up the newspaper she'd been reading. "Frankie doesn't want you to come in."

"Why? Was I that bad? Am I fired already?"

"No, you did fine. Help yourself to some coffee." Marge nodded toward the pot and a clean mug set next to it. "Frankie doesn't want you anywhere Braxton might think to look."

Piper helped herself to the coffee and pulled out a chair across from her hostess. "I appreciate his concern. But he's overreacting."

"You're entitled to your opinion. But he's serious. You are not to show up at the Sheriff's office, and you are not to go home. Frankie said he'd be by later to check on you."

"What time?"

"He just said 'late this afternoon'. He's got a full schedule today."

"So I'm under house arrest?" Piper hadn't intended to sound snotty, but there was an edge to her voice.

Marge grinned. "No. Just don't go anywhere your husband

might be."

Piper played with her spoon. "I'm sorry about putting you out like this. I wouldn't be too happy to be awakened in the wee hours and find a houseguest dumped on me."

Marge held her hand palm up. "Not a problem. I've done it before for my kid brother. I'm sure I'll do it again."

"You're Frankie's sister?"

"Yep. Everyone's related to everyone else around here. You never know whose cousin you're talking to. Keeps you on your toes. Well —" Marge got up and rinsed out her mug. "I'm holding down the office today. Please make yourself at home. And if you need anything, call."

After Marge left, Piper's restlessness became so overwhelming that she paced the small house like a caged animal. She needed to hear a friendly voice, be somewhere familiar, to feel like she belonged with someone, belonged somewhere.

She needed Ren.

She reached her limit within an hour, and contrary to all the arguments she could make against doing so, she took off in search of him. She couldn't bear standing idly by, doing nothing. She couldn't shrug off Keysa's warnings as nonsense the way Frankie did. Keysa had the same kind of prescience her own grandmother had possessed. It was foolhardy to discount such ancient knowledge as 'hocus-pocus.' And as she had decided the day before, she would start at the gorge.

The closer she got to the river, the more apprehensive she became. She missed Raven, kept looking around for him, but to no avail.

Coming from town, she approached the gorge from a different direction than she'd ever before used and realized, for the first time, what a vast network of trails there were. Hikers, sightseers, fishermen and hunters had all beaten down paths, some easy, some quite challenging, all of which seemed to intersect the largest trail, the one which skirted the precipice.

The higher she climbed, the stronger the wind blew and the more frigid the air became. By the time she reached the pathway paralleling the gorge, her face felt raw and chapped, her lips stiff. She peered over the rocky banks to the river below. The water level was down, yet what remained ran furiously, frothing and spewing over the rocks, eddying into swirling pools in the cradles.

Pulling the collar of her jacket up over her chin, she continued up the path. By the time she reached the flats, her feet tingled with cold. When she approached the fork in the path, she stomped her feet to get the blood circulating.

The stomping reminded her of Raven, how he shifted his weight from foot to foot before settling on her shoulder. Were his feet cold? Was that what prompted the gesture? The corner of her mouth lifted into a bittersweet smile.

She panned the sky again, searching for Raven. There was nothing but the wind whipping through the chasm, tearing her eyes. She moved on.

After wandering only a little way, she spotted what looked like a pile of discarded clothing. She approached slowly. *Why would clothes be heaped —*

A wave of numbness washed through her. Her legs froze.

A mound of what appeared to be partly flesh, partly plaid, lay to the left of the path. Something about it struck her as familiar.

Then the pieces fell into place.

The plaid.

Ren's shirt. She stumbled toward the mound.

Then stopped.

Susannah.

Or what remained of her.

Relief surged through Piper like a wave. *Thank God it wasn't Ren.* Then shame flooded her, guilt that she could feel relief because it was a young woman dead rather than her lover. But relief was undeniably what she felt.

Something brown and furry scurried across the path on the far side of the bloated mound.

Susannah's head was covered by Ren's shirt. Ren had found his daughter's body. But where was *he?* He wouldn't leave her here, he would have —

An eerie sensation enveloped her, as if her mind was a wide angle camera lens, slowly, smoothly zooming into a narrow focus. The sounds of the wind and river receded, leaving only a silence broken by the dry, scuttling sound of a crisp leaf blowing across the path.

The gray of the sky and the brown of autumn-bald trees were suddenly that much grayer, browner. The daylight brightened, and the smallest details of the landscape stood out in sharp relief: A vein of quartz networked across a boulder fifty feet past the pathway, a deer rub on the oak tree to the left, the dried, once slimy track of a slug trail across a basswood leaf, the pores on the naked leg in front of her.

Her nostrils flared, and she inhaled the aroma of crushed pine needles, leaf mold, putrification, spoor and the wet cleanliness of the rushing water below.

Her fingers flexed and rubbed against her jeans. The denim felt as rough as an emery board, and the sound of flesh against cloth was as raspy as a knife buttering toast.

Every sense sharpened, intensified. She was an extension of the trees and rocks.

Ancient memories? The blurring of man and Nature like grandmother used to talk about?

A new scent tickled her nose. Metallic. Familiar and strange. Then it came to her.

Blood.

Her eyes narrowed, sharpening her sight even more. She panned the area, slowly, methodically, from left to right. There was a small indentation a little way up the path from the body.

Head down, shoulders hunched, she walked toward it slowly, eyes sweeping back and forth over the path. There. A track. Three toes and part of a pad. Headed toward the gorge. She followed.

Another track. Whatever made the imprint had been running. This one was complete, four toes and the entire pad. Like a cat's paw, but larger. Much larger. Still headed toward the gorge.

Part of a boot print. Facing away from the gorge. Facing the running feline.

A droplet of blood, dried brown against the faded green of a crushed blade of grass. A space as large as a small tract house bedroom where the grass was trampled. Flattened.

Where the grass gave way to the well-worn dirt path, she found an area where the dirt was freshly gouged and scraped.

Something had happened here: the scent of blood was stronger.

She knelt, traced over scratch marks on the hard-packed earth with gentle strokes of her fingers. A large dark stain — she leaned close and sniffed. More blood. Soaked into the ground. Scuff marks, something dragged, something rolling, something —

She looked over the edge of the gorge. Spatters of dried blood clung to leaves on a small tree part way down the bank. Scrape marks. A sapling, its roots curled around an outcropping three quarters of the way to the river — snapped, where something heavy had fallen on it.

She rocked back on her haunches, the damp cold settling over her, heavy. Oppressive. Like a great weight on her chest preventing the expansion and contraction of her lungs. The cold seeped through her layers of clothes and layers of skin and joined a core of ice starting deep within, until every molecule in her body was cold. Numb.

Ren had fallen into the gorge. It was *his* blood spattered all over.

She reconstructed the entire scenario in her mind, from his discovery of Susannah's body to his encounter with the predator. Bobcat? Mountain lion? Did it matter?

No. Ren was gone. Nothing else mattered.

She gave herself up to the cold.

CHAPTER TWENTY-FOUR

Piper tossed pebbles into the water, watching as they sank into the swirling eddies and frigid froth. An occasional shout drifted from the top of the precipice as Frankie and his men took care of Susannah's remains.

She had stayed with them for a while, plucking at Frankie's sleeve, pointing out the evidence that supported her theory of what happened to Ren.

He'd looked closely at the tracks, had asked the forensics people to photograph the trampled grass and the blood-spattered leaves, the claw marks in the dirt and the broken sapling well down the side of the gorge.

But he made it clear that his priorities lay with Susannah. He seemed to think Ren was invincible, incapable of stumbling into harm's path. Once she'd answered all of his questions, he'd returned his attention to the crime scene.

Forgotten, she'd wandered a quarter-mile or so down the trail to where the land sloped gently toward the river. She picked her way to the water. Her glance raked over the rocks and shrubs, looking for signs of Ren.

She found what she'd been looking for directly below the site where Susannah's body lay.

Several black feathers lay glistening in the sand. One floated on a rock-bordered pool of stagnant water. They were blacker than the night with a metallic brilliance about them. Raven feathers.

The world slipped into slow motion. A heavy lethargy commanded her limbs and her mind. She was empty, a shell, incapable of doing anything but sitting there turning the feathers in her hand, feeling their softness, their warmth.

Suddenly, a hand clamped on her shoulder.

"You okay?" Frankie asked.

She nodded. "Why don't you believe me?"

"About Ren?"

"Yes."

"Piper, you made some valid points back there. Damned good points. I wish my deputy was as observant as you are. But I don't buy the theory that Ren went over the cliff. I don't buy the theory Ren was carrying Susannah at all."

"But I showed you the boot print and the cat tracks. You saw the broken sapling and blood spatters yourself." She licked her lips, trying to make them more flexible. "And Ren's shirt, wrapped around Susannah. How much proof do you need?"

"Piper, I —"

"Can't you check the print against his shoes? Or do DNA tests or something?"

Frankie squatted, bringing himself down to her eye level. "We aren't the L.A.P.D. We're a small town police force —"

"That didn't stop you from spouting some pretty sophisticated theories about haematodipsia —"

"That's not fair. I told you that your descriptions triggered some alarms in my head, stuff from Abnormal Psych classes, stuff I haven't thought about in years. That's why I checked into it. I'm not saying Braxton *has* haematodipsia — I said it was a possibility. You've got to understand that we don't have the resources of a Los Angeles or New York. We're dealing with a very complex, very remote crime scene. It's going to get dark shortly, and the State boys have only just arrived. Of course we'll take impressions of the tracks and prints, but probably not until morning."

"And the shirt?"

Frankie ran his fingers through his hair. "I'm going to try to find Mary Beth again. Maybe she can identify it. Trouble is, damn near every man in the county has a red and black plaid shirt. It's the 'good old boys' uniform."

Piper tried to sound reasonable. "If you don't think Ren found the body, what *do* you think?"

Frankie stood up and stretched his back muscles. "You don't want to know." He jammed his hands in his pockets and looked out at the water.

"Yes, I do," she said, surprised at the strength in her voice. She stood up, her back to the river, and put her hand on his forearm. "I need to be convinced Ren isn't in the river somewhere."

He tugged on his jacket. "After I sent you away from the scene, and the photographer finished taking photos of the position the body was in when you found her, the medical examiner rolled Sus — the body — over. She'd been...eaten."

"Eaten?" Her voice sounded like a little girl's.

He nodded, his eyes still staring at the water. "I think the cat tracks you spotted were from a bobcat or something that was feeding on her."

"Those tracks were too big for a bobcat."

"Okay, maybe a mountain lion. We don't have many, but there's been a few around over the years. I think another predator wanted in on the feed and they fought. Those scuff marks in the dirt are consistent with rolling, scrabbling animals. I think they continued to battle over the kill, got too close to the edge of the gorge and went over."

"Then were are they? Their bodies should be on the rocks below. Or at least there would be a lot of blood even if they both survived the fall — which is unlikely. And what about the boot print?"

"It was old. Actually, I found several others after you left. Some smaller, possibly female, maybe even Susannah's, and some sneaker treads."

Piper stopped trying to sound reasonable. "That print was fresh."

Frankie spun around, eyes blazing. "What makes you such an expert? Okay, you made some good observations up there, but that doesn't make you a forensics expert. As for Ren, personally I think he's with Mary Beth. I'll — what are you looking at?"

Piper's gaze had swept across the face of the cliff, then riveted on something caught in a small cedar tree dangling upside down by a slim reef of bark still connecting it to its root. But for that thread of bark, the trunk would have been severed in two.

Her blood turned cold. All the moisture in her mouth seemed to dry up at once, and she thought she might be sick. "There," she mumbled, and she pointed toward the suspended tree with a shaking finger. "In that cedar tree."

"What? I don't see anything."

The cedar tree blurred in her eyes, bubbled, as if she were looking through an aquarium.

"Ren's amulet," she said, wiping her eyes, trying to clear her vision. "To the left of the trunk, half way up." She turned to Frankie. He was squinting, staring at the tree.

"I don't see anything."

"Go get it," she said. "It's there. I swear it."

He glanced at her, uncertainty written on his face for a fleeting moment.

Then he moved off and began climbing the steep face of the bank. The bottom ten feet or so were almost a sheer vertical drop and he had to angle over to the injured tree from the side and approach it from above. Frankie dislodged several small rocks as he dug his boots into small toeholds in the crevices, and Piper prayed the plants he used as hand holds were sturdy enough to support his weight.

Frankie reached down and plucked the leather pouch from its resting place, pushed it into his pocket and began maneuvering down the cliff.

When he rejoined her on the bank, his face was ashen, and the hand holding the amulet out to her shook.

"Now do you believe me?" she asked, taking the amulet in her hand and curling her fingers around its warmth.

"I — I don't know what to think," he said.

But the truth was written all over his face.

"Have you ever seen Ren without his amulet?" she asked.

He bit his lower lip, then shook his head, no. "Come on. I'll give you a ride back to Marge's."

"No. I'm staying here for awhile."

"Absolutely not. It'll be dark in less than an hour. You're coming with me."

"I'm perfectly safe here. And I'll be back at Marge's before dark. I promise."

"No. Come on." He put his arm out help her, but she shrugged him off.

"Piper, dammit, we've got a murder victim on our hands, two people missing —"

"I thought you said Ren and Mary Beth were probably together somewhere."

"I know what I said," he snapped.

"But you don't believe it, do you? Especially now. Especially after this." She held the amulet out.

He opened his mouth to say something, then apparently thought better of it and dry-washed his face with his hands instead. "I'm so tired I don't know what to believe." He paused for a moment and scrunched his eyes together as if to clear them. "But I know this: I have a murder victim, two people who should be around who aren't, an abusive husband quite possibly suffering from some form of necrophilia and other neuroses, who has also disappeared." His eyes locked onto hers. "You're *not* staying here by yourself."

Piper shrugged her shoulders. "As you wish, *Sheriff.*"

The ride back to Marge's was a silent one.

Piper waited until the squad car disappeared from view, then slipped out the door and walked back to the gorge, careful to stay away from the hustle of the crime scene.

The sun had started to dip behind the top of the mountain. The surrounding sky was a bright orange that faded to salmon at the outer edges of its range, then blended into the faded light blue of afternoon. The wind, as it did most every day at sunset, died down, as if it, too, wanted to appreciate the sun's light show.

Piper slid her hands into her jacket pocket, keeping the fingers of her right hand curled around the raven feathers and amulet as she walked, drawing comfort from them.

She glanced up. The sky was bruised now, a dark purply-blue that faded to a sickly yellow in the remnant of the sun's path. It spoke to her wounded heart, stopping her feet as she watched it. Suddenly, the sunset's remains blurred, quivering and fuzzy. The tears had started again, welling over her lashes and rolling down her cheeks.

Her fingers touched the tears.

She sank down on her knees, too tired to go on. If nature

abhorred a vacuum, perhaps something would fill the void in her. The nothingness was, inch by inch, sucking her into a black hole.

She heard a *crack* behind her.

The image of Susannah's corpse flashed through her mind.

The fingers of her right hand clutched the amulet and feathers tighter, as if gathering strength from them, as if their heat would protect her.

Why hadn't she stayed at Marge's?

She turned her head, preparing herself to face a killer cat — muscles flexed, ready to pounce — that was stalking her.

It wasn't a cat. It was worse.

She scrambled to her feet. "Braxton!"

CHAPTER TWENTY-FIVE

Piper clamped her mouth shut to smother the scream she felt building. More than just terror welled up inside her, there was a gut-wrenching sadness. Compassion. "What's happened to you?"

His hair — usually so soft and fine — was matted and filthy. It stuck out in clumps on one side of his head, glued close to his scalp on the other, as if flattened by his lying on it. His clothes were filthy — bloodstained and tattered. One sleeve hung by a small section of seam at the shoulder, the knees of his pants were ripped and frayed.

"What are you staring at?" he growled.

"You — don't look like yourself."

He stopped, cocked his head to one side, and waited. His eyes were strange, almost as if he didn't recognize her.

It was too much. God forgive her, but she couldn't deal with Braxton's troubles now.

A soft wail escaped her, and she sank to her knees, dropping her face into her hands where the amulet still lay. She felt her black hair draping around her like a shroud, as if to keep her sorrow in.

She knelt on the thick carpet of scarlet, gold and orange leaves, rocking back and forth, as if she were trying to comfort herself. Ren was gone.

Gone!

"Piper?"

Her head snapped up when she heard her name. She clutched the amulet to her chest. Braxton! — or some semblance of Braxton. She'd forgotten he was there.

"Piper?" he asked again, approaching slowly in a lop-sided old man's gait, so different from his usual, cocky strides. His voice sounded rusty, but there was an intelligence — a recognition — in his eyes that hadn't been there a few moments ago.

He put his hand on her shoulder. She didn't flinch from his touch, but her gaze lingered on his heavily ridged fingernails, long and unkempt. Yellow.

He tapped on her temple with one finger. "Knock, knock, anybody home?" he asked, then reached toward her folded hands and tried to uncurl her fingers.

She jerked away.

His hand shot out quickly and snatched the small deerskin purse from her. He turned it over, gasped as he saw it's design. His yellowed nail traced over the tiny beads — minuscule, shiny black beads — embroidered into the shape of a raven's head.

He loosened the leather thong that drew the amulet closed, opened it, and dumped the contents into his hand.

A glossy black feather lay on his palm, tinged with metallic glints. A small, smooth quartz pebble, and a trickle of dirt joined the feather.

He glanced up from his upturned hand and locked onto Piper's eyes.

She swiped at the tears flowing in a steady stream down her face, tracking over her cheekbones and dripping onto her red sweatshirt where they soaked into the fabric, staining it a deep scarlet.

He shook his head, rubbed his eyes with one grubby fist as if trying to clear his vision of some unsettling image. When he dropped his hands back to his side, scattering the remnants of Ren's tokens to the ground, his eyes were vacant again. Predatory.

She scrambled for Ren's mementos, scooping up the feather and pebble with earth, sand and leaves, stood up, and stiffened, started to back away.

Braxton's hands suddenly shot up to his ears, covering them, his eyes wild. A strange gurgle sounded in the back of his throat that quickly changed into an agonized scream.

"Braxton?"

Whirr.

Louder than before, overwhelming, deafening. Pain shot through his head from one ear to the other.

The bitch with the onyx eyes was backing away from him, her thin brows arched so high they looked as if they might fly away. She looked...terrified.

The hum softened somewhat. Became tolerable. No more than the buzz of an angry fly.

He looked down at himself, at his tattered shirt, his chest criscrossed with scratches peeking through the rips in the cloth. Blood bubbled and seeped through the fabric.

Nails raking at him, hands trying to ward off his blows.

He saw his bare feet — scraped, raw and stinging as if he'd run miles across rocks and thorns.

He held out his right hand. His cuticles were caked with dried blood, mud smears on the back of his knuckles; the hair on his arm was matted and half-hidden in blood. He turned his hand over. The underside of his nails were caked with tissue.

Bent white fingers reaching for his eyes, clawing him, raking down over his belly.

Whose fingers?

Ah. The woman in the housecoat.

But he'd washed her off of him. Had he met her again?

He looked into the whore's eyes, darker now, darker than her black heart. She should have been crying black tears, but she wasn't. The tears were as silver white as the froth on the water below.

She watched him strangely. Cautiously. Then her puzzled look changed, turned to one of...disgust? Revulsion?

"What have you done?" the woman whispered. "Braxton, what have you become?"

Whirrr.

He reached for her.

She stepped back. The black eyes were wary. Alert.

His fingers tingled, ached, wanting to wrap themselves around the slender shaft of her neck and squeeze, longing for that crunching *snap,* yearning for the suspicion in her eyes to turn to fear, to terror. Yielding to his power and might.

No, not wanting it. Needing it.

His hands reached out.

She backed up farther, half-crouched, as if waiting for him to charge.

But then, inexplicably, the flow of her tears stopped, and she straightened up. Her eyes cleared. She looked at him as if she were seeing him for the first time. And she didn't like what she saw.

"You're no longer human," she said. "Your spirit is gone. I don't have to feel any guilt. Not anymore."

She turned from him and began to walk away.

Whirrrrrrr.

"Don't turn your back on me!" he screamed.

She kept walking.

Just like his mama had done.

He lunged. He grabbed her by the shoulder and spun her around.

"Don't you dare turn your back on me. Ever."

"I'm ashamed to share your name," she said and tried to turn again.

He held her.

She wrenched away.

He couldn't breathe. He cringed. The buzzing in his head got louder, changed into voices, indistinct, shadowy. They increased to a deafening pitch.

"I'm ashamed of you!" they cried. Mama cried. Or was it the whore yelling?

"You're worthless, like your no-good, do-nothing father!" they screamed. "A piece of shit!"

"Bastard! You've made my life hell!"

Whirrrrrr.

He had to shut her up. Nothing was more important than to quiet her.

He reached. His hands dashed for her throat. No pushing this time. No lunging shove.

She jerked away from him, twisting...

And fell.

She launched over the edge of the precipice, cartwheeling. She fell more quickly than mama had. Mama had bumped and thumped down the stairs, and her pink curlers had burst open when her head slammed on the bottom step.

But this woman, this — she was mama! turned over and over, a rag doll in a flowered housecoat, pirouetting in a macabre death dance.

Blinding burst of white light. *Whirrrrrr.*

Splat!

Splattered. Broken like a porcelain doll.

Shattered.

She sprawled, arms and legs akimbo, her head at a peculiar angle to her neck.

Lolling.

Like the pink serpent.

A shadowy stain spread from beneath her hair. In the fading light, it looked almost black.

It trickled into the water, dyeing the froth eddying around the rock, dispersing around the base of the rock, expanding, coloring the spume black.

The whirlpool spun faster, coalescing into a cylindrical, revolving shape like a miniature water spout, twirling around the boulder's waterline, skimming the surface until it had circumnavigated the rock.

The vortex left the water, slowly at first, its elevation increasing in unison with the accelerating revolutions, rising higher. The cyclonic shape started to spread, seemed to be dissipating, but the he realized it was regrouping itself into...

The beating of wings — flap, flap, glide. Flap, flap, glide — demanded his attention. It sped down the gorge, descending lower into the water, the hilt of a kitchen knife stuck between its eyes.

The raven!

It glided ever lower, its path straight as an arrow, unwavering, heading for the coalescence that, even as he watched, rearranged itself into another raven.

The first raven's screech echoed off the walls of the chasm. It circled the still solidifying bird, screeched again, circled, and banked off in the direction from which it had come.

The smaller raven followed, caught up to the first, and after a brief touching of wing tips, the pair flapped off down the gorge, rising ever higher until they flew out of sight.

He stared at the sky, awaiting the raven's return.

There was nothing but the encroaching black of night.

A flash of red along the bank.

Gone.

A streaking shadow across the treeline.

Disappeared.

Whirr.

He looked back toward the river. The boulder was empty, deserted, holding no souvenir but the black stain that still trickled over its contour and flowed into the rushing water.

What exactly happened there? What am I looking for?

He couldn't quite remember why he was there at all, or where that woman with the big black eyes had gone. Or the other one, the one who was to take care of him. The one with the curlers.

But the stain called, a siren call summoning him, enticing him with a cry so seductive that it blocked all other thought from his mind.

The call, only the call, the summons awakening something in his belly, a burning hunger that needed to be fulfilled.

He lowered himself over the edge, hand over hand, from bush to sapling, answering the call of the stain.

CHAPTER TWENTY-SIX

There was one small segment of her brain that wasn't seized by panic, and that part wondered — since she was about to die — why wasn't her life flashing before her eyes?

A sideward crash into the icy water drove the air out of her lungs while engulfing her in frigid froth. She quickly plunged through the swift current near the surface to the more peaceful water near the bottom of the deep pool. The shock of the cold water snapped her out of panic into pure animal instinct.

Survive!

She kicked, aiming for the top. At least, she hoped she kicked. She intended to, but she couldn't feel her feet and legs, so she wasn't sure if they responded. Then the water brightened, and she was caught in the stronger surface currents.

Air!

She gulped down greedy swallows of air, sucking in froth, too, sputtering, before the current slammed her sideways into a boulder — *crack!* A flash of pain coursed through her arm like a lightning bolt.

She flailed for a ledge, a crevice, anything to grab on to.

Nothing.

The water pinned her against the slicked surface by sheer force, spun her around till she faced the boulder, then she slid hand over hand across its rocky face until she reached the rounded end. There, she was swept helplessly away by the current once again.

The world consisted of twilight sky, spewing water, blurring rocks and an occasional frantic swallow of air for how long? Seconds? Minutes?

Suddenly, she was propelled into a tangle of branches and twigs, enmeshed in them. The current tugged at her legs, working to sweep her farther downstream, but her upper body was held fast by the branches of a river birch felled by some long forgotten storm.

Piper dangled there until she caught her breath and her heart decelerated to something nearer normal.

The threat of hypothermia loomed in her mind. Her left arm hung useless at her side, but she shook off exhaustion and propelled herself down the tree trunk by hooking her leg over it, and used her right arm to shimmy toward the massive tangle of roots protruding from a clump of earth on the bank.

About four-feet from the shore, she unhooked her leg and dropped into the shallow water, collapsing.

She shifted onto her knees and crawled toward the bank, glancing upriver.

Braxton was silhouetted against the graying sky, a hundred or so yards upstream and at the top of the gorge.

Her heart stopped. She caught her breath and held it for a moment, as if he could hear her raspy intake of air from so great a distance, then began scrabbling for her footing. She slipped and slid on submerged rock ledges like a dog skidding across freshly waxed floors, until she reached the bank, and heaved herself behind a large rounded boulder.

Her heart still raced as she cowered behind the rock, rubbing her legs with her good hand, accelerating the circulation, then shuffled them back and forth against the dirt. She had to get moving. She was shivering so violently she was afraid she'd shake loose whatever body parts had remained intact after her plunge into the river.

She peered over the top of the boulder, but she couldn't see where Braxton stood from this vantage point.

Inching along the boulder, she looked again. Braxton was working his way down the precipice, hand over hand, from sapling to outcropping. He reached the water's edge. Instead of running down the shoreline after her, he rock-hopped out to a large flat boulder almost in the middle of the river — the one on which she'd so recently sunbathed — dropped to his hands and knees and lowered his head to the rocky surface.

What the hell was he doing?

Curiosity overcame fear, and she watched, stunned, as he knelt, his lips moving as if in prayer. His head cocked first one way and then the other. When he began to lap at the rock with his tongue like a cat huddled over a bowl of cream, she shuddered and turned away.

She glanced back in time to see him bolt from the rock and begin to make his way back to shore.

She had to start moving, not only to distance herself from Braxton, but also to get warm.

As it was, she stumbled through the last of twilight, maintaining her bearings by keeping the roar of Crooked Creek to her left and feeling her way through the almost-dark like a blind person. She never shifted her weight to her forward foot until she was certain the footing was solid.

She'd forgotten how intense country darkness could be: blackness so thick it looked as if it had been painted on. When the stars began to appear, they served by contrast, to make the rest of the sky appear blacker still.

She was exhausted, depleted by cold and trauma. She had to find someplace to spend the night, a place sheltered from the wind, a place Braxton wouldn't stumble on.

A hundred-yards farther downstream, she found a sheltered spot between two large humpbacked boulders that was filled with a thick layer of pine needles, shed by the pines dotting the overhang above.

She scraped out some of the needles with her good hand, lay down in the depression and covered herself with the displaced needles. It wasn't the most efficient bed, but the pine needles trapped at least some of her body heat.

Enough to prevent hypothermia?

Probably not, but she didn't know what else to do. Her arm throbbed. Jagged bolts of pain shot through her as she tried to find a comfortable position. She couldn't stop shivering. Her teeth chattered so unmercifully she was sure they'd soon be worn down to nubs.

The thought of sliding slowly into shock and slipping unknowingly from shock into death seemed less frightening than facing reality.

Ren. Braxton. Ren and Raven. Right and wrong. What's real? Life or death. Feathers.

As her mind slid toward blackness, she embraced the dark.

Frankie was beside himself. He hadn't slept all night, not since Marge called to ask him where Piper was.

Armed with battery-operated lanterns, he and Warren returned to the top of the gorge. They crawled over the crime scene on their hands and knees, searching for the slightest trace of Piper, some faint piece of evidence. Even a hint.

Nothing.

He returned to the Wyatt house. It remained untouched, unvisited.

He checked at the motel. Nothing.

He pounded on Ren's mother's door until Jeff, rubbing the sleep from his eyes and with his hair sticking up like a cockatoo's crest, opened the door.

"Have you heard from Piper?" Frankie asked, stepping into the warmth of the front hall.

Jeff shook his head, yawned hugely and scratched his scrawny bare chest. "Was I supposed to?"

"What about your parents? Have you heard from either of them?"

"No, sir. Not that I know of. Gram might have, but of course she was already asleep when I got home from my buddy's house."

Frankie shook his head and sighed. "Go wake her up for me, please."

"It's three o'clock in the morning!"

"I know what time it is," Frankie snapped.

Jeff went down the hallway to Keysa's bedroom.

When he returned, the kid was wide-eyed. "She's not there."

"Where is she?"

"I don't know. Her bed hasn't been slept in."

"Didn't you say she was asleep when you came home?"

"I thought she was," Jeff said.

"What time did you come in?"

"About nine." He gulped, and his Adam's apple looked huge in his slender neck.

"Either she was there or she wasn't."

"I didn't open her bedroom door to look, Sheriff. I assumed she was asleep because she wasn't out where I could see her. She's usually in bed by nine or so."

"Where could she have gone?" Frankie asked.

"Wherever she went, she walked. She doesn't drive anymore. Or maybe someone picked her up." Jeff's face lit up. "Maybe dad came and got her."

"Goddammit! Another Wyatt missing. The FBI couldn't keep track of this family. Who the hell knows where any of you Wyatts are? Except for you and Susannah."

"Susannah? You found her? Is she okay?"

Oh, shit.

CHAPTER TWENTY-SEVEN

Suddenly a presence penetrated her sleeping mind and prodded it into awareness. Piper's eyes flew open. A human head, hair askew, loomed over her, outlined against the first faint gray of pre-dawn. She tried to scream, but it came out as a squeak.

A hand promptly clamped down on her mouth.

"What're you screaming for? Don't you know any better than that?" Keysa whispered. "When I take my hand off your mouth, you don't make one peep. Understand?"

Piper nodded. Keysa was the last person she expected to find hovering over her. Was she still asleep?

"Good," the old woman said and removed her hand.

"What on earth are you doing here?" Piper whispered.

"Waking you up. Come on."

"No, I mean, why are you down here? At the river?" Piper sat up, wincing as pain shot up her arm and across her shoulders.

Keysa stared at her in disbelief, as if Piper had asked something stupid. "Come to get my boy."

"Ren? Have you...have you found him?"

Keysa nodded, then jabbed the end of her walking stick into the ground and used it for leverage to hoist herself to her feet. As Piper waited for the details, she noticed a large lump-like growth on the old woman's back. In the faint light, she couldn't make out what it was. Suddenly she realized the old woman was tottering off.

"Where is he?" Piper cried, scrambling to her feet and taking off after Keysa.

"Shush." The old woman pointed downstream.

"Is he okay?"

Keysa shook her head.

Piper's breath caught in her throat. "Is — is he alive?"

"For now. You must help me get him home."

Piper drew abreast of the woman. The hump on Keysa's back was a backpack with a peeling picture of Tinkerbell on it.

Tinkerbell?

"Shouldn't we call an ambulance? Or Frankie?"

Keysa stopped and looked over at Piper with her mouth open. "Frankie? Frankie's a nice boy and a good friend to my son, but Frankie can't find his way out of his own bed. Why would I call Frankie? We take care of our own."

Piper wasn't going to argue that point. She dropped back as they squeezed through a narrow opening between a boulder and another fallen tree. "How did you find me?" she asked when she was able to walk at Keysa's side.

"Hah! A blind man could have found you. You left sign all over the gorge. Blood, footprints, broken twigs all over the place." The old woman shook her head in disgust. "Shoddy work, Pippi."

"Piper."

"Pippi, Piper, whatever. No name for one of The People." Keysa came to an abrupt stop. She cocked her head and held her hand up, signaling Piper to silence.

"What is it?" Piper asked.

Keysa turned and glared at her. "Sssh!"

Piper cocked her head and listened. Nothing.

Only the ever-present roar of water rushing the gorge. Even the birds weren't awake yet.

And then she heard it...a rustling, something moving heavily between the trees.

The two women stared at the spot above them where the rustle had originated, halfway up the hillside.

Keysa sidestepped behind one of the boulders and motioned for Piper to follow. They hunkered down behind the rock and watched and listened.

A flash of something appeared through the trees: a man, auburn haired.

"Adahy," Keysa whispered as Piper said, "Braxton!"

They followed his fleeting form, sometimes a shadow, sometimes invisible except for the tall weeds and grasses that bent as he passed, moving in the same direction in which they were headed.

"Hurry! And stay hidden," Keysa said, taking off at a surprising clip. "Ren is vulnerable. He cannot withstand an attack by Adahy."

Adahy?

No, it was Braxton. Even with his hair sticking out like a bushman's in the outback, it was definitely Braxton. Or a disturbing facsimile.

"That's not Adahy. That's Braxton," Piper said as she caught up to the old woman. "Or what *used* to be Braxton. He pushed me over the cliff. I don't know what he'll do if he finds Ren. How much farther?"

"Not far," Keysa said. Then her foot went out from under her, and she started to fall.

Piper grabbed the woman's arm with her unbroken one and stabilized her.

Keysa flashed her a look that offered both thanks and reproach. The look startled Piper for a moment, and then she almost smiled. She could imagine the frustration of being a young warrior trapped in an old woman's body.

Glancing frequently at the hillside, Keysa skirted the edge of a promontory, then grunting with effort, worked her way down to her knees, and crawled beneath a large fallen branch that straddled two rocks.

Tinkerbell snagged on a twig, halting Keysa's progress, and Piper worked to free the knapsack.

"What's in this pack?" she asked as she worked.

"My healing things. Herbs, scissors, knife, Band-Aids. Hurry up."

"Tinkerbell, huh? Not very professional for a shaman."

Keysa glared at her. "Maybe not professional, but frugal. It was Susannah's when she was little."

Piper finally broke the green twig on which the sack was tangled. When she was free, Keysa stayed on her hands and knees and crawled crab-like beneath an outcropping.

"Ren!" Piper cried, spotting the sheen of his silvery hair, glistening in the first sunlight rising over the eastern ridge. She scrambled over to him and touched his shoulder with her fingertips.

One side of his face was deeply gouged — clawed, with a small chunk of his cheek missing. Some kind of ointment had been packed into the wound. His left eye was swollen shut, and a small patch of his hair had been snipped away. A jagged line of black stitches crossed the newly sheared spot like railroad tracks. His leg was splinted on a slender tree limb three inches longer than his leg. His opposing arm was also splinted. A small fire burned near him, aromatic with sweet cedar and sage.

"Oh, my God, Ren," Piper whispered, surveying the visible damage.

"Quiet, Pippi. Adahy is nearby," Keysa warned.

"What're you doing here?" Ren asked.

"I came looking for you," Piper answered. "But I ran into Braxton. He...he —"

"Pushed her over the cliff," Keysa finished for her. She turned to Piper. "Now, I fixed Ren up good, huh? He can walk, I think, but he'll need to be supported. And I'm not as steady as I once was. That's where you come in. Help him up."

Hoisting a man as tall as Ren to his feet from a prone position with one leg immobilized by a tree limb was a daunting task — especially with Piper's broken arm — but they eventually heaved him upright.

Not without a cost.

The wrenching movement ripped open the clawmarks on Ren's chest, wounds that Keysa had carefully stitched together, anointed, then covered with her blanket. Piper's eyes filled with tears as she watched the blood start trickling down Ren's chest and his face contort with pain.

Ren leaned heavily on Piper and used the walking stick on the other side. Keysa carefully smothered the fire, gathered up her remaining herbs and stuffed them into her backpack.

They'd taken only a few steps when something crashed nearby in the woods.

All three stopped until it was evident whoever had been running through the woods had bypassed them.

"Who was that?" Ren asked.

"Custer, if we're lucky," his mother replied and motioned them forward.

They skirted Crooked Creek even farther downstream, to where a gully cleft the hillside at a gentler incline, then followed the gully back up to the top of the gorge.

Using the walking stick, Keysa pushing her son from behind while Piper supported him at the side, they made it to within fifty yards of the road that skirted the gorge to that point.

And twenty-feet away from Braxton.

CHAPTER TWENTY-EIGHT

For the briefest moment, nobody moved, as if all four were actors in a bizarre tableau.

Braxton's mouth was drawn dramatically down at one side. He breathed rapidly, rattly, his chest rising and falling as he gulped air. He stood hunched over, like a third-rate actor in a grade-B caveman picture. Piper half expected him to grab her by the hair and drag her to his lair. There was something empty about his expression, as if the soul within had given up tenancy.

Then he blinked. His nostrils flared, and he sniffed the air. His eyes narrowed and a feral expression, devoid of human compassion, filled them. The whites of his eyes were yellow.

He wiped a thin stream of spittle from his mouth with his forearm. His lips curled back from his teeth like a Rottweiler warning off an intruder.

Keysa screamed, "ADAHY!"

He stepped back, startled by the old woman's noise, then hunkered down into a semi-crouch.

Braxton was fast.

Ren was faster still.

Bracing himself by jabbing the protruding limb splint into the dirt, he twirled the walking stick like a baton with his good arm and used it as a stave, holding it horizontally in front of the women like a barrier.

But Braxton crashed into the walking stick, sending it twirling away, and sent Ren toppling backward, Braxton riding the injured man to the ground.

Keysa was fumbling in her backpack as Piper grabbed the stick, and swinging it like a baseball bat, Piper brought it down on Braxton's head as he lunged toward Ren's neck with his teeth bared.

Braxton rolled off Ren's body and into the underbrush. He

looked dazed.

With an agility amazing for a woman half her age as she slid her knife from the backpack, Keysa charged forward, an inhuman cry tearing from her throat that sent a chill rippling down Piper's spine. The old woman gripped her knife like a dagger and lunged at Braxton, still trying to untangle himself from the bushes.

"No!" Piper screamed.

Braxton tucked himself into as small a target as possible and rolled farther into the brush.

But Keysa caught him in the calf, the knife piercing his flesh. His scream reverberated through Piper's ears.

Keysa pitched forward, toppling over him, her knuckles white around the knife handle. The embedded blade ripped downward and Braxton rolled free of the old woman.

Braxton's scream rose an octave until he was howling like a wounded animal, a shrill braying that echoed off the ridge and bounced around them. His eyes were as wild as a rabid dog's, a sickly green against their yellow background.

Piper rushed to Keysa, fumbling in her pocket as she ran. She pulled out Raven's feathers, no longer soft and silky, but clumped together in spikes from the wet, and peppered with grains of sand. Bending to the old woman, she threw the feathers at Braxton.

His eyes widened farther in horrified recognition as he stared at the raven feather drifting toward his forearm. He glanced at Piper, nostrils flared. For a fraction of a second, she thought there was a glimmer of recognition flashing through his eyes, a trace of sorrow.

Then the look vanished. His eyes glinted hatred, the fear of a cornered animal. He flicked the feather from his arm as if it were a hot ember, then scrambled to his feet but stayed hunkered over, his fingers splayed around the knife that still protruded from his calf.

He wrenched the blade from his flesh, nostrils quivering, and in the blink of an eye grabbed Piper around the neck from behind and yanked her backwards, dragging her toward the edge of the gorge.

She couldn't breathe! The pressure around her windpipe was excruciating.

Knowing her throat would collapse at any moment, and with her vision dimming quickly, Piper scanned from left to right, wanting — needing — her final image to be of Ren's face.

She found him.

He'd thrown back his head, mouth wide open, and screeched horribly, an unearthly ululation, that was quickly overridden by the sound of her pulse pounding through her head.

A shadow fell over her vision.

Was this death? Shadows?

She closed her eyes to give herself up to the inevitable. Another strange noise. Beating. Wind bursts, close to her face. A strange, animal howling from behind her.

And suddenly she toppled over backward, collapsing to the ground. Air rushed through her mouth and down into her lungs, clearing her vision and stilling the roaring in her head.

But the beating breeze continued. The howling grew louder.

She rolled onto her knees and looked up into blackness. Metallic blue-blackness.

Wings — flapping, beating wings and glittering black eyes. An enormous mound of birds — ravens — muffled Braxton's animal-like howling. They surrounded him, were on top of him, and the sky grew dark as even more ravens arrived, blotting out the sun. Fifty. A hundred. Joining their comrades on the ground — the mound a hill of hammering beaks, ruffled neck feathers.

The howling stopped.

"Stop them!" Piper screamed.

The undulating mound of ravens broke apart, splitting off like sparks from a fire until there was only the crumpled form of a still-writhing man and a dozen or so ravens.

"Stop!"

Flapping their great wings, the ravens became airborne. Braxton's body was lifted by both arms and a leg, slowly at first, then he was soaring, carried aloft by his black bearers, high, higher over the gorge, over the river.

And they let go.

"NO!" Piper screamed.

In slow motion, like a discarded doll, Braxton spiraled to earth, his body an "X" against the sky, cartwheeling, spinning, down, down until he crashed onto a boulder in the middle of Crooked Creek.

Piper dragged herself to the edge of the gorge, sobs racking her, threatening to tear her apart. Ren hobbled over to her, put his arms around her, held her, as she stared in disbelief at the broken body of the man she had once loved.

Braxton sprawled on his back, eyes wide, unseeing, mouth still gaping open as if he'd been trying to scream when the impact cracked him.

It seemed to take forever until she could stop sobbing enough to speak. She turned to Ren. "Can't leave him there. Can't. Got to get down. It's not right. He might still be —"

Ren closed his eyes for a moment and shook his head.

"He's dead, Piper. I promise you. His neck is broken. We need to call Frankie."

Keysa joined them. Piper tore her gaze away from her husband and glanced over her shoulder at the old woman. "Are you okay?"

Keysa was dusting herself off and trying to look dignified. She was panting like a woman in labor. When her breathing slowed, she looked at Piper. Her voice was without expression and her face unreadable. She jerked her head in the direction of Braxton's body. "That's your husband?"

A cold fist flexed icy fingers in Piper's heart, then reached outward. "No. My husband is dead. That is Adahy, grandmother."

The old woman nodded, satisfied.

Piper looked back at Braxton. The froth swirled around and crashed over Braxton, cleaning him even as they watched. Piper tried to look away. She couldn't. Her eyes seemed riveted to Braxton's body, both fascinated and horrified by the circumstances of his death. She slumped back into Ren's warmth, her mind struggling to comprehend what had happened, and even while she tried to make sense of it, something more bizarre happened.

Something that clogged in her brain, as if a comb had been working its way through her thoughts and stumbled on a tangle.

The churning water bubbled furiously. Roiled. The waves crashed in on each other from every direction, like a storm at sea. Froth and spray splashed over the dead man.

The waves grew bigger, surging over him, ebbing away from

him. And every time the water receded, it peeled away years from the body's face. The ravages of time and hard living melted away. His clothes were soaked, but no longer tattered rags. His wet hair clung tightly — silkily — to his scalp. He looked much as he had when they'd first met.

"What the —"

As they watched, a loosely formed mist began to seep from his opened mouth, from his ears and nose, leaking from the corners of his eyes and from his many wounds. The thin threads of mist joined together above him, forming a small cloud over his face, faintly at first, then as dense as fogfire. The cloud billowed, stretched, lengthened, higher, wider.

For a brief moment — little more than a flash — Piper thought she saw a face in the mist, the way animal shapes appear in the clouds, a strange, angular face with menacing eyes.

She blinked, and the face dissipated, melded back into nothing but gray fog. The mist drifted away from Braxton, glided above the surface of the water, churning up a small, agitated wake on the water's surface, till it reached the shore and disappeared behind a boulder.

She glanced from the boulder to Braxton.

"I — I don't understand," Piper whispered.

"I don't either," Ren said. She glanced at him and he looked as puzzled as she felt.

"If you ask me," Keysa said, "that was Adahy's spirit leaving your husband's body."

"What?"

"I think Adahy took over your husband. He probably possesses someone for a little while until they are no longer any use to him. Now, perhaps he'll look for someone else."

Piper opened her mouth to speak when something scuffled through the woods just out of their sight. All three heads turned toward the sound. Piper's comment died in her throat. Something large crashed through the underbrush, running away from them, heading deeper into the mountains.

A familiar weight settled on Piper's shoulder. Raven lifted one foot, then the other as he settled onto his perch. He jerked his head a few times in her direction, as if wanting her attention. She reached up and stroked his chest feathers, leaning her head against him.

"What now?" she asked Ren, glancing at him.

He staggered, clutching his chest, his face gray. The blanket had fallen from his torso as he had wrangled with Braxton, and his chest wounds were bleeding freely again.

Piper braced him up. "He can't go on, Keysa. Is there something you can do?"

The old woman nodded, slipped off her knapsack and started pulling out her healing things. "Straighten him out," she ordered.

Piper eased Ren down, pillowing his head in her lap.

"I need something to bind his chest after I dress it," Keysa said, "to stop the bleeding."

"Take my sweatshirt," Piper said.

"Too stretchy." Keysa ripped around the hem of her corduroy dress.

Ren lifted his head from Piper's lap. "Are you going to hit me up for a new dress, mother?"

"You bet," Keysa answered, glancing at her son. Her eyes sparkled, as if she were relieved he was able to joke. "And a pricey one, too. I've already picked it out." She looked at Piper. "Hold those gashes together with some pressure, here and here." She pointed to the worst wounds, then returned to her work. Within a few minutes, she had two long bandages about six inches wide. Her slip hung down past the end of her skirt by a foot.

Ren licked his lips as if to moisten them.

"Do you want some water?" Piper asked.

His eyes widened, then narrowed. "And have you go alone to the river for it? I don't think so." He managed a feeble smile. "You just keep on being my pillow and holding my skin together so my insides don't slide out."

"You're not hurt *that* bad," she said.

"Feels like I am."

Keysa withdrew some clean cotton squares from her pack and used them to daub away Ren's blood. Then she smoothed some ointment across the wound and dusted the entire wounded area with a gray powder from a sandwich bag. "The air must cleanse the wound for a while before we can bandage it," she said, then rocked back on her haunches.

She tapped Ren's shoulder with a gnarled forefinger. "It is the law of The People that retribution must be made in kind. If a man steals your horse, you must take his, or stock of equal value. If a man steals your good name, you must take his."

"An eye for an eye, mother?" Ren asked. Even through his obvious discomfort, he managed to sound wry. "Besides, we aren't of 'The People'. We're Tlingit, remember?"

"When in Rome..."

"Why Braxton?" Piper asked. "Of all the people around here, why would Adahy choose Braxton?"

"Maybe his creativity made him more vulnerable," Ren said. "An easier target than most. Or perhaps guilt is the funnel that permits evil to enter. I don't know."

Keysa pulled in her lip thoughtfully for a moment, then said, "The debt must still be paid. I don't think you have to mutilate anyone. But you must take something of equal value. Adahy took your daughter's life from you. What can you take in return?"

"Braxton's dead," Piper said, staring off into the woods. "He was insane toward the end — you saw him. He'd lost his humanity. He had no idea what he was doing. Isn't that punishment enough? A man as brilliant as he once was died as...something less than human."

"Adahy will never be caught," Keysa said, winding the skirt-bandage around her son's chest. "He is destined to wander the mountains until the final day."

Keysa tucked the edge of the bandage into the wrap and turned to her son.

"Can you go on now?"

"Just a few minutes to rest. Please. And may I — may I speak to Piper for a moment? Alone?"

Keysa didn't look pleased, but she nodded her head, brusquely, and walked off a few feet.

"Piper," Ren whispered.

She lowered her head to his.

"Are you going to be okay?" he asked.

She nodded. "I'm confused. I can't say I really understand what I just saw — what I think I saw — but in many ways,

Braxton has been dead to me for a long time. But if — and I'm not saying I believe it, but *if* it was the spirit of Adahy that turned Braxton...that way...why does there have to be retribution? And how can you take retribution from a spirit? Besides, nothing can bring back Susannah. What's the point? "

His eyes brimmed with sorrow for a moment. He looked as if he were going to say something, then changed his mind. Instead, he pulled her to him and kissed her.

For that brief moment, Piper felt fused, unsure of where she left off and Ren began, as if the lines between them had blurred so completely they'd stopped being two separate entities.

Keysa returned, her eyes darting upriver, gesturing with her hand for them to get moving. Distant shouts pierced the early morning air, so far upriver that it was impossible to guess who was shouting or how many people there might be.

The whine of a siren grew louder, stopping near the point where the voices seemed to be coming from.

Ren's face went ashen from the effort of getting upright.

"Can't you give him something for the pain?" Piper asked as they started toward the road.

"Yep. Soon's we get home." Keysa stole a sideward glance at her son, a small hint of a smile playing around her mouth. "I'll steep up some of that wild cherry tea that'll knock him from here to Sunday."

The grin faded. Keysa stopped as suddenly as if she'd rammed into an invisible wall.

"What's wrong?" Piper asked.

The old woman appeared not to have heard. Her face was puzzled and as Piper watched, Keysa fished her amulet out of her shirt, and held it while tears overran her lids and traced down over her weathered cheeks.

"What is it, mother?" Ren asked. "What do you see?"

"Help him down," Keysa ordered Piper. When Ren was settled, she turned to Piper. "Go toward the voices. Frankie is there. Bring him and his medical people to my son. I'll wait here with him."

Ren watched his mother as she gave Piper her instructions. His face turned even more gray as he listened to her words, as if he suspected the truth behind them. "Mother?"

"Our days of sorrow are not yet over," she said, lowering herself beside him. She pulled his head into her lap. "Go!" she told Piper.

Piper stumbled onto another crime scene. Searchers — exhausted from their long ordeal — shuffled dejectedly around the perimeter of a small clearing. A body was being loaded into an ambulance as Piper crossed the clearing toward Frankie and put her hand on his arm.

"Piper, thank God. You're okay." Frankie's cell phone rang. He answered it, gesturing for Piper to wait. "Yeah, Marge, what's up?" He listened intently, glanced nervously at Piper, then said, "Call me back if there's any further news."

He clipped his phone back onto his belt. "Piper, there's no easy way to say this. The fingerprints we found on the small cooler near Susannah's body match Army records for Braxton, and a bite mark on Susannah's breast correspond to Braxton's service dental records. I have to arrest him."

"He's dead."

"What?"

"Dead. At the bottom of the gorge."

"What happened?"

"You won't believe me. I'll let Ren tell you."

"Where's Ren?"

"With Keysa. About half a mile that way." She pointed in the direction from which she'd come. "He's in rough shape, Frankie. You need to get your EMS guys over there. Who's dead?"

He grabbed her arm and steered her toward the edge of the clearing. "It's Mary Beth. I found her Bronco this morning when I was combing the woods looking for you or Ren or Keysa."

Piper nodded. Bit her lip.

"You don't seem surprised."

"Nothing surprises me anymore."

Frankie took a deep breath. "I'll have to tell Ren. This is going to destroy him completely — a wife and daughter within thirty-six hours."

"He knows."

"What? How can he know?"

"I think Keysa is explaining it to him now. Get your medical boys and come on."

EPILOGUE

Piper set the mug of coffee on the corner of the desk, leaned over and kissed the top of his head, her amulet brushing the back of his neck. The amulet matched his own new one, both of them adorned with Keysa's stylized black-beaded ravens. Piper tapped the manuscript box. It was already addressed to Everett A. Palmer of The Palmer Literary Agency. "Well?"

He smiled and covered her hand with his. "Finished. It's been a long haul."

"Congratulations! When do I get to read it?"

"You can start right now." Ren pushed back his chair, and hoisted himself out of his chair, offering Piper his seat.

He leaned against the wall and looked through the window to the spring green countryside. The ravens perched in the large oak tree at the edge of the woods, shifting their weight from foot to foot, watching crows fight over a raccoon's carcass that had shown up before dawn.

He glanced over at Piper. She had taken the manuscript from its box and stacked it neatly on the desk before her. She sat, staring thoughtfully at the title page, tracing the byline with her finger.

"What's wrong?" he asked.

"I — I'm still not sure how I feel about this."

He hobbled to her side and scooped the heavy veil of hair from the side of her face. "There are times when there is no right or wrong, when there are neither truth nor lies, black nor white, but only shades of gray. This is one of those times. Braxton took my wife from me."

"And so you took his wife."

"Are you unwilling?"

"No, but —"

"He took my children."

Julie Anne Parks

"Susannah. You still have Jeff," she answered softly.

"I don't have Jeff. Not really. The boy still grieves for him. Between mourning his mother and sister, and missing Braxton, my son is as good as gone to me."

She couldn't argue that. Jeff had never seen Braxton as anything but his mentor. Nor was the boy there at the end, when Braxton had shed his humanity like a snake sheds its skin.

Ren pressed on. "He tried to take your life. And mine."

She spun on her chair toward him. "It wasn't his fault. He was crazy. Possessed maybe. Crazy definitely. Don't you think he paid the ultimate price?"

"I'm not responsible for that, Piper. No one is."

She looked down at her hands. "I know."

"And he took my stories, so I have taken his name."

"It still doesn't seem right."

"It's the *only* way, my love. Look at it this way. If we *don't* do this, Braxton will be remembered as a writer who burned out quickly, falling from fame to shame. His achievements will be overshadowed by his end." Ren put his hand beneath her chin and lifted it gently, forcing her to look up at him. "But if we go through with this, his last mention in history will be a positive one. And his debt to me will be paid."

She nodded, squeezed his hand briefly, then turned the title page over.

She took a deep breath and began reading the first page:

Chapter One

It seemed a sinister place, a dark and brooding landscape of steep slopes and craggy chasms. Black clouds roiled above wooded peaks, plunging the hillsides below into shadows like a spreading stain of darkness. It was a place where a creative mind might easily slip from the mundane to the macabre, where even the most unimaginative soul might be goaded into believing the unbelievable.

It was perfect.

ABOUT THE AUTHOR

Julie Anne Parks has worked as a flight attendant, administrative assistant, executive secretary, freelance writer and newspaper reporter, turning to fiction in 1995. She's had a dozen short stories published in mainstream and genre presses as well as several essays. She lives in North Carolina with her husband, Chuck, and the youngest of her three children, Tim. The two oldest children, Michael and Shannon, have flown from the nest. The Parks household is filled with pets, most senior of whom is "PJ", a German Shepherd.

With what little leisure time remains after writing and a full-time job, Julie reads voraciously, loves movies, boating, and travel — particularly long weekends in the Carolina or Tennessee mountains where *Storytellers* is set — or to the Carolina coast. There she wanders the beach searching for shark teeth, Piña Coladas, and new story ideas.

She is a member of the Horror Writers Association and the Writers Group of the Triad.

Storytellers is Julie's debut novel.

THE KISS OF DEATH
An Anthology of Vampire Stories

Sixteen writers invite you to welcome their own dark embrace with these tales of vampires old and new, frightening and funny, provocative and arousing. Each tale is its own cool embrace, its own delightfully dangerous kiss of death.

Sandra Black
Tippi N. Blevins
Dominick Cancilla
Margaret L. Carter
Sukie de la Croix
Don D'Ammassa
Mia Fields
D.G.K. Goldberg

Barb Hendee
C.W. Johnson
Lynda Licina
Kyle Marffin
Deborah Markus
Christine DeLong Miller
Rick R. Reed
Kiel Stuart

Trade paperback, 304 pages
ISBN 1-891946-05-6
$15.95 US ($19.50 CAN)

Available from your favorite bookstore or on-line bookseller.

SHADOW OF THE BEAST
by Margaret L. Carter

Margaret Carter has been a fixture in dark fiction for nearly thirty years, with anthologies, critically acclaimed non-fiction books and her own long-running horror fiction periodical to her credit. And here is her long awaited horror novel debut.

It begins with a hellish night of bloodshed and horror. A nightmare legacy arises from Jenny Cameron's past — destroying her family, threatening everyone she loves — and now it's come to claim her in an orgy of violence and death.

A beast roams the dark streets of Annapolis, Maryland, a terrifying creature more animal than man. And the only way Jenny can combat the evil from her past is to surrender to the dark and violent power lurking within herself. Her humanity is at stake, and much more than death may await her under the shadow of the beast.

Trade paperback, 256 pages
ISBN 1-891946-03-X
$15.95 US ($19.50 CAN)

Available from your favorite bookstore or on-line bookseller.

NIGHT PRAYERS by P.D. Cacek

Stoker Award winner P.D. Cacek's debut novel is a wryly witty romp that introduces Allison Garret — thirtysomething, biological clock loudly ticking and perpetually unlucky in life and love — who wakes up in a seedy motel room...as a vampire! In a rollicking tour of the seamy underbelly of L.A., Allison hooks up with a Bible-thumping streetcorner preacher, but they'll both need more than a night full of prayers to escape the clutches of a catty coven of strip club vampire vixens out for blood.

"Further proof that Cacek is certainly one of horror's most important up-and-comers."
Barnesandnoble.com

"The novel works...Cacek exhibits a winning sense of humor."   **Hellnotes**

Trade paperback, 224 pages
ISBN 1-891946-01-3 $15.95 US ($19.50 CAN)

Available from your favorite bookstore or on-line bookseller.

CARMILLA - THE RETURN by Kyle Marffin

Kyle Marffin's provocative debut is a modern day retelling of LeFanu's classic 19th century vampire novella. Gothic literature's most notorious female vampire — the seductive Countess Carmilla Karnstein — stalks her unsuspecting victim through darkened city streets to the desolate northwoods and back to her haunted Styrian homeland.

"Marffin's clearly a talented new writer with a solid grip on the romance of blood and doomed love."   **Locus**

"If you think you've read enough vampire books to last a lifetime, think again. This one's got restrained and skillful writing, a complex and believable love story, gorgeous scenery, sudden jolts of violence and a thought provoking final sequence that will keep you reading until the sun comes up."   **Amazon.com**

Trade paperback, 304 pages
ISBN 1-891946-02-1 $15.95 US ($19.50 CAN)

Available from your favorite bookstore or on-line bookseller.

THE DARKEST THIRST
A Vampire Anthology

Sixteen disturbing tales of the undead's darkest thirsts for redemption, power, lust and of course, blood. Includes stories by:

Michael J. Arruda	Barb Hendee
Edo van Belkom	Paul McMahon
Sue Burke	Kyle Marffin
Margaret L. Carter	Deborah Markus
Stirling Davenport	Julie Anne Parks
Robert Devereaux	Rick R. Reed
D.G.K. Goldberg	Thomas J. Strauch
Scott T. Goudsward	William R. Trotter

"Succeeds quite well where so many anthologies have failed...approaches its subject with the enthusiasm and vigor lacking in collections filled with jaded veterans."
BookLovers

"If solid, straight ahead vampire fiction is what you like to read, then The Darkest Thirst is your prescription."
Locus

Trade paperback, 256 pages
ISBN 1-891946-00-5
$15.95 US ($19.50 CAN)

Available from your favorite bookstore or on-line bookseller.